D. J. Pierce

About the Author

MICHAEL CRAVEN is an award-winning advertising writer who has worked for some of the most creative agencies in the country. His career has taken him from New York City to Los Angeles, to Boulder, Colorado, where he lives and works. Michael grew up in Jacksonville, Florida. *Body Copy* is his first novel.

BODY COPY

BODY COPY

MICHAEL CRAVEN

HARPER

NEW YORK • LONDON • TORONTO • SYDNEY

HARPER

This book is a work of fiction. The characters, incidents, and dialogue are drawn from the author's imagination and are not to be construed as real. Any resemblance to actual events or persons, living or dead, is entirely coincidental.

BODY COPY. Copyright © 2009 by Michael Craven. All rights reserved. Printed in the United States of America. No part of this book may be used or reproduced in any manner whatsoever without written permission except in the case of brief quotations embodied in critical articles and reviews. For information address HarperCollins Publishers, 10 East 53rd Street, New York, NY 10022.

HarperCollins books may be purchased for educational, business, or sales promotional use. For information please write: Special Markets Department, HarperCollins Publishers, 10 East 53rd Street, New York, NY 10022.

FIRST EDITION

Designed by Laura Kaeppel

Library of Congress Cataloging-in-Publication Data is available upon request.

ISBN 978-0-06-165716-0

09 10 11 12 13 OV/RRD 10 9 8 7 6 5 4 3 2 1

BODY COPY

CHAPTER 1

Donald Tremaine, the ex-pro surfer, the ex-husband, the current private eye and Malibu trailer park resident, looked in the mirror and said, "Happy birthday, old man."

He was thirty-nine. He didn't feel thirty-nine, though. He didn't. He felt forty-six. But that was because he'd celebrated the night before with a couple friends and more than a couple cocktails.

Tremaine dropped to the floor and cranked out fifty push-ups. As he finished number fifty, he said, "Ouch."

His morning routine hurt a little more than usual. That was also because of the previous night's activities, not because he was officially one year older. That's what he told himself, anyway.

Still down on the ground, he looked over at his ancient English bulldog, Lyle, sleeping in the corner. Back in the old days, Lyle would come over and lick his face when he did push-ups, but not any more. Nowadays, Lyle would just look at him then go right back to sleep. He wouldn't even consider trotting over.

"Where's the love?" Tremaine would say.

But Tremaine knew Lyle was just old, a lot older than thirty-nine. At least on the dog scale.

Tremaine was in a good mood despite the sting in his head. He was giving himself a nice birthday present. Real nice. Two months in Australia surfing the best waves the continent had to offer. He needed it, too. He'd worked a lot of cases in a row, and he was tired and ready to get out of L.A. for a while.

Nice thing about being a private investigator, you could usually get out of town when you needed to. When business was slow or when he wanted to clear his head, Tremaine would hop in his car and drive down or up the coast—sometimes just for the day—and surf the California spots he'd been surfing all his life. But not this time. This time he was headed across the globe to ride waves he hadn't seen since he quit surfing professionally.

How long had it been, man, fifteen years?

Tremaine, up on his feet now, looked down at his big surfboard bag. All packed. Clothes and equipment for two months, and three different surfboards. All he had to do was drop Lyle at the neighbor's and head to the airport. But not yet. It was only 9:00 A.M. He had some time to kill before his flight. So he grabbed the *New York Times*—the Gray Lady—and a cup of coffee and walked outside. He then climbed the ladder on the side of his trailer, coffee in one hand, paper under his arm.

Tremaine stood on the roof of his trailer looking due west. He had a clear view of the ocean, just one of the perks of living in the Old Colony Trailer Park in Malibu, California. Sure, you could also see a McDonald's and a row of Dumpsters just off the Pacific Coast Highway, but boy, could you see that ocean. The Pacific. Big—giant— and right there. Just down the hill and across the two-lane highway. The vast, blue-green mass was practically his backyard.

Tremaine had a couple chairs and a table set up on the roof, so he sat down and got to the paper. First up, the front page. Then sports, then the arts.

It was quiet. The wind rustled his paper a little, and a car or two zoomed by down on the PCH, but for the most part it was quiet. Nice and quiet. Just Tremaine, his paper, his coffee, and his slowly disappearing hangover. Then that quiet was broken.

A black Volvo station wagon pulled up next to his trailer and parked in the guest spot. A young woman got out of the car and looked up on the roof at Tremaine, who was looking at her.

"Excuse me, I hope this isn't a bad time. I'm looking for Donald Tremaine. Are you Donald Tremaine?"

Tremaine looked at the stranger. A brunette, early to mid-thirties, a shadow across her face as she shielded her eyes from the sun. And, Tremaine couldn't help but notice, attractive. Quite attractive. He was a P.I.; he noticed these things.

"Shit," he said under his breath.

"Excuse me?"

Tremaine thinking, this is someone coming to me with

3

a case. It sure as hell wasn't a groupie from his old surf tour days. The random groupies had stopped showing up a while ago. Shame about that. No, this had to be a case. Tremaine normally didn't turn down cases, almost never, but he was going on vacation no matter what. Yes, she was attractive, but that absolutely did not matter. That wouldn't affect his decision. It wouldn't.

Tremaine said, "Yes, I'm Donald Tremaine. How can I help you?"

"I wanted to talk to you about hiring you. Should I come up?" she said.

Tremaine liked that she wasn't afraid to do business on the roof of a trailer. But it might be a little more professional to talk inside, even though he wasn't taking the case. He stood up and said, "I'll come down."

CHAPTER 2

Standing in front of the trailer's door, the woman said, "I'm Nina Aldeen."

Tremaine gripped her extended hand and officially introduced himself, "Donald Tremaine."

Tremaine observed her, processing his first impression. He noticed he was wrong about her being a brunette. Well, she was a brunette, but her hair was very dark, almost black. It accentuated her slightly pale skin and pretty blue eyes. Pretty blue eyes, Tremaine noticed, that held a hint of sadness.

Tremaine said, "Come on in. Would you like a cup of coffee?"

Inside, Nina sat down, sipped her coffee, and said, "I have to say, I don't think I've been in a trailer before, but this is quite nice. I didn't realize they came with hardwood floors."

"I put them in when I moved in. It came with sky blue shag carpet."

Nina said, "Like you see in somebody's basement."

"Or van, even."

"I bet you got it out of here immediately," she said.

Tremaine had lived with it for more than three years.

He said, "Yeah, right away."

Nina looked around a bit more. Tremaine looked at her looking around. At the floors, at the art on the walls, at the book collection. Tremaine thought, no need for the tour now, she's seen everything.

She said, "I really like it in here."

She meant it, he could tell.

"Thanks," he said.

"It's nice and spare. I always let things pile up."

Tremaine nodded and said, "How'd you hear about me?"

"From John Lopez."

"Great guy. Great cop. We grew up together."

"He told me that."

Then Tremaine said, "I don't want to hear anything about the case."

Some surprise registered on Nina's face and she said, "Oh. Why not? John told me you'd take the case if I paid you your fee. He told me what it was, I'm fine with it."

Lyle, who had been in a deep sleep, picked his head up and looked in the direction of the woman. Lyle considered the stranger, squinting his eyes at her and sniffing the air in her direction. Within seconds, his head was back down and he was off to sleep.

"That's Lyle. You probably thought he was dead."

"It might have crossed my mind," she said. "Why don't you want to hear about my case?"

"Because I can't take it. I'm going on vacation. See that big bag over there?"

"I was wondering what that was."

"Those are my surfboards," he said. "I'm going on a surf trip."

"John said you were a surfer. He said you used to be a pro."

"Yeah, a pretty long time ago."

"He said you were the world champion."

"It was a pretty long time ago."

Tremaine felt some anxiety in his chest. He didn't want to talk about the tour, didn't want to hear the question that people always seemed to end up asking: *Why'd you quit?*

She didn't ask.

She said, "Well, it's okay if you're going on vacation. I'll hire you when you get back."

"I'm leaving for two months."

Nina thought for a second, but no longer than that, and then said, "It's been a year since my uncle was killed. I suppose I could wait two months, if that's what it takes to hire you."

"I know other P.I.s."

"John Lopez told me not to waste my time with a bad P.I. who isn't going to get anywhere. This is a case the police couldn't solve. By the way, John told me to tell you he hadn't worked on the case."

Tremaine laughed at that.

Nina continued. "He told me you'd solved cases the

police couldn't figure out. That you'd done it a couple times. And if I was going to hire someone, I should hire you."

"Lopez said that to you? He never says nice stuff like that to me."

Tremaine wanted to ask her what her uncle's name was, but he knew that if he did, he wouldn't be going to Australia. He knew that if he started getting details on the case, particularly knowing he was going to work on it when he got back, it would ruin his trip. He'd be out in the waves, dropping in on a big one, but instead of enjoying the freedom of being thousands of miles away from home and the rush of gliding down a wave, he'd be thinking about the case he knew he was coming back to. What happened, why it happened, and who did it. He simply couldn't help it.

He looked at Nina. That smooth, pale skin and that dark, almost black, hair. The way she sat in the chair, comfortable, but with her feet together, and her arms crossed, looking a little reserved. She had the perfectly tailored, expensive clothes, but then a necklace made of little bright blue and yellow glass beads that might have been made by an artist in the East Village of New York City. And just that hint of sadness in her eyes. It was all working for her; she had the mix just right. And, no, not attractive. A knockout. Yeah, that's what his investigative skills told him. She had the kind of beauty that hurt you a little. Made you want to drop to the floor, get in the fetal position, and just sob.

Tremaine was considering doing that now. But instead, he asked Nina a question, *the* question. His curiosity had gotten the best of him.

"What was your uncle's name?" Tremaine said, knowing now for sure, now that he could hear the words coming out of his mouth, that his trip to Australia was officially postponed.

"Roger Gale," she said.

"I remember the case. He was the advertising guy. Started the big agency over in Playa del Rey."

"That's right. I'm surprised you remember. It made the papers, but after like a day it stopped showing up in the press."

Tremaine grabbed the *New York Times* that he'd brought in from the roof. "These guys did an obit."

Nina nodded and said, "I still have it."

Tremaine began to think back about the obit and the couple other articles he'd read about Gale. He said, "He was found in his agency—in his office—right?"

Something—pain, sadness, confusion—showed on Nina's face, and she took a breath before she said, "Yes. They found him at his desk. Sitting at his desk. Dead. He had a head wound, but they realized later that he had been strangled."

Tremaine paused for a moment. Then switched gears and said, "Roger Gale. He came up with the famous campaign for Rogaine—*Just admit it. You want your hair.* Right?"

"Yeah, that's right," Nina said, smiling.

"Where everybody in the commercials was admitting stuff that they really thought but were afraid to say."

"That's the one."

"That's a good campaign," Tremaine said. "Funny. Smart."

"Will you help me when you get back from your vacation?"

"I'll help you right now."

9

"You really don't have to cancel your trip. I can wait."

"I'm not canceling it. I'm postponing it."

She said, "I kinda feel bad. I know that feeling right before a vacation, it's a good feeling."

"Don't feel bad. If I went on the trip knowing I had a case to get back to, I wouldn't be able to relax. I would be looking at a kangaroo and thinking about Roger Gale."

"I understand. I'm like that with my work, too."

"What do you do?"

"I teach Italian and art history at UCLA"

"Do you teach John Lopez's brother?"

"Yes. He's the person who put me in touch with John. You are a good P.I."

Tremaine now thought, a beautiful woman, a college professor, *and* a sense of humor. I'm glad I took the case. Even though none of those things caused me to take the case. I'm a professional, for Chrissakes.

"Here's the way I work. I'll need a few days to do some research before I talk to you. I want to know more before I start asking you questions."

Nina nodded and said, "Something I want to ask you . . . One of the reasons I wanted to look into this was because I felt the police just gave up. My uncle was kind of a big deal, you know? A prominent member of society. Not that that should make a difference, but it does. Anyway, the case is still technically open, but nobody's doing anything about it."

"Cold."

"Excuse me?"

"The case is cold. That's what they call it. What's your question?"

"Does that surprise you? That the police aren't paying any attention to a murder? I mean, a man was killed and the case is just sitting there."

Tremaine walked over to the coffee pot and poured himself another cup, number three, or was it four? He was beginning to get that shaky feeling—that shaky feeling he kind of enjoyed.

He said, "The LAPD has to deal with an enormous number of cases. And, to your point, the fact that Roger Gale was a well-known person does give his case more attention. But that doesn't mean it can be solved. Sometimes the police work is bad, sometimes the workload is just too overwhelming, sometimes it's a combination of both. And sometimes . . . sometimes the case just can't be solved."

Nina nodded and said, "Well, I'm glad you're going to give it a try."

"There's almost always something that can lead you somewhere," Tremaine said. "It might be very hard to pinpoint, but it's almost always there."

Nina stood up and pulled a card out of her purse. She handed it to Tremaine and he looked at it, focusing on the name. Nina Aldeen. It had a nice sound to it.

"Call me or e-mail me when you want to talk," she said. "I really appreciate your taking this, and again, if you want to go on your trip, I can wait."

"I'll call you in a couple days."

Tremaine walked Nina out. They both stood just outside the trailer, right where they had been when they first introduced themselves to each other.

Tremaine said, "So, was there another reason you wanted to look into this?"

Something happened in her eyes, and she waited just a second too long to talk.

"Another reason?"

"Yeah. You said the cops not doing anything about it was one reason. Is there another one?"

"I said that? I guess I meant . . ." She cut herself off and again paused before she spoke. Tremaine looked at her eyes. Something far away was in there, and he almost thought she was going to cry. But then he saw something else, a quick but fierce fight within her that showed she wasn't going to let that happen.

She said, "I don't know what I meant by that. I think it was just a figure of speech. But in thinking about it now," she took a breath, "I guess there was another reason. I guess I meant that some people in our family wanted to hire someone like you, but just couldn't bring themselves to do it. Roger's wife—his widow, Evelyn—or my mom— they were too hurt by it all to open it up again. If that's even really what they wanted to do. I guess I felt like I could be the one to take some action, you know? Even if it was just hiring someone. As sad, as tragic as it was, the murder I mean, I was less emotional about it than they were—you know?"

"Yeah," Tremaine said. "I'll talk to you in a couple days."

And then he watched Nina turn and walk to her car with her arms crossed and her head pointed just slightly down.

CHAPTER 3

The first person Tremaine needed to call was his old buddy at the LAPD, John Lopez, not just to thank him for the referral but to get some information from him on Roger Gale. But before he did that, he'd have to take care of something else, something fairly important to him: the Daily Jumble. That game in the paper where you unscramble the words, then figure out the clever little riddle at the end. It's very popular with the over-eighty crowd—Tremaine knew that. He would often say to himself, Jesus, Tremaine, you're not even forty and you're doing the Jumble every day like an old man. Start devouring Jell-O and yelling at the neighbors, and you'll *be* an old man.

Tremaine liked to pretend the game helped keep his mind sharp, but he knew it was just a dumb puzzle that he was addicted to. Even more compulsive than his doing it every day was the fact that he timed himself. His best time ever? Thirty-seven seconds, start to finish. It was almost pathetic that he was proud of that. Extremely proud of that.

Tremaine had planned to do the puzzle on the flight to Australia, but since that wasn't happening, he had to do it right away, before the day got away from him. The Jumble wasn't in the *New York Times*, so Tremaine produced his copy of the L.A. *Times*. Not a bad paper—a good one—but he only subscribed for the puzzle.

Now he was ready. Pencil, stopwatch, puzzle. Tremaine sat at his kitchen table, pressed start on the stopwatch, and got started. The four unscrambled words were MYRIG, TEAGA, TOLBET, and WHALLO. The riddle was: *What it takes to wear the latest designer clothes.* The blank answer looked like this. A _ _ _ _ _ _ _ _ _ _.

Tremaine was off to the races. The first one, MYRIG, was easy: GRIMY. He wrote it down. Then he knocked out TOLBET and WHALLO: BOTTLE and HALLOW. TEAGA? What was that? TEAGA. Hmm. Got it: AGATE.

He took the circled letters out of the solved words: The M and the Y out of GRIMY. Both A's and the E out of AGATE. Both T's and the E out of BOTTLE. And the H, an L, and the W out of HALLOW.

The new unscrambled word looked like this: MYAAETTEHLW. *What it takes to wear the latest designer clothes . . .* A what? A . . . A . . . Tremaine looked at the stopwatch, already over a minute. Shit. A . . .

Got it: *A wealthy mate.* Those clever bastards. Tremaine hit the stopwatch. One minute, forty seven. Not a terrible time, but not even in his top fifty.

All right, Tremaine had had his one minute and forty-seven seconds of fun, now it was time to get to work. To go on the real clock. He picked up his cordless and dialed.

"Lopez. Tremaine," he said.

"I figured you'd be calling after I sent Nina Aldeen your way."

"You ruined my vacation."

"What vacation?"

"I was off to Australia today for two months."

"You don't tell your friends when you're leaving the continent for two months?"

"Oh, I tell my friends."

Lopez said, "Hey, you better start kissing my ass. I'm assuming you want me to send you the police report on Roger Gale."

"I'll buy you a steak."

"No, you won't. You'll buy me a steak and several drinks."

"Fine."

"Several *expensive* drinks."

"Fine."

"I mean like Belvedere and Maker's, minimum."

"Fine."

Then Lopez said, "Did Nina mention that I didn't work on that case?"

"No, she didn't."

"Bullshit."

Tremaine said, "I appreciate you sending the work my way, John. Really. And not just because Nina's the kind of girl you'd sell your soul for."

"My pleasure. We go back a long way."

"Indeed."

"Remember those days?" Lopez said. "Growing up? We pretty much just surfed, chased girls and got high."

"We got in a few fights as I recall. Out there in the water defending our turf."

"Had to, those guys down in Huntington were mean. That is, till you became the local hero. You had a nickname, what was it? Something about you being a crazy bastard."

"You're funny, Lopez. Say, what do you do these days without me to protect you?"

"I thought I protected you. For a P.I., you don't have a great memory."

"Selective. But I do remember the good old days. I think about them often," Tremaine said.

"Your life hasn't changed much, has it, buddy?"

"Not as many girls."

"But the grass?"

"You're a cop. I can't tell you that. Now you're the one not remembering anything."

"I'll get you some stuff on Roger Gale in a couple days."

"Thank you, sir."

"Oh," Lopez said, "Happy Birthday."

"Should I be expecting a present?"

"The police report, the investigation files, the autopsy report. Those are your presents."

"But I'm buying you a steak and drinks for that stuff."

"Yeah," Lopez said, "I know."

CHAPTER 4

Tremaine went for another cup of coffee and thought, no, can't do it, done for the day. Starting to see spots. Oh, what the hell, it's my birthday . . .

He got online and started to look around for information on Roger Gale. His life, his career, his history. The first thing he did was find a picture of the man. A picture of the man as he had looked just before he was killed. Tremaine stared at the image on the screen. Short white hair, blue or maybe even gray eyes, and a tan, a California ad man. He looked alive, alert. Younger than his fifty-nine years.

Information on the guy's career was a snap to find. He was all over the Net, his achievements in the world of advertising being nothing short of huge.

Roger Gale began as an ad writer, a copywriter, and started a small direct-mail ad agency with an account executive named Ted Parker. Both men had been in the business only a few years, but they hung a shingle anyway in San Clemente, California, and started chasing business. Knowing they wanted a more high-profile agency, they moved the shop north to L.A. With its new home, the agency began to grow and moved around Los Angeles as it expanded.

And expanded. Gale/Parker began growing at a breakneck pace, hiring top-notch creative and account management people from the best agencies in the country. With Roger Gale and Gale/Parker becoming synonymous with cutting-edge campaigns, many of the people who joined the agency came knocking without solicitation.

The agency got huge and, as the years passed, opened offices all over the world. But the flagship office, where Roger Gale had been found murdered, was right down the road from Tremaine, in Playa del Rey, California.

In various articles, Roger Gale was referred to as a "visionary," a "genius," a "workaholic," and a "brilliant advertising mind." The *New York Times*, in the obituary that Tremaine had read more than a year earlier, said, "Roger Gale was the West Coast's single most influential advertising person and, in fact, ranks right up there with the all-time giants, David Ogilvy, Leo Burnett, and Bill Bernbach."

A lot of the campaigns Roger Gale had created Tremaine remembered. They were famous. Stuff for Old Spice and Panasonic and Puma and, of course, Rogaine, the campaign he had discussed with Nina. *Just admit it. You want your hair.*

But the main focus in nearly every piece Tremaine found wasn't the specific campaigns Roger Gale had created. It was Roger Gale himself. The maverick, the innovator, the leader. This wasn't just a guy who created some memorable commercials. This was a guy who changed the way the industry operated. Under Roger Gale, there was no such thing as proper work attire, you could wear what you wanted. Out were the suits and loafers; in were the T-shirts, ripped-up jeans, and flip-flops. And you didn't have to sit at your desk. You could work outside in a tree if you felt like it.

Just as long as you were willing to die for your ads.

Roger Gale's employees, as a result of this new attitude, saw him almost as a god. Even though they were made to work long days, nights, and weekends, they deeply respected him and were fiercely loyal to him. They respected his passion, his commitment, and the fact that even as a living legend, he walked around the office carrying a red pen and would stop mid-stride to excitedly jot down an idea, sometimes on his hand or arm.

The Gale/Parker agency—the physical appearance of it—got almost as much attention as Roger Gale and the work his agency produced. The agency's headquarters was a massive old airplane hangar that had been turned into a state-of-the-art ad agency. No traditional offices, just a gargantuan, wide-open space with clusters of work centers everywhere, bright orange walls, and a full-size basketball court *inside*.

Tremaine looked at the agency on the Gale/Parker Web site, where they offered a virtual tour. On the outside, the building looked like nothing more than a massive orange

19

warehouse. But inside, it was an irreverent, modern office space to say the least. It was the physical manifestation that Roger Gale's agency did things differently. In Gale's words, it was "built to fuel creativity and show prospective clients that contemporary thinking is literally the foundation of the place." And, Tremaine thought, if prospective clients wanted to play a little five-on-five, they could do that, too.

On a personal front, there wasn't much interesting stuff about Roger Gale. At least not on the Net. Tremaine did find out a little, though. Roger Gale's first wife died in an automobile accident, he had no kids, and he was survived by his second wife, Evelyn Gale, his sister, Rita, must be Nina's Mom, and a stepson, Peter, who lives in Los Angeles.

Tremaine took a break from the computer and sat thinking for a moment, processing his cursory investigation of the great ad man who had been struck down by murder. Tremaine thinking, all this praise, all these achievements, all the respect from the people who worked for him, yet someone wanted him dead. And someone made him dead. He was getting excited about examining the specifics of the actual crime, the killing. Who found him, who did the police detectives talk to, what was the evidence? Tremaine's brain was starting to send him questions, send him signals that it was cranking up, getting ready to start looking around. He sat there realizing if the day had gone as planned, he'd be getting on a plane in a little while. But it hadn't gone as planned, so he was investigating a murder instead.

CHAPTER 5

Tremaine walked over to his neighbor's trailer. The guy who lived there was a twenty-five-year-old struggling actor named Marvin Kearns. Tremaine needed to tell Marvin, before the day got away from him, that he no longer needed a dog-sitter for Lyle.

Tremaine had come to know quite a bit about Marvin Kearns. For one reason, mainly: Marvin told him. Marvin had a staggering number of things to say. He was a walking diatribe. And his language, it was crazy, almost formal at times, full of dramatic phrasing and unusual word choice. Contrived, maybe, but Tremaine didn't care. He liked him, liked his company, admired his dedication to pursuing something he wanted to do.

Tremaine knocked on Marvin's door.

Marvin almost immediately opened the door and said, "Donald Tremaine!"

Before Tremaine got to the matter at hand, he had to acknowledge two things. The first was Marvin's new haircut, a totally shaved head. Marvin always wore his hair short—he was balding and liked to keep it tight—but now there wasn't a speck of hair on his head. His large head. Not particularly out of proportion, though. Even though he was only five-three, Marvin was a pretty big guy. All of his parts were big and bulky. Big arms, big legs, big chest, and a big bald head.

Marvin Kearns was a stump. And now, a bald stump.

Tremaine said, "So you went ahead and just took it all off, huh?"

"This morning. I got shaving cream. I got a razor. And I shaved it off. It's a superior look. HAIR GETS IN MY WAY! And I don't have time to be in-between anymore. If you're going to do it, do it. You don't stick your toe in the pond, you jump in."

"Okay," Tremaine said.

"Okay!" Marvin repeated with glee. "That is such a large response."

Marvin rated almost everything he came in contact with. If he liked something, it was either "superior" or "large." If he disliked it, it was "soft" or "insufficient."

Most of the stuff that Tremaine did received high ratings from Marvin simply because Marvin had a very high opinion of Tremaine. Although Marvin was relatively young, he had a full knowledge and appreciation of Tremaine's surfing career. He was one of those twenty-five-year-olds with a real appreciation for what came before. In fact, he liked what came before more than he liked what was around right now. He was like an old man in that way.

The second thing that Tremaine had to acknowledge was that Marvin was wearing fatigues.

"What's your audition for?" Tremaine said.

"Extra in a war movie."

"You're showing up fully in character for a part as an extra? That's not sticking your toe in, that's jumping in."

"Headfirst, Mr. Tremaine. Headfirst."

"Marvin, I came by to tell you that I'm not going on my trip. I postponed it because I got a case."

"Is that why the beautiful woman was at your place this morning?"

"What, are you spying on me?"

"Not you, her."

"I can't say I blame you."

"I'm sorry I won't be looking after Lyle. He is, as you know, a superior animal."

"I'll tell him you said that. He might not hear me, but I'll tell him."

"If you need any help on the case, just let me know."

"I will."

Marvin always asked Tremaine if he could help him on his cases. Tremaine didn't mind his asking, but he'd never taken him up on it, not yet, despite many, many requests. Tremaine said good-bye and started heading back to his trailer.

Then Marvin said, "Happy Birthday, Mr. Tremaine."

"Thanks, Marvin," Tremaine said, looking over his shoulder at the bald stump clad in camouflage.

Eight hours later, Tremaine got in his car, a sky blue 1971 Oldsmobile Cutlass Supreme two door, and drove to Venice. He was going to wait until he'd read the police reports before he talked to Nina, but he had a question that was ready to be asked now, just not to her face. It was seven, dusk, almost dark, and still quite a bit of traffic as he took the Pacific Coast Highway south, through Santa Monica into Venice, the great, the one and only, Venice, California. Expensive these days, really expensive, but man, still the best. Still had that bohemian feel, bright-colored California beach bungalows right next to the more modern architecture of the too-big-for-their-lots houses that the rich people had built. It made for an odd combo, the invasion of money into Venice. You'd see a brand-new Beemer parked right next to an old-school VW Thing with a bunch of surfboards on its roof. Tremaine wondering, will the dough eventually strip it of all its charm? Strip it of every last bright blue shack with some guy with a three-foot beard living in it, sitting on his porch playing the flute in a housedress and cleats, yelling at passersby about hidden messages in Blue Oyster Cult lyrics?

Impossible. Some of that would never go away, Tremaine hoped. You could certainly still feel the history, see the real locals crawling the streets, feel them looking at you all wild-eyed as you entered their turf. Tremaine thinking, they especially didn't like it when you surfed their waves. He smiled thinking about that, knowing he got welcomed into their breaks because of his history.

He called information and said, "Venice, California. Nina Aldeen please. And I just need the address."

Got it. 424 Rialto. A great street, one of the most charming, very close to where he had lived with his ex-wife. It still made him a little sick to think about it, to examine even just a moment of their cohabitation.

Still.

He drove right past Nina's house. Looked at it, though, as he went by, tried to glean with a quick—real quick—look whether anyone was home.

Tremaine parked two blocks away, behind a caramel-colored '89 Chevy Chevette and in front of a sparkling silver Lexus. He got out and began heading back toward Nina Aldeen's house.

Tremaine thinking, why did Nina say there was more than one reason to look into this, then pretend that she didn't? Is there something there, something she isn't telling me?

True story. Tremaine had a client once, in his early days, Jeff Creswell. Real early days, right after Tremaine had gotten his P.I. license and his license to carry a firearm. Jeff came to Tremaine, hired him to follow his wife, said she was cheating on him. From the beginning, Tremaine sensed something off in Jeff, something troubled, something dishonest. But he took Jeff at his word and took the case. Mistake. Here's what happened. Tremaine followed Jeff's wife, Trudy, to a hotel. Trudy went in the hotel with a man. Through the lens of his camera, in the window of the hotel room, Tremaine could see violence. Trudy's body being slammed up against the window, the blinds being pulled and torn. In an instant, Tremaine was in the room. Instead of finding the man beating up Trudy, he found the man, Trudy, Jeff, and briefcase full of cocaine. Jeff's plan was to shoot Tremaine, take the blow, then tell his suppliers that *two* men had come to the hotel to steal the coke, and that he had gotten one of them, but the other one had gotten away with the blow. Then Jeff and Trudy and the guy posing as her lover would take the coke, sell it, get rich, and retire. Jeff wasn't very smart. Tremaine shot him in the shoulder, took his gun, and called the cops.

As a result, when Tremaine thought a client was bullshitting him, was hiding something, he was careful. Very careful. Because not listening to himself in the past had almost gotten him killed by a half-wit criminal named Jeff.

Was Nina looking into this for some other reason? When she said "one of the reasons," was that a slip-up? A window into something darker? Had her rich, successful uncle promised her a bunch of money then gotten killed before changing his will, and now Nina wanted some answers? Or was there something else, something he couldn't even fathom with the information he had at this point?

Who knows? Point is, she told him something then tried to pretend she hadn't, then tried to scramble an answer together while possibly holding back tears.

Or maybe she was just talking normally, saying things like *one of the reasons* just off the cuff. And maybe that faraway look in her eye was just because she was upset, made to think about her dead uncle, right in that moment, in a way she hadn't in a while. And now Tremaine was overthinking things.

Tremaine thinking, overthinking things? That's what I *didn't* do with Jeff . . .

Was Nina lying?

Maybe not. But maybe.

He wanted to try and find out, needed to try and find out.

These days, a little older, a little wiser, still alive, his motto was *Sometimes the best person to look into is the person who hired you.* Not particularly clever; Roger Gale wouldn't have written it. But it was true, and that's all that mattered.

Tremaine laughed at this as he slid through the shadows, down the quiet streets, past houses with evening activity and lights on inside, with dogs barking occasionally but not obnoxiously. Nobody noticed him.

He walked right in front of 424 Rialto looking right at the front door. Great little house. Not really ranch style, but maybe California-ranch with a beach flair. Brown wood with bright blue shutters. The contrast looked good. There was a little yard in front with a little fence that bordered the sidewalk. Once inside the fence, you walked up three steps to a great little porch with a swing.

Tremaine wanted to move in. Despite his suspicion, he liked Nina, wanted to trust her, could feel there was something real about her. He could picture himself sitting there on the swing with her having a beer, listening to some tunes, maybe rubbing Lyle's back with his foot.

Concentrate, Tremaine. You never know with people.

He kept moving, walked right by the house, then past one more house, which was on the corner. He went right, around the corner, onto a perpendicular street. He stopped amid the shadows of a bush hanging over the high fence of Nina's next-door neighbor. He stood, still, looked around. No one.

He walked in the same direction he'd been going. Halfway down the block he went right, into the alley behind the block of houses on Rialto. He passed her neighbor's, then was directly behind Nina's house. There was a high, sturdy-looking gray wooden fence. He looked around. Clear. He slowly pulled his head up over Nina's fence and looked into her small backyard. There was a deck and a sliding glass door off the deck.

In one move he pulled himself over the fence and into her backyard. Then, quickly, he darted into the small side-alley formed by the edge of her house and the chain-link, waist-high fence that ran between her house and her neighbor's.

He looked, carefully, into every window on the side of Nina's house. Some lights on, but no activity. No Nina. He looked through a window that allowed him to see the inside of the front door. No alarm. Chalk one up to luck.

He stood still for fifteen minutes, then looked in every window again. Unless she was lounging in the tub, she wasn't home.

Lounging in the tub. He thought about that for a minute longer.

He walked over to a small door that led out to the little side-area where he stood. He looked under the mat for a key. Nothing. He tried to reach the inside doorknob through a little cat door, but couldn't. Too tight. He ran his hand along the wooden ledge at the top of the door, nothing. Would he have to pick it? It'd been a while, but he could swing it. Then he looked up into the shadows of the little aluminum awning above the door. It was painted blue, just like the shutters, as was the wood that supported it. There was a little light from the inside the house, but it took a second for his eyes to adjust. When they did, he spied a little nail sticking out of a piece of the blue wood. The nail was painted blue. And on that little blue nail was a little blue key. He grabbed it, unlocked the door, replaced the key, went in, shut the door, locked the door. It always amazed him how easy it was.

Inside. Unpretentious yet sophisticated. Lined with books and rugs and artwork and a redone kitchen with lots of copper and cooking supplies. Wine, cookbooks, garlic cloves.

He looked around. One big room in the front. Then a sort of side room with a big dining room table on one side and a bookshelf built into the wall on the other. This side-room led to the kitchen, which then led one way back to an office and the other way to a little hallway that went to the bedroom and the door he just came through.

He walked back to the office and opened the sliding glass door that led out to the back deck a foot and a half.

Then he walked back up to the main room in front and stood there not knowing exactly what he was looking for. He felt something rub his leg and he jerked his foot up. His heart was in his throat. He looked down at a red-orange cat looking right at him with big, mesmerizing, green cat-eyes. He knelt and scratched the cat's head and looked at the cat's name tag. It said DARRYL.

He moved on. He looked in a couple drawers in the front room. Nothing interesting. Some cards, some pictures, some change.

He looked through the dining room, then went in the bedroom. He looked in the drawers, the closets, under the bed, then the drawers again. And here's what he found: stuff that's usually in drawers and closets and under beds. He walked back into the office.

There was another bookshelf full of books. Some writers he really liked. A real mix. Mark Twain. Joyce Carol

Oates. Elmore Leonard. Is that *La Brava*? Great book. But he didn't have time to look at them; he had to keep moving. He looked through her desk drawers, carefully. There were bills, papers, notes, old notebooks. But nothing to do with Roger Gale except some photocopies of a few different obituaries.

Then he saw some kind of manuscript, a big stack of typed pages. Was she writing a book? Only some of the manuscript was there. The top of the page that was face-up said 213. Tremaine picked it up, started reading. This is what it said:

And you can't quite describe the feeling because there are so many feelings. They come in waves. Sometimes it's simply that you can't believe your marriage broke up. You can't believe you are one of the failures. But that's not so much a feeling as it is a thought-through realization. The feelings are more erratic. Sometimes you're happy—happy it's over, happy you're out of a difficult situation. Sometimes you're introspective, analyzing the divorce from an almost clinical, outsider's perspective. Sometimes you're nostalgic; a random memory can hit you from nowhere at any time. But the hardest one, the one I don't even like to acknowledge, even when it's just me and the feeling, is the feeling of being lost. Not just lonely. Lost. Lost at sea, with no connections back to the mainland that is your life.

Nina had gone through a divorce and was writing a book about it. Tremaine felt the blood move in his body.

He knew what she was writing about. He'd been married. And divorced. He liked that she was putting into words a feeling he had had. He looked back down at the page.

> You are locked in to another person, to a life to-gether, and suddenly it's gone. And you don't know what to do with yourself. You don't know who you are or who you're still connected to. With me, I had pulled away from my family. My husband was my family. I actually felt strange in my new single role talking to my own parents. Everything in my life seemed strange, seemed wrong. I desperately needed to reconnect—with my family, with my life. I needed something good.

Tremaine heard the front door opening.

In one move, he put the manuscript back on the desk and went sideways out the open sliding glass door. He ran toward the fence, jumped, put one foot in the middle of the fence, his hands on top of it, pulled himself over, landed quietly on the pavement in the alley.

And he ran.

Not toward the street but deeper into the alley behind the row of houses. He reached the street on the other end of the block, went right onto the sidewalk, and walked, back in the shadows again, to his car.

Driving home, windows down, cool beach air in his face, he thought about Nina. That's what she left out at the trailer. That's what the pause was about, the look in her eye. This was the other reason she was looking into Roger Gale's murder. She needs to do something good. She needs some answers that make sense. She needs to reconnect with her family in some way.

She needs to reconnect with her life.

Tremaine thinking, and I suspected her of something less real, something less innocent. I suspected her of maybe having some impure reason to look into this killing.

Then he thought, remember Jeff Creswell. I'm a P.I., for fuck's sake, and that's what I do. I suspect people of stuff that's less innocent.

Now back on the PCH, heading north to Malibu, Tremaine thought about what Nina was doing right now. He knew what she was doing right now. She was looking at the sliding glass door, thinking, I can't believe I left that open; anybody could have just waltzed in here. He would never hear about it, he knew that too. She'd never know he'd been there. But the most important thing that Tremaine knew was that he didn't feel Nina was hiding something, and he was looking forward to helping her out.

CHAPTER 6

The next day, a big packet arrived via messenger from the LAPD, from Lopez. Tremaine emptied the contents onto his desk, leafed through them, and took out the specific things he wanted to look at. Then he went up on the roof.

Sunny and nice again. Shocker. Southern California could be like *Groundhog Day*. Tremaine knew he shouldn't complain, but every now and then a little rain or something would be nice. A drop or two. Jesus, Marvin could come over and spray him with a hose and it would be a nice change.

Tremaine took off his shirt and lit up a smoke and suddenly he was glad again that it was warm and lovely. Tremaine didn't smoke a lot, but when he was just starting to think about a case, a smoke was nice. And when he was driving, a smoke was nice then, too. And after surfing, they weren't bad either . . .

Tremaine looked at the police reports he'd brought to the roof. They included everything from autopsy information to statements from people interviewed about the murder to crime scene information to notes from police detectives. John Lopez, good man.

Tremaine began by reading the specifics of the murder. Just over a year ago, Roger Gale was found dead at approximately 6:30 A.M. on a Saturday morning; however, the time of death was estimated at approximately 12:30 A.M., much earlier that morning. Gale was found by an employee of Gale/Parker named Mary O'Shaughnessy, who had come in to work that morning. A go-getter, Tremaine thought— 6:30 on a Saturday. According to Mary, Roger Gale was sitting upright at his desk with his eyes open, then, out of nowhere, he slammed down onto his glass desk. She witnessed this fall.

She's quoted in the report as saying, "I was looking in his office at him, wondering if he was in some sort of creative trance. Then, he just slammed down onto his desk."

This fall cut his head and certainly added drama to the situation, but it had nothing to do with why he died. No, when he was killed some six hours prior to his being discovered, he'd suffered another blow to the head. But the thing that killed him? Asphyxiation. The conjecture in the report was that the blow to the head knocked him out, then the murderer calmly and easily plugged up the old air holes.

Roger Gale, Tremaine read in numerous statements,

had definitely left the office the Friday night before he was found. So he had either returned and been killed in the office, or he had been killed elsewhere and deposited at the office.

No one saw him return. But, as Tremaine learned poring over the statements, Friday night was the one night people didn't work till the wee hours. It was the one night the employees got out of there, were encouraged to get out of there. Many of them came in on weekends, as Mary O'Shaughnessy had, but Friday night the place was relatively empty. So, if he'd come back late that Friday night, he could have gone unseen. It wouldn't have been unusual.

Tremaine wondered, did the person who killed him know Friday nights were slow, or did they just get lucky?

The agency did employ a twenty-four-hour security service, but the two guards who worked the night shift weren't there to determine who could and who could not enter the agency. They were just there to make a statement. Officially, the agency's doors locked at midnight, but everyone who needed a key had one and knew the alarm code. Roger Gale wanted the agency to be accessible anytime anyone might have a creative surge. Gale himself came and went at all hours—always had. The security guards really just stood around outside, ostensibly guarding but rarely questioning, rarely even noticing, the people who came and went.

The guards on duty the night in question claimed not to have seen anything. Claimed that they never saw anyone, Roger Gale or otherwise, come in that Friday night after the last person left around nine. A note in the report indicated that both the security guards were fired shortly after the murder. They'd become friends while working together and had been caught leaving their posts to get alcohol. So, Tremaine thought, the night of the murder, they could have been three sheets to the wind. Probably were.

Tremaine continued to peruse the information and began to see why the police never got anywhere. There was essentially no evidence. Nothing at the scene, no unusual fingerprints, no indications of someone being in Roger Gale's office who shouldn't have been there. And Roger Gale's past? Looked clean. No business deals gone bad, no affairs. Officers had asked many of the employees and his family members about Gale's irregular hours, but everyone just said Roger Gale worked hard. No one had any reason to believe he was involved with anyone other than his wife. There was never an official suspect named.

There was, however, a person of interest listed: a man who held the position of Creative Director at a rival Los Angeles ad agency, a man named Tyler Wilkes. He had been questioned extensively and was, according to many Gale/Parker employees, jealous of Roger Gale—really jealous. Tyler Wilkes had built his agency in El Segundo, a neighborhood close to Playa del Rey, home of Gale/Parker. He'd also built it to physically resemble Gale/Parker. And, according to the report, he was "constantly" comparing the two shops, constantly trying to compete with the legend of the ad man down the road. "Obsessed" was the term one cop used. But the police could never get anything on Wilkes. It was simply their only lead.

Tremaine wondered, do people in the advertising business kill each other? You got that in certain worlds—drugs, politics, possibly. But advertising? Tremaine had always considered advertising to be something of a prestigious field. Martini lunches, teams of people in black turtlenecks, location shoots. But murders?

You never know, Tremaine thought. He was always surprised at the reasons people found to kill each other. Reasons that often seemed stupid, silly, insane, impossible. Yes, shit between people, or in people's heads, can escalate; it just can. And ad agencies have relationships with enormous companies. That means lots of money. And that's what a tremendous number of murders are about: money. So what makes advertising different? If an agency down the street is winning all the business, getting all the respect, wouldn't it be nice to have the creative force behind that agency gone forever?

Maybe.

CHAPTER 7

Tremaine and Nina Aldeen decided to meet at noon at the Rose Café in Venice, a casual breakfast and lunch spot where you could sit outside on the patio, in the sun. Tremaine arrived, looked around, didn't see Nina. So he made his way out onto the patio and sat down at a table in the corner. He ordered a cup of coffee and sat there, his head still, his eyes scanning the lunch crowd from behind his glasses. People-watching—always a good way to kill some time.

A few minutes later, Nina entered the patio. As she ducked underneath a tree that sprouted up through the patio bricks, Tremaine thought, yeah, just as I had remembered, beautiful. He got that feeling, the one you get when you see someone for the second time, and they're better than before. He stood up as she arrived.

"Hi, Donald," she said.

She was wearing bright red lipstick. Tremaine noticed it and noticed again the little glimmer of sadness in her eyes. This time he knew where it came from.

"Hi, Nina."

They sat down. A waiter came over, and Nina, too, ordered a cup of coffee.

Tremaine said, "I've done a little research on your uncle. He was an impressive guy."

"Thank you. His whole life was advertising."

He couldn't tell if she was implying something.

"I don't mean that in a negative way," she said.

There was his answer.

"When I was little," she said, "I used to come out here in the summers, and he'd just let me hang around the agency while he worked. It was great because there was all kinds of stuff to play with. Tons of pens, and all kinds of paper and scissors and things. And lots of people, too."

"Did you stop coming out after a while?"

"High school, you know. I felt that spending time with my friends in Connecticut was more important than spending the summer in an ad agency. Hindsight is twenty-twenty, but I'm sure I would have learned more if I had kept coming out here. All we did in high school was talk about boys and try to get people to buy us beer."

"Same. Except replace boys with girls and beer with beer, booze, pot, and cigarettes."

Nina said, "You can smoke cigarettes and still surf competitively?"

"I didn't smoke that many cigarettes."

"What about the other stuff?"

"Let's get back to the case."

Nina smiled.

Tremaine said, "What about after college? Did you keep in touch with your uncle then?"

"He offered me a job. But I was married by then, living in Connecticut."

She paused for a second and said, "I'm not married now. I got divorced pretty recently."

She paused for another second and said, "That sounded weird."

"It's okay. I've been married. And divorced. It never sounds right when you talk about it."

"Thank you. People don't realize that. I'm actually writing a book about it. That's the length I'll go to so I don't have to talk about it and sound weird."

Tremaine laughed. And did his best not to indicate that he, in fact, had read some of her book.

Nina said, "Anyway, I'd talk to my uncle on the phone and stuff still, but at the time of his death, it had been years since I'd seen him."

"What about your mom? Did she see him?"

"Not really. They were friendly, but my mom was seven years younger than Roger. And lived three thousand miles away. After she married my dad, she started raising a family, and my dad was working long hours and Roger's ad career was always going a million miles an hour ... Everybody was busy. The years went by and they just kind of got used to not really seeing each other. It's kind of sad when I think about it. You know, I'm sure they loved each other, but they didn't see each other much."

"So neither you nor your mom really knew him—in a personal way—at the time of his death?"

Nina paused and then said, "Yeah, that's true. I had never thought of it that way, but I'd say it's true. We knew his history, and we knew a lot about his business, his agency, partly because we talked about it a lot after the murder. But you're right, we didn't really know him anymore. I could see how hurt my mom was when Roger was killed. Maybe there was some regret."

Tremaine said, "At the time of his death, your uncle held two titles at his ad agency. I know he came up with ad campaigns, but what exactly was his role?"

"It's confusing, kind of, if you haven't worked in the business. Ad agencies, basically, are split into two sides, the business side and the creative side. Roger was the head of both. He was the president and the creative director. But really, he was the creative director. Which means he was the boss of all the writers and art directors."

"And those are the people who sit around all day throwing a football, coming up with ideas for beer commercials?"

"Yeah. Roger determined which of those ideas got presented to the clients."

"And from what I've read, he came up with a lot of stuff himself."

"Yeah. Constantly."

"So, if Gale/Parker was presenting an idea for a commercial to somebody, your uncle either thought of it or approved it."

"Yes. And he would go and present the work himself. The bigger stuff anyway."

"What about the business side? What was his role there?"

"In terms of the number-crunching and investing and loans and taxes and all that stuff, he basically just signed off on things. He had people doing that for him. What he did do a lot, though, was chase new business."

"He was a legend. I imagine it was pretty easy for him to get a meeting."

"Yeah. A lot of times, clients would just give the agency business because of its reputation. Because of his reputation. But most of the time, even if you're really famous like Gale/Parker, agencies have to come up with something good, then put on a song and dance. And that was his specialty."

The waiter came around. Nina ordered a Cobb salad. Tremaine, the eggs Benedict.

"So, bottom line," Tremaine said, "if Roger Gale weren't around, Gale/Parker would get less business?"

"Maybe not at first. Because there are a lot of talented people at every good agency. But over time, business would wane because there are only a handful of people as passionate and good as Roger was." Nina looked at Tremaine and said, "When the investigation was going on, the detectives looked into a work-related connection."

"Right," Tremaine said. "Tyler Wilkes, the guy from the other ad agency."

Tremaine didn't tell her how he knew this, that he'd obtained the police report. She didn't ask. If she had asked, he still wouldn't have told her.

"Yes," Nina said. "Tyler Wilkes was their only lead."

"Mine too. So far." He then said, "What about Ted Parker? Is he still around?"

"No," she said. "Ted Parker left Gale/Parker about ten years ago. He'd made his money, he was ready to get out. So he moved to Hawaii to relax. And, after one month there, he had a heart attack and died."

Tremaine shook his head and said, "Life can provide some dark twists." He knew this to be true.

"But the name stayed?" he said. "Gale/Parker?"

"Yeah. The agency was famous by then, but more than that, Roger wanted Ted's name to stay."

Tremaine said, "And that meant it was going to."

The waiter came back around, this time to deliver their lunch. He put their plates down and said, "The salad for the lady, and the Benedict for Insane Tremaine."

Tremaine managed a polite enough smile.

Nina said, "What does that mean?"

"I have no idea."

Nina gave him a sly smile, "What is that, a nickname?"

"I have no idea how he knew my name or why he decided to make a little rhyme out of it."

"Come on."

"All right. When I was surfing professionally, some guys made a video of me called *Insane Tremaine*."

"Why did they call it that? What was insane about it?"

"Some of the waves were large. I never liked the title."

"Why? Trying too hard?"

"Yeah. And I never felt insane when I rode those big waves. I felt scared, but not insane."

"If you were scared, why'd you do it?"

"I liked it. It was challenging. And, even with the fear, I always felt like I could do it, make the drops. Of course, I was often wrong. I was often very, very wrong"

"What happened when you fell?"

"It could be pretty ugly. That was the main reason for the title of the movie. There was a section of the film that was just a montage of one wipeout after the next. I got absolutely pulverized many, many times. People enjoyed watching that for some reason."

"I think I'd like to see that."

Tremaine smiled.

Then Nina said, "How long were you the number one surfer in the world?"

"Not long. The year I received the number one ranking, I quit the tour."

He knew the question coming next, but he was prepared.

"Really? Why'd you quit?"

"I'm the P.I. here. I ask the questions."

"Seriously, why did you quit? All the time you must have put in, you were probably still very young."

"I was twenty-four years old."

"So, why did you quit?"

Tremaine took just a hair longer than normal to say, "It was time."

Nina didn't ask again.

After lunch, Tremaine walked Nina to her car.

Nina said, "So, I'll call the office manager at Gale/Parker. She's great. She'll make sure you talk to all the right people. When do you want to go over there?"

"As soon as possible. Gale/Parker's the first place on my list."

"You'll like Laurie. Laurie Donnelly's her name. She was one of the first employees. She's worked there for twenty years. And has the attitude to prove it."

"Attitude?"

"Not toward people she likes. And she'll like you, because I hired you. And I'm related to Roger Gale, whom she's totally loyal to."

"Who doesn't she like?"

"Laurie's seen the agency go from a small little shop to a global force. Nowadays everyone at Gale/Parker is hipper and holier-than-thou. So, if some hotshot with dyed hair and a really good résumé tries to tell her how things should be at the agency, she lets them have it. By the way, she's also a big flirt, so be prepared."

Tremaine laughed at that.

Then Nina said, "Not to pry, I know you know what you're doing, but you said Gale/Parker is first on your list. What else is on your list?"

"Tyler Wilkes is on my list. Roger's widow, Evelyn, is on my list."

"Right. Check out his work life and his home life."

"Bingo. And, by the way, you're allowed to pry. You're the boss."

Nina got in her car, the black Volvo, and she sat in the passenger seat talking to Tremaine through the open window.

"I hope Evelyn is helpful. She's very buttoned up and old-fashioned."

"That's okay, it's always good to meet people, even

people who don't like talking. You never know what they're going to give you, even if it's by accident."

Nina thought about that and nodded. And Tremaine looked at her, sitting behind the wheel of the sleek black Volvo wagon. She was strapped in by the seatbelt, and he couldn't help but notice again how her features all fell together so nicely. The dark hair, the pale skin, and the red lipstick. In that moment, looking at her looking great behind the wheel of the car, Tremaine wanted to just get in the passenger seat and drive off to no place in particular.

CHAPTER 8

Two days later, Tremaine got up, went for a surf, fed Lyle, then got into his Cutlass and hit the road, headed toward the famous Gale/Parker advertising agency.

He hung a left at the Lincoln-Longfellow intersection in Playa del Rey, then took another left down a short little side street called Flower Avenue. And there it was. A giant remodeled airplane hangar, with a second story attached, lots of enormous windows, and a bright orange paint job. Atop the second story, a flag flew, a flag that said GALE/PARKER with a stick of dynamite between the two names.

He pulled the Cutlass in between two three-series BMWs. He noticed each of the cars proudly bore Gale/Parker bumper stickers. The bumper stickers had the

Gale/Parker logo, dynamite and all, and underneath the logo, it said THE HARDER YOU WORK, THE BETTER THE WORK.

Tremaine said, "Yeah, I guess so," and got out of the Cutlass and walked toward the entrance. The entrance was on the second story. You had to walk up some outdoor steps to get to the door, and Tremaine could see from down on the ground that there was a little reception area once you got inside. That was the only thing the second story was for—the reception area. Once inside, Tremaine assumed, you headed down the slightly declining tunnel that was connected to the agency. Tremaine thought, up to the second floor to get to the first floor?

The door to the balcony outside the reception area swung open and out came Nina Aldeen.

She waved from up on the balcony and said, "Donald!"

Tremaine looked up, waved, walked up the stairs to greet Nina.

"You found it okay?" she said.

Tremaine considered saying something like "hard to miss," but figured everyone probably said that, so he just said, "Yeah, no problem."

"Great. Let's go inside."

Nina and Tremaine walked into the reception area. Nina thanked the receptionist and guided Tremaine toward the tunnel that led into the hangar, the agency. The tunnel was white on all sides and Tremaine could see activity at the end of it, people walking by, an office in full swing. Tremaine remembered the modern style from the virtual tour, but now he was seeing and feeling it firsthand. It felt interesting, different, impressive.

Nina said, "Roger helped design the agency, so when you see it for the first time, it's revealed to you all at once."

At that, they exited the tunnel and entered the agency proper. It was truly a sight to behold, the virtual tour he'd taken did not do it justice. Wide open spaces, full-sized billboards touting ads that Gale/Parker had created. An enormous cutout poster of the smart-ass hound dog that they'd created for Alpo. Punching bags hanging everywhere, things that must be desks but sure didn't look like desks . . . And there was the basketball court, right in the middle of it all.

But what struck Tremaine most were the people. Young people everywhere. Some of them were walking, some trotting, some zooming this way and that on roller skates and skateboards, humming across the smooth concrete.

Tremaine stood there and just observed them. Dyed hair, nose rings, tattoos. It was like being at a punk rock show—without the anger.

And the clothes, they definitely ran the gamut. You still had your older people in all black, but you had many more younger people in jeans and ironic *Happy Days* T-shirts. Hell, some people barely wore anything at all. Like that beautiful girl over there by the water fountain. What's that she's got on, a napkin? And, man, did most of them seem young.

"So you can dress like this and drive one of those Beemers out there?" Tremaine said.

"Scary, isn't it?"

"Maybe I should go into advertising," he said. "Except, I'm like twice everybody's age."

"Maybe even three times," Nina added with a sly grin.

"Let me show you around a little, then we'll go meet Laurie."

Nina led Tremaine around the agency, explaining how each account had its own section. A dog food account got its own chunk of floor space, a running shoe account, a car account. Tremaine looked at the billboards that were up inside the hangar and recognized almost all of them. Television monitors were all over the place, too. On each of them, a series of commercials ran over and over in a loop. Commercials created by Gale/Parker.

Nina led Tremaine to the middle of the agency, where there was a room with two big glass walls and two big orange metal walls that didn't look inhabited. Inside it sat what looked to Tremaine to be awards. Little gold statues and plates.

"This was Roger's office. Nobody felt right about taking it over, so they use it to house all the awards the agency wins. I guess it's kind of a tribute because Roger had won so many himself."

"What do you mean, awards?" Tremaine asked.

Nina laughed. The laugh of someone who just realized that there's no possible way the other person in a conversation could know anything about the subject at hand.

Nina said, "The advertising industry is very self-congratulatory. They hold awards shows every year to honor things like the best TV commercials or the best magazine ads."

"Do people from outside the industry have an interest in these awards?"

"Not really. It's basically just advertising people congratulating each other."

"Keeping score."

"Exactly."

Nina and Tremaine moved on and now entered another unusual room within the open space created by four wood walls, each a different height. The wood walls had windows cut into them. There wasn't a ceiling on top of the walls, but rather an open view to the top of the hangar. An attractive woman with blonde corkscrew hair stood up from behind her desk. She looked to be about forty.

"There you two are," she said.

She walked around her desk and approached them. Her skin-tight, dark blue jeans rubbed together on her way over. Sticking out her hand, she said, "I'm Laurie Donnelly."

Tremaine, shaking her hand, replied, "I'm . . ."

"Donald Tremaine. You were quite a surfer," Laurie said.

"You've done some research," Nina said.

"Yeah, when I heard he was coming in, I looked him up."

Laurie looked at Donald. "Still have your looks, I see. Still have the blonde hair. Not as long though. Looks a little like Redford's in *Butch Cassidy*."

Tremaine smiled, embarrassed.

"You'll have to excuse Laurie," Nina said. "Like I said, she's an incorrigible flirt."

"I'm not sure I know what that word means," Laurie said. "Nina's an intellectual. I just tell it like I smell it."

"With that, I'll leave you two alone," Nina said.

"You sure he'll be all right?" Laurie said.

"He's a private eye; he's been in dangerous situations before."

"Not this dangerous," Tremaine said.

"Oh, he's got a sense of humor, too," Laurie said.

"I wasn't kidding."

Nina said good-bye to Tremaine and Laurie and left.

Laurie Donnelly was the kind of person Tremaine needed. She had a position of stature at the agency and was happy to use it to help him out.

Laurie said, "Who do you want to talk to first?"

"How 'bout you?"

"Let's do me last. I've got a few things to do, stat. But I can get you started and all set up for a full day."

Tremaine said, "Why don't I start with the girl who found Roger, Mary O'Shaughnessy?"

Before he had even finished his sentence, Laurie was on her phone.

"Mary, it's Laurie Donnelly. The gentleman I was telling you about earlier is going to be coming by to talk to you shortly. Be as cooperative as possible and answer all his questions."

It's not possible that Laurie heard Mary's response because the receiver was already back in its cradle. Slammed abruptly down.

Then Laurie looked at Tremaine and said, "She's ready when you are."

Laurie set up some other interviews for Tremaine, told him who he was going to talk to, then winked at him and said she'd see him later.

CHAPTER 9

Mary O'Shaughnessy and Tremaine sat in a small conference room that had a small table, some chairs, and no windows. Tremaine looked at Mary, probably twenty-six, attractive, but desperate to be taken seriously. She was sitting so upright that it had to hurt, and she had her hands tightly clasped in front of her, almost like she was praying.

"So you wanted to talk to me first?" Mary said.

She couldn't contain how impressed she was with herself over that fact. Tremaine nodded at her question.

"I thought it would be good to talk here," Mary said. "This is called a solitary room. It's for people who want to take a break from the action of the agency, and just sit in here and think. You don't have to be a creative to use it. Like, I use it sometimes, even though I'm an account executive."

"A creative?"

"Yeah, that's what they call the writers and art directors. Creatives."

Tremaine wondered if they called her group Kind-of-Annoyings. He said, "Account executive. Laurie said you were an assistant account executive."

He had to point it out. Look at this girl, with the ridiculous posture and the little up-and-comer smirk. He just had to.

"Well, I am, but that won't last long. I've already been promoted once. I started as a receptionist."

Tremaine moved on. "So, you found Roger Gale that Saturday morning?"

"Yes!" she said.

She was so proud of it. Proud of being the one to find a dead guy.

"He was sitting there at his desk, it was very early in the morning. I was the only one in the office, the first person here. Well, other than Roger, obviously."

"But he was dead, so that doesn't count," Tremaine said.

"Exactly," she said.

She didn't take his comment as a joke, she wanted credit for being the first person in. Mary was talking, describing the scene. Tremaine was sort of listening but knew within seconds that he wouldn't get any information from Mary that wasn't in the police report.

He asked her a few questions anyway; she was, after all, giving him her time. Even though, as each second passed, he became more cynical about his first interviewee.

"So, you saw Roger's head crash down on the desk, and you went in his office to find out why that had happened?"

"Yes," she said. "And I called out his name a few times, and when he didn't answer, I felt his pulse, like they do in the movies. And when I had my fingers on his neck, some blood from his head, where it had hit his desk, dripped on my hand. It was really weird."

"Then you called the cops?"

"Yes," she said. "And I remember my fingers stained the phone with blood."

Tremaine thought about saying, please, save the imagery for your screenplay, but he didn't.

Instead, he remained relatively polite and said, "Did you know Roger Gale? On a personal level?"

It hurt Mary to respond to this question, Tremaine could tell.

"No," she said. "I'd only talked to him once in my life."

"And what did you talk about?"

"Not much. I said hi."

"And what did he say."

"He smiled."

Tremaine said, "Thanks for talking to me, Mary. You've been helpful."

"I have?" she said.

Tremaine smiled.

Tremaine, after leaving Mary, sat down with a young copywriter named Matt Bishop. A creative. They sat in Matt's "office" a room with three orange steel walls and an opening on one side that looked out into the agency. Matt had a goatee and his fingers were bejeweled with several cheap-looking rings. His dark hair and dark goatee set against pale Iowa skin gave him sort of a sinister look. But within seconds of talking to him, Tremaine realized, Matt Bishop was a genuinely nice and helpful guy behind the wannabe-rock-star exterior.

"Thanks for talking to me," Tremaine started.

"No problem," he said. "Lots of people would be really glad if the person who murdered Roger was caught."

Tremaine noticed an ad hanging on the Matt's wall for Häagen-Dazs ice cream. It showed a woman sitting on her couch crying and eating from four different cartons of ice cream. The headline on the ad read: *The breakup was really bad. That's why our ice cream is really good.*

"Is that a real ad?" Tremaine asked.

"No. We pitched it to the client, but they didn't get it. Typical."

"Too morbid for them?"

"Yeah, they said it gave their product a depressing image."

Tremaine thought, they were right.

"This would have won a ton of awards," Matt said. "Instead, they took the straight approach. We always run into that with clients. They never want to take risks."

Tremaine shifted the subject and asked, "So, you worked with Roger Gale?"

"Some, but not enough. But I was working with him on the H&R Block pitch at the time of the murder. So, the time I did spend with him was right around the time of his death."

"Did you like him? As a boss? As a person?"

"He was the best mind this business has ever had."

"But did you like him? Was he fair? Was he a straight-shooter?"

"That was his best quality. Even above his talent. He respected anyone who came to work every day ready and willing to come up with new ideas. No matter who it was. That's why he liked me. I had an idea for the H&R Block pitch, so I got up the nerve to introduce myself to him one day at lunch. So I told him my idea, and he liked it, and the next thing I know, I'm working directly with him. Every day. Coming up with ideas for the pitch. He never asked me about my credentials, where I had worked before, what I had done while I was at Gale/Parker, anything. I don't even think he knew I was a copywriter at first. He just liked the idea and said let's do it."

"What about if he didn't like your ideas? How did he act?"

"He told you. There were plenty of suggestions of mine that he didn't like. Believe me, plenty. He'd just say so."

"When you worked with him, did you get to know him at all, personally?"

"Not really. It was actually kind of funny. We'd work all day and never really do any small talk. Nothing. I tried to get him to talk about stuff other than work, you know, what he did on the weekends or whatever. He'd just kind of look at me. All he wanted to do was work. He was just totally consumed. It was amazing."

"Did you ever see him outside the office?"

"No. I couldn't get him to *talk* about stuff outside of work, much less make plans with me."

"No, I mean, did you ever just run into him randomly?"

"Once. I saw him at a restaurant."

"Who was he with?"

"His wife. I didn't say hi. I was too intimidated. It was before the H&R Block thing."

Tremaine considered this kid, Matt Bishop. Just a young successful guy who has a tremendous amount of respect for Roger Gale. Tremaine wondered, though, if Matt was just going to tell him a series of Roger Gale Was Great stories. Stuff he could read in an ad magazine or online. But this kid did know the man, a little. He certainly offered more insight than Mary.

Matt was still talking. He said, "You know how committed Roger Gale was?"

Tremaine shook his head no.

"Okay, check this out. Roger found out Gale/Parker was going to be invited to the Ford pitch. This was years ago, when Gale/Parker was just starting to really explode. Anyway, they weren't going to be formally invited for a month or so, but Roger knew they were getting the nod. So, to research the company, to get a feel for it, Roger moves to Detroit and gets a job in one of the Ford plants. Not on the assembly line, nothing too technical, but still, doing manual labor in a plant. Busting his ass forty hours a week, working for Ford. He kept the job for more than a month, lived in Detroit, hung with those guys, the whole deal."

Tremaine looked at Matt. Watched him as he told the story of his idol with enthusiasm, even passion.

"Then the pitch rolls around," Matt said. "And Roger moves back to L.A. so he can work on it. Everybody here goes gangbusters for another month or so to prepare the creative. Then, the actual presentation rolls around. Roger presents the work, then goes on to tell the top brass at Ford how well Gale/Parker knows their business. And how he knows—personally—how hard the guys work to put the cars together. The grand finale was Roger pulling out his pay stubs, showing everybody that he'd taken a job at their company. Showing everybody that Gale/Parker wasn't full of shit when it came to understanding what goes into making Ford cars."

Tremaine said, "I'm assuming you guys won the business."

"They awarded the account to Gale/Parker that day."

Tremaine thought about the story, thinking, man, that's really going far out of your way to communicate your passion. Dramatic too, Roger Gale using the fact that he worked for Ford as an exclamation point to his pitch. Ta-da! Expecting a big guffaw from the room, almost. Not even considering that this might seem a little obsessive, a little invasive, a little weird. Maybe he just didn't care what it seemed like.

Tremaine said to Matt, "That's an impressive display of commitment. Risky, too. You never know how someone's going to respond to something like that."

"Yeah," Matt said. "Passion, creativity, with a little risk thrown in. That's what Roger Gale lived for."

Tremaine talked to some of the other creatives, some account execs, and Roger Gale's long-time assistant. They added to the image of Gale forming in Tremaine's head but didn't give him anything to sink his teeth into. No real knowledge of the man outside the halls of Gale/Parker.

That changed when he sat down with a man named Jack Sawyer.

CHAPTER 10

Jack Sawyer was a man Laurie had told Tremaine he had to talk to. When Tremaine got to Sawyer's office—his three orange steel walls—he was surprised to see an older man, maybe fifty-five, maybe even older, in jeans and cowboy boots sitting at an old polished wooden desk, one that had clearly been brought in.

"Excuse me," Tremaine said. "Are you Jack Sawyer?"

In a rusty, gravelly voice, the guy said, "That's me."

Sawyer stood up, bowlegged, a little bent over. This guy was an old cowboy working with a bunch of kids.

"I'm Donald Tremaine."

"Yeah, I know who you are," Sawyer said. "Donnelly told me you were coming. And I remember your old surf video. You were a crazy bastard."

Tremaine considered explaining that, no, he wasn't crazy, but why get into it? This guy seemed like a character, somebody who might tell him something he hadn't already read in the reports or online.

They shook.

"Have a seat," Sawyer said.

Tremaine did.

Sawyer said, "So, Nina hired you to figure out who killed Roger?"

"Yeah."

"Well, I can tell you, almost for sure, that nobody in these halls did it. I was one of the first employees hired here, and I know everyone who's ever worked here. There were people who got sour over getting passed up for a promotion or something. But nobody wanted Roger dead. Everyone respected him too much. The cops kept asking questions about whether he cheated on his wife because he kept such crazy hours, and there are women everywhere you look here. Have you noticed?"

Tremaine said, "Maybe."

"Maybe," Sawyer said. "I like that. But crazy hours, leaving the agency at midnight, grabbing a drink somewhere, things like that, that's advertising. That doesn't mean he's banging some broad in a broom closet. I suppose if he was having an affair with someone who worked here and she got pissed, she might have done it, but I don't think that happened. If he was having an affair, he wouldn't have been doing it here."

"Why is that?"

"Ad agencies are worse than sewing circles. Everyone knows everything about everyone. And if the big guy was involved with anyone, people would have found out. You know how you tell if two people at an agency are doing it?"

Tremaine shrugged.

"They don't talk to each other. The people flirting with each other, they're just having fun. The people ignoring each other . . ."

"They're having lots of fun," Tremaine said.

"Yeah," Sawyer said. "And it happens all the time in agencies 'cause you're here all the goddamn time. That's one of the reasons I got in the business. But Roger? I don't think he ever had that kind of fun, not here at least. I never heard anything like that. Never."

"What about outside the office?"

"I don't know. I don't really know what he did outside the office. He didn't socialize with people from the agency much."

"Who did he socialize with?"

"Fancy people. That was important to his wife."

"What do you mean? Hollywood types?"

"Not really. Old-money people. People down at L.A. Country Club. People who look down on Hollywood."

"That doesn't sound like Roger Gale's kind of crowd."

"I don't think it was, but why do you say that?"

"Well, I didn't know him, obviously. But the image I have of him so far is that he was an artist, a guy who cared about creativity, about substance. It doesn't seem like he'd be concerned with status that much. It seems like his work was his big passion."

"It was his big passion. That's why he was here all the time. That's why he went to some of the lengths he went to do great work. That's why he still wrote body copy at fifty-nine years old."

"Body copy?"

"Yeah. Body copy is . . . let's say you have a magazine ad. Well, there's the big headline up top. Then there's a couple paragraphs below it explaining all the great things about your product. Writers hate writing that shit 'cause nobody reads it. So they make the junior writers do it for them. But not Roger Gale. He still wrote it himself, even as head of the agency. He didn't care if no one read it; he wanted it to be perfect. That's passion."

Tremaine said, "So, back to the country club crowd . . ."

"Yeah," Sawyer said. "Roger's work was his passion. But his wife, she had her say, too, and she's a strong woman. And, like I said, that world was important to her."

"Right," Tremaine said. "When you're married, it's a give and take. I've been married. I know that to be true."

"Look at me." Sawyer said. "Do I look like the kind of guy who wants to go to Linens-N-Things this weekend?"

"No, you don't," Tremaine said, "but I bet that's what you're doing."

"That would be a smart bet. Because I love my wife."

Tremaine nodded and said, "Did Roger Gale love his wife?"

"I don't know," Sawyer said. "He acted like he did. But Roger Gale was a master manipulator. It's what he did for a living."

"And it's what he lived for."

"That's right," Sawyer said.

Tremaine liked Jack Sawyer, got a kick out of his candor, felt like he could ask him real questions.

Tremaine said, "Who, if anyone, do you think I should talk to?"

"It's a tough call. Nobody seems to know anything. I'm sure you'll talk to Evelyn, but she won't tell you much."

"Do you think she has much to tell?"

"I doubt she's hiding anything, but she didn't like the attention the murder brought. You know, nice people down at the club don't get murdered. So, even if there are little things that might help you, personality traits and whatnot, they'll be tough to pull out of Evelyn."

Tremaine said, "It always helps me to talk to people who knew a victim, even if they don't have much to say. I might find out later that they gave me more than I realized. This guy Matt Bishop, he basically just told me how great Roger Gale was . . . But he might have helped me. I just don't know yet."

"Well," Sawyer said. "I don't want you to find out later that I helped you. I want to help you now. There's this ad hack right down the road, Tyler Wilkes, that's who everybody thinks might have done it."

"I'm hearing his name a lot."

"Tyler runs an agency in El Segundo called Think Big. You'll love this guy. You think you've seen some poseurs around here? This clown's so caught up in competition and advertising, he might have been able to convince himself that Roger needed to die so he could win himself a sneaker account. Wait till you see his agency. He ripped off the design of this place just shamelessly. And did a bad job at that. He's also got a blow habit, so maybe he's crazy."

"How do you know about the blow?"

"The whole industry's a sewing circle, not just the individual ad agencies."

Tremaine kept talking to Sawyer. Turned out, Sawyer ended up asking as many questions as Tremaine. Wanted to know about his surfing career. Specifically, the parts where girls in bikinis came up out of nowhere and propositioned the world's number one.

"I thought you were married," Tremaine said.

"Doesn't mean I don't want to hear."

"It didn't happen that often," Tremaine said.

"Just lie to me and tell me it did."

Tremaine laughed and said, "Okay, it did."

Sawyer got a faraway look in his eye and said, "Really?"

On his way out, almost not believing he hadn't asked him yet, Tremaine said, "So, Jack, what do you do here?"

Sawyer said, "I'm just an old hack, now. Back in the day, though, I used to be a pretty good art director. Used to partner with Roger on all the early stuff."

Tremaine respected the old guy, still doing his thing after all these years.

"These days, though," Sawyer said. "I just come in here to make sure the place doesn't go to shit. Make sure it doesn't get too phony."

"I bet Roger would have appreciated that," Tremaine said.

"I hope so."

CHAPTER 11

Tremaine walked back to Laurie Donnelly's office after a long day at the agency. He was looking forward to talking to her, but he was really looking forward to *finishing* his talk with her, for no other reason than he wanted to go back to the trailer and catch an evening surf. He entered her space, with the four walls each a different height, and almost ran into her as she was on her way out of her office.

Now, standing right in front of him, she said, "Want to grab a beer?"

It took Tremaine off guard a bit and he said, "Now?"

"No. In a month. Yes, now."

She had that playful smile, the one she'd had when he'd first met her.

"Well," Tremaine said politely, "I was thinking of interviewing you here, then heading home for a surf."

"You can go for a surf anytime," Laurie said. "But I might not ever ask you to have a beer again." She smiled again and said, "Come on, it's a change of scenery. Plus, I have a joint."

"You're assuming just because I'm an old surf pro that I smoke pot."

"Yes," she said.

"Good guess."

She said, "Do you know a bar down the street called Brennan's?"

"Been there many times," Tremaine said.

"Well?" she said.

Having a drink with an attractive, mischievous, fortysomething woman whom he was interviewing for a case could lead to trouble.

So Tremaine said, "I'll meet you there."

At the bar, a nice, dark little dive, three beers and one joint in, Laurie said, "You know, to find out who killed him, it'd be nice."

"Nice?"

"I was very sad for a long time, I still am. But it's been a year and I can think about it now without that feeling of shock. I'm curious; I want to know why. Who hated him enough to kill him? You know?"

"You said you never saw him outside of work . . ."

"No one really did. Roger and his wife, they were society people. Big shots, even for L.A."

"Jack Sawyer told me that, said they hung around with the old-money crowd."

"Right," Laurie said. "Roger wasn't from that world, but he could fit in anywhere, and he used his charm on those people to get their business. Bank clients. Things like that. But I did know Roger pretty well because he worked all the time, so I was around him a lot. He didn't invite me down to the club, but when you're around someone that much, you get a feel for them. And I liked Roger Gale. I really liked him. He was so smart."

Laurie finished her beer and held her empty glass up to Tremaine to see if he wanted another. He did.

Tremaine said, "What about this guy Tyler Wilkes? Everybody seems to be talking about him."

"He's a poseur. A successful poseur but a poseur. No, not even successful, he was handed his agency by someone else who built it up. So he's always fighting that. Tyler's just one of the many creative directors in the business who was jealous of Roger. He's into drugs supposedly, too. He might have thought that if he killed Roger he could be the ad king of L.A. That people would start to respect him. That means a lot. There's a lot a money in advertising."

They sat there at the bar for another hour, talking about Roger Gale, to be sure, but moving off the subject, too. Talking about other things . . . Life.

Tremaine looked at Laurie. Into her forties, but still really sexy. She'd kept her figure up, and the corkscrew blonde hair fit her just right. It was wild, like her. Tremaine found himself now not so much looking at her as checking her out. He imagined what she looked like naked, standing in front of him.

The beers—and the joint—were sending his mind in a different direction, clouding his judgment. He liked it.

Tremaine snapped out of his daydream and said, "Did you ever notice anything unusual about Roger?"

"What do you mean?"

"What I mean is, was there ever anything, anything, that struck you as odd? I understand he was an unusual guy to begin with, taking a job on a Ford assembly line and things like that. But, did you ever have a moment where you said, that's *interesting*, even for him. It could be small, inconsequential, anything."

"Yes and no," Laurie said. "I got to work one morning really early. I was the first one in."

"Even before Mary O'Shaughnessy?"

Laurie laughed and said, "I know, she's such a climber. Anyway, I found Roger in his office asleep. In the same clothes from the day before. He woke up, right as I walked by his office."

"He'd slept there?"

"I guess. Now, we all worked late a lot. But we always went home eventually, even if it was five A.M. You know, go home, take a shower, come back around ten. That's why I said yes and no. Because it was kind of unusual, but on the other hand, Roger Gale was a workaholic, so who knows?"

Tremaine thought, maybe Roger did leave, but instead of going home he came back to work so it *looked* like he spent the night. But he didn't say it.

Two beers later, Tremaine said, "Laurie, it might be time to head home. I've got an old bulldog to walk."

Laurie looked at Tremaine and narrowed her eyes a bit. "When you walked in my office this morning, I got a little excited. I saw your old pictures online, but I still didn't expect you to be so cute."

"Oh, well, that's awfully nice of you to say."

"Don't be modest."

"It's my nature."

"Sure." Then Laurie said, "Want to come over? I live right in Santa Monica."

"I don't think that would be a very good idea," Tremaine said.

"Oh, yeah? Why not?"

"I don't want our relationship to be awkward. I might have to talk to you again about the case."

"Tremaine," she said. "I'm an adult. I'm not going to call you tomorrow and ask you to take me out to dinner."

"Laurie," Tremaine said, looking at her looking right at him. "You're very convincing. And I won't lie to you. I've thought, just during our time here, about what it would be like to go spend a little time together and possibly play a game or two of Twister. But I'm only good for a couple of nights. Then I run home to my trailer and my bulldog."

"I'm not looking for two nights," Laurie said. "Just one."

Laurie moved closer to Tremaine, her face was inches away from his, and her breasts were now pressed against his arm. He took a deep breath.

She said, "We don't even have to go to my house. Why don't we just go get in my car right now."

"What kind of car do you have?"

"A Honda Accord."

"It might be a little cramped," Tremaine said.

"Well, then we'll just have to move our bodies into interesting positions."

Tremaine downed his beer and said, "I have been taking yoga."

CHAPTER 12

The next morning, Tremaine woke up in the trailer, slammed some coffee, slammed the *New York Times*, slammed the Jumble, then called Evelyn Gale, Roger's widow.

"Hello," she said.

"Hello, Evelyn?" Tremaine said.

"Yes, who's calling?" she said.

"My name is Donald Tremaine, I'm a private investigator."

"Yes, Nina said you would be calling."

"Is this a bad time?" Tremaine heard some anxiety in Evelyn's voice, that unmistakable tone people exude when they want the other person on the line to know that it is indeed a bad time.

"No," she said. "It's fine."

"If you would be willing, I'd like to talk to you about your former husband."

"I don't think I can tell you anything that I haven't already told the police. Can't you just ask them?"

"Yes," Tremaine said, "but it would help me more to talk to you."

"So you can determine whether or not I had anything to do with it?"

Evelyn's comment was terse; she was on the offensive. She had the speech, even the voice, of a well-bred woman. And like so many well-bred women, she could inflect her words with an authoritarian edge and make it clear that she was not to be challenged by anyone.

Tremaine said, "Yes. So I can determine whether or not you had anything to do with it. And, so I can determine if you can help me determine who did have something to do with it, if you didn't."

Evelyn said, "I didn't mean to be rude, I know you're just doing your job. But we're finally putting all of this behind us. It's very painful to have a loved one killed. You may not understand this, but you can get to a point where you don't even care who did it; you just want it to be over."

"I'd like to talk to you in person, will you talk to me?"

"I suppose," she said. "By the way, the other detectives called me Mrs. Gale."

"Is that what you want me to call you?"

"I'm just wondering why you didn't?"

"Evelyn's your name, right?"

"Yes."

"That's why I didn't."

All right, Tremaine had made contact with Evelyn Gale, but he hadn't heard back from Tyler Wilkes. He'd called him twice and hadn't heard anything. Talked to his assistant—Heather, nice girl—but had gotten no confirmation through her of a meeting. And no call back.

Tremaine, at his desk, Lyle at his feet, thought about the fact that this guy Tyler Wilkes, this guy who lots of people were pointing the finger at, hadn't called him back. In his time as a P.I., Tremaine had learned a number of things to be true. One of them was that when people are contacted by a cop or a private investigator, they call back. And damn quickly, nine times out of ten. That one time out of ten that they don't call? It's usually because they've got something to hide. Occasionally, occasionally, someone is extremely busy or for whatever reason doesn't get the message. Or, in the rarest of cases, the person is so confident that they have nothing to hide, they're content to just wait until the investigator contacts them again. That's very rare, though. Like, bloody.

People when they're contacted by a P.I. immediately think something is wrong. They think *they* have done something wrong. They've forgotten to pay some bill or that some obscure, wholly unintentional misdoing from their past is coming back to haunt them. The initial reaction to a call from a P.I., whether innocent or guilty, is a defensive one. *This must be some mistake. I'll call that P.I. back right now.*

Another frequent scenario is, a person will think he or she is being contacted to provide information on a case. As a result, a sense of self-importance is created. The person will think, of course this P.I. wants to talk to me, I'm the kind of sensitive, intuitive thinker who will help them crack this case.

It's very similar to the reason reporters often don't have trouble getting people to talk to them. People *want* to talk to them, they want the attention, they want to obtain that feeling of importance and know that when the case is done or the article is written, they contributed.

But seldom do they not call back. Unless something is up.

So, Tremaine put in a call to John Lopez. He had a question for him, a question about Tyler Wilkes. He knew this question was going to cost him a steak dinner, they always did, so that night they decided to have just that, a steak dinner, at Taylor's, just west of downtown. Tremaine's treat.

When Tremaine entered Taylor's, John Lopez was already sitting down.

"Insane Tremaine," Lopez said as he stood up, Tremaine now within earshot.

"You know I don't like that nickname," Tremaine said.

"Yeah," Lopez said. "That's why I use it."

"Lopez," Tremaine said. "It's good to see you. Wait, no, actually it's not."

The two sat down, in the dark back booth that Lopez had selected. The AC was on full blast, it was damn near freezing in the place. Perfect. It had been a hot day, it felt good. There was a cold Budweiser on the table for Tremaine, another plus. Lopez had one too, his half drunk.

Tremaine and Lopez caught up, got a couple beers down, ordered.

About halfway into their steaks, they began to discuss the

matter at hand, Tyler Wilkes. "I looked into Wilkes for you. Looks like he may not be such a great guy," Lopez said.

"Surprise, surprise," Tremaine said. "Like I said, I got no call back from him after two messages."

"As you know," Lopez said, "he was never officially named a suspect in the Roger Gale case. And he was questioned pretty extensively by some of the detectives."

"Yeah, I read that. Larry DeSouza and Bill Peterson."

"Right. You can call them if you want. I told them about you."

"Cool."

"Peterson's actually in Atlanta now," Lopez said.

"What, he transferred?" Tremaine said.

"Yeah, I know, it's rare for detectives to transfer."

"Won't he have to start at the bottom? What does he know about Atlanta?"

"Usually that's the case. But Peterson knows the captain down there. He was able to keep his position and make more dough. I probably would have made the move, too. Cops don't make P.I. money."

"That's why I'm getting dinner," Tremaine said.

"No, you're getting dinner because I'm giving you privileged information on Tyler Wilkes."

"Oh, yeah," Tremaine said.

Lopez said, "DeSouza said Tyler Wilkes was really jealous of Roger Gale."

"Yeah, Wilkes has an agency down the street that doesn't get half the respect Roger Gale's place does."

"Right," Lopez said. "Everyone thought Wilkes might have been obsessed with Roger Gale. His agency looks like Roger Gale's, he used to always talk about him . . ."

"On top of that," Tremaine added, "no matter what Wilkes does, the rest of the ad community always accuses him of just copying the stuff Roger Gale did."

Lopez took a big swig of his beer and said, "They could never really get anything on him, though. You know that already. But the detectives then didn't know what I'm about to tell you. It hadn't happened yet. And it doesn't pertain to the Roger Gale thing."

"Before you tell me, let me tell you my suspicion," Tremaine said. "He talked to the cops at the time, willingly and regularly, right?"

"You saw the report. They grilled his ass."

"Well, I haven't told Wilkes why I'm calling. So he must not think I'm calling about that. Because even if he is hiding something about Roger Gale, he's figured out his spiel regarding that matter. He's got no reason to duck me. He didn't duck the police, why would he duck me? So maybe he's worried about something else."

"That's why you make the big bucks, Tremaine."

"Like I said, I'm getting dinner." Tremaine continued, "And if he is worried about something else, maybe I can confuse him into telling me something about Roger Gale before he figures out what exactly I'm going for."

Lopez grinned. "I'll tell you what I know."

"I'd appreciate it."

"Guy's been to rehab a few times. Probably into drugs and running a little paranoid."

"Good to know."

"This next piece of information, well, it's confidential."

With that, Tremaine flagged down the waitress.

"What do you need, boys?" she said.

"Get this gentleman a scotch on the rocks, top-shelf."

"My pleasure."

The waitress scurried off.

"Go on," Tremaine said.

"Tyler Wilkes made a huge investment in a cement company called L.A. Stone. This was after the Roger Gale investigation went cold. Here's the thing. A guy named Paul Spinelli started the company."

"Don't know the name."

"He's a guy we've suspected—we know—is involved in a tremendous amount of organized crime."

"How involved?"

"Very. He runs the show. He's the head guy."

"Family?"

"Not by blood. It's just an organization. And he's at the top. But for all the same reasons we always have trouble with these fucks, we've never been able to prove it."

"Tell me more about L.A. Stone."

"It's a real company and a total bullshit company all at once. Spinelli is connected to lots of the builders around town. So, knowing that, he creates a real cement company, hires some people who actually know what they're doing to run it, and then seizes all the business he can. Most of his employees just think they're working for the most successful company in town. Little do they know, the mob is arranging all the contracts they get. Other companies go through the bidding process, but L.A. Stone has a certain knack for obtaining business."

"So you don't know whether or not Tyler Wilkes has any knowledge of what he's into?"

"No one knows and no one cares. Regarding this issue,

no one is concerned with Tyler Wilkes. He's a pawn. But the reality is, Paul Spinelli approached Wilkes with a win-win business proposal. And Paul Spinelli, when you see him, when you look at him, he's scary. He's shady. You can tell. I'd bet a lot of money Wilkes has some suspicions of his own. He may even know exactly what's up. That he's in bed with some serious people. Either way, your having that information could frighten him a little bit, keep him off balance."

"Let me ask you this," Tremaine said. "How scary is Spinelli? How scared would Tyler be if he thought he'd pissed off Spinelli?"

"Very," Lopez said. "They call Spinelli the Shark. For three reasons. One, he goes after business like a shark. Two, he's always moving. And three, he kills with no remorse."

"Well then," Tremaine said, "that's the perfect nickname for him."

"Yeah, it is."

Tremaine looked at Lopez.

"What?" Lopez said.

"You parting with this confidential information? Lemme guess, some of the higher-ups down at the old station house are involved in this whole bullshit and are intentionally making it difficult to make a bust. And it's pissing you off."

"You said it, not me."

"You're a good man, Charlie Brown," Tremaine said. Lopez didn't respond. He just downed his top-shelf scotch on the rocks.

CHAPTER 13

Tremaine's hangover, from his night with Lopez, made the Jumble slow-going. He sat there, at his desk in the trailer, big cup of coffee, medicine, sitting never too far away. The words were: MYAIT, DAHYN, CABEEM, and BOEDUL. The riddle was *What the hairdresser did when the rack of clothes went on sale. He "_ _ _ _ _ _ _" _ _ _ _.*

It took him almost three minutes to turn MYAIT into AMITY, DAHYN into HANDY, CABEEM into BECAME, and BOEDUL into DOUBLE. It took him another forty-five seconds to get the riddle. To turn MTHDECMOBE into COMBED THEM. *What the hairdresser did when the rack of clothes went on sale. He "combed" them.*

Tremaine looked at the stopwatch. Pathetic. Almost four minutes. His worst time in years.

Trapped in a hungover daydream, he was a little startled by his cell phone ringing. "Donald Tremaine," he said, after hitting the "talk" button.

"Hi. This is Heather, from Tyler Wilkes's office."

"Sure. How're you doing?"

"Oh, fine. Sorry it's taken a few days to get back to you."

"No problem."

"Tyler would like to schedule an appointment with you."

Tremaine thought, it's about time. Then he thought, I'm actually glad he waited a few days. Sure, it gave *him* time to prepare, but it also gave *me* time to prepare.

"Good," Tremaine said. "When?"

"How 'bout tomorrow morning at ten?"

"I'll be there."

The next day, at five till, Tremaine pulled the Cutlass into Think Big Advertising. Everybody's right, he thought, place looks a little like Gale/Parker. But not quite as . . . cool. Tremaine got out of his car and found the reception area. There, too, he thought, Think Big's aesthetic mirrored Gale/Parker's. But just a little off.

Tremaine sat in the reception area, waiting. On the coffee table, scattered about, were trade publications— *ADWEEK, Ad Age, Electronic News*, and the *Hollywood Reporter*. He noticed there were an abundance of *AD-WEEK*s and only one copy of the others. Must be the most important one.

So he picked it up. That's when he realized why there

were more of this particular trade than the others. Tyler Wilkes was on the cover. Clad in black with blue-tinted glasses, even though in the photo he sat inside at a conference table. Above the vanity shot of Tyler there was a headline that said: THINK BIG IS GETTING BIGGER. Then underneath the headline, in much smaller type, it said: BUT DO THEY GET RESPECT?

Tremaine flipped through the magazine and found the article on Tyler Wilkes. It said Tyler Wilkes hadn't come up through the ranks like most ad guys. Five years ago, it said, he was a mid-level copywriter at a tiny agency in San Diego when his cousin married Bob Means, the sixty-five-year-old founder and creative director of an L.A.–based ad agency called Think Big. Think Big, at the time, was in a twenty-five story building in Westwood and was sturdy and profitable, but far from glamorous. Health care accounts, insurance accounts, and car dealerships. Tyler Wilkes and Bob Means met at the wedding and hit it off. Wilkes was into his forties, but Means thought of him as the son he never had. Six months later, Means retired and announced the new creative director: Tyler Wilkes.

Wilkes promptly moved the agency to an open-space warehouse in El Segundo and hired younger, "hipper" talent all in an attempt "to change the culture." The article noted that the space Wilkes built was "clearly influenced" by nearby Gale/Parker and didn't really fit with the work or the clients Think Big had. Most surprisingly, the article questioned both Tyler's advertising history and his creative abilities, pointing out that he had a reputation for being arrogant, and that the recent growth of the agency was mostly the result of one of their insurance accounts merg-

0

ing with another company. The piece all but came out and called him a poseur.

Tremaine wondered why Tyler would have this magazine on display. No such thing as bad publicity?

He finished the article and was sort of half-reading the rest of the magazine when he heard, "Are you Mr. Tremaine?"

Tremaine looked up to see what can only be described as an absolute vision of a young woman. Shockingly, distractingly gorgeous. Playboy Bunny, but better, more sophisticated. Tremaine thought, how could one describe this woman and do her justice? Got it. Long blonde hair, big tits, perfect ass. Crass, maybe, but there was simply no other way. How can you have that up top and that down there? He was asking himself this seriously; he really wanted to know. This one, she simply defied physics. She was a work of art. Tremaine was trying desperately not to just stare. Or run, headfirst, into a wall. But it was hard. She was incredible, magical, standing there, black pants, black shirt, big white smile.

"Yes," Tremaine said. "I'm Donald Tremaine."

He stuck out his hand and stood up. She shook it and smiled. Tremaine felt her hand in his. Soft, a little cool. Man, this woman was incredible. Tremaine was entirely polite. Again, just making an observation . . .

"I'm Heather," she said. "Tyler's assistant."

"Nice to meet you," he said.

"Tyler is ready to see you. I'll take you to his office."

The two walked into the agency. Donald looked around and again noticed the similarities between Think Big and

 0

Gale/Parker. The fact that the aesthetic of this shop was an imitation of Gale/Parker was just plain obvious. No wonder everybody said it. It was true. It was the stepchild version of Gale/Parker. The open spaces weren't quite as open. The exposed steel was painted an oddly depressing bright green. And, off in a corner, there was, almost unbelievably, one of those basketball shooting games you see in bars. It all contributed to an ersatz feel, like it was *trying* to be hip. Granted, the Gale/Parker space was itself a bit contrived, but it was really good contrived. Really well done, impressive, and, above all, original. This place just missed. Like a knockoff of a popular brand. Close, but no cigar. It reminded Tremaine of his surfing days when a company would rip off a shaper's design. The board would basically look like the custom-shaped one, but if you looked close you could tell. And if you took it for a ride, baby, it was night and day.

They arrived at a big, centrally located office, very similar to the awards room that used to be Roger Gale's office at Gale/Parker.

"Here we are," Heather said.

Tremaine looked in Tyler Wilkes's office and saw Tyler wearing an outfit that resembled the one he had on in the picture on the cover of *ADWEEK*. Except this time he had red-tinted sunglasses on. Tyler was on the phone and he held up a finger indicating to Tremaine and Heather to hold on a sec, he'd be off the phone in a minute.

Heather went back to her desk, a few feet away from the entrance to Tyler's office, and sat down. A young guy with a shaved head slowly slid by on a skateboard, the skateboard making that great sound on the exposed cement floor. As he passed Tremaine, he said under his breath, "We call her Drop-Dead Heather."

"Huh?" Tremaine said. But the skateboarder was already ten feet away, out of earshot.

Then Tremaine looked at Heather sitting there at her desk and thought to himself, oh, right, Drop-Dead Heather.

Tremaine looked back into Tyler Wilkes's office. Tyler hung up the phone and got up from his desk. Tremaine expected to be greeted at this juncture, but instead Tyler put up his finger again, indicating hold on one more second. Then Tyler went into a separate, closed-off room that adjoined his office. Probably a bathroom. Tyler shut the door, then reemerged thirty seconds later. Odd.

Tyler walked out of his office to where Tremaine stood. "Tyler Wilkes," he said, extending a hand.

Tremaine was now seated in a chair in front of Tyler's massive black desk.

"Do you like our offices? They're pretty new still," Tyler said. Tremaine looked at this guy, his cocky smile.

"They remind me of the Gale/Parker offices," Tremaine said.

"But not in a way that looks like we ripped them off, right?" Tyler sucked in air through his nose.

The bathroom trip.

Tyler continued talking. "We didn't copy them, their style, I mean. Their style in terms of the office is what I'm saying. Or their style in terms of advertising! We would never do that. And the ad community knows that."

Tremaine didn't say anything. Tyler asked him another

question. "So what is this about? The Roger Gale case from a year ago?"

"Sure," Tremaine said. "We can talk about that."

"Hey, I've already answered those questions. I had nothing to do with that guy getting killed. I've got nothing more to say on the issue. If you want to hear the things I said, you can just go look at the police files. P.I.s can do that, right? I talked to the cops over and over. I've told them everything I know. Which is nothing."

Man, Tremaine thought, this guy's wired out of his tree. He must have gone into the bathroom and stuck his nose in a pile of blow.

"Listen," Tyler continued. "I'm a busy guy. I'm running a six-hundred-million-dollar ad agency. A six-hundred-million-dollar agency that's growing. And the ad community knows that. So, like I said, I really don't have anything more to say about Roger Gale."

"Could you tell me your relationship to him?"

"Look, I've got nothing more to say. I figured this was why you were coming to talk to me. Anyway, I said it all a year ago. Why don't you go talk to his wife. He used to cheat on her, that's what I heard."

"I'm going to talk to his widow. But right now, I'm talking to you."

"Well, I'm through talking about that."

"Then let's talk about other stuff."

Tremaine looked at Tyler Wilkes, looked right through those red-tinted glasses and said, "Tyler, do you do any investing?"

Tyler now studied Tremaine. He looked caught off guard, worried.

"Yeah, I invest," Tyler said. "That's how you make money." Tyler paused and said, "Look, what do you want to know about Roger Gale? I guess I can go over it again."

Tremaine said, "What was your relationship to him?"

"We were business competitors."

"Would you say you were equals?"

Tyler Wilkes shifted in his chair. "No. Roger Gale was a legend. But, right now, my shop is damn close to outbilling Gale/Parker."

"Did you build your shop to look like Gale/Parker?"

"No, and no one in this business thinks that."

"The ADWEEK article I just read indicated that people in the business do think that."

"That ADWEEK writer wants to be doing what I'm doing. He's just jealous. No one who matters thinks that."

Tremaine looked at Tyler, some perspiration forming on his forehead, above the glasses. Tremaine said, "So, what kind of stuff do you invest in? Companies?"

Tyler didn't answer right away. He looked out his window, maybe at Heather, maybe into space.

"Tyler?" Tremaine said.

"I invest in all kinds of stuff. The market, companies, my own company."

Then Tremaine said, "Would you say that advertising is a cut-throat business?"

"What are you here to talk to me about?" Tyler said.

"Roger Gale," Tremaine said.

"Okay. Yeah, I would say advertising is a cut-throat business."

"Do you think someone in advertising would kill someone else in advertising over billings, over money? Is it that cut-throat?"

"I don't know what you're implying, Tremaine," Tyler said, a little more self-assured now, back to where he was when Tremaine first walked in.

"I'm asking you a question," Tremaine said. "Is it that cut-throat?"

"I don't know," Tyler said. "I know *I* would never do that. I don't need to. Look at my agency. It's huge. We win accounts just based on our work, nothing else."

"When you win an account," Tremaine said, "do you usually get to know the owner of the company?"

"Yes. If it's a private company, of course. That's who gives us the business."

"So, you have relationships with lots of company owners?"

"Yeah, I do."

"Do you know owners of other companies? Ones that you don't do ads for?"

"What's this about? Is this about Roger Gale?"

"We can talk about that. I already told you that."

"So ask me a question about Roger Gale?"

"In a minute. Give me the name of someone who owns a company who you know, but don't do ads for."

"Why?"

"Why not?"

"What does this have to do with Roger Gale?"

"You tell me."

"What?"

"I've got to go, Tyler. Thanks for talking to me," Tremaine said.

"You're done?"

"Do you have something else to tell me?"

Tyler Wilkes stood up. Tremaine stayed seated. In the same position he was in for the entirety of their conversation.

Tremaine said, "If you do have something you want to tell me, just call me."

He pulled a card out of the breast pocket in his shirt and threw it on Tyler Wilkes's desk. It said DONALD TREMAINE, PRIVATE INVESTIGATOR. Underneath that it had two phone numbers and an e-mail address.

Tremaine got up and headed for Tyler Wilkes's office door.

"Tremaine," Tyler said.

Tremaine turned around.

"Why did you ask me about my investments and about company owners and all that bullshit?"

"Why do you think?"

"I don't know, that's why I asked."

"That's what P.I. work is, Tyler. Taking all the things about a case or a person and trying to connect them." Then Tremaine said, "Where are you from, Tyler? Where'd you grow up?"

"Phoenix," Tyler said.

"Hmm," Tremaine said and walked out.

Out in the parking lot, Tremaine opened the door to the Cutlass and heard, "Donald." It was Heather, Tyler's assistant, heading toward him. She trotted up and, jeez, he couldn't help but notice again, wow, the body, the hair . . .

She was one of those women you see in magazines, but not in life.

"Hey, I've got a question for you," she said.

"Yeah."

"Stand like this," she said. And she put her left foot out in front of her and then she held her hands behind her back. Tremaine, playing along, did what Drop Dead Heather said to do.

Heather looked at him and said, "Yep. You're him. You're Insane Donald Tremaine. My brother, my *older* brother, had that poster of you from a long time ago where you were standing kinda like that."

"Yeah, right," Tremaine said. "At Pipe, in Hawaii."

"I thought I recognized the name when you first called, but it's been a long time since I've seen that poster. But my brother happened to call while you were talking to Tyler."

Tremaine nodded. There was some silence, awkward maybe.

"Do you still surf?" she said, moving a step closer to him.

"Yeah, sure." This girl was unbelievable. Part blonde beach babe, part high-style executive type.

"I used to look at that poster all the time," she said. "The way you were standing on the board like it was so easy."

"Give the credit to the photographer. He captured a moment of calm in a pretty intense situation."

"I remember the bathing suit you were wearing. Red with a lightning bolt down the side. They were kind of short-shorts, too."

"That was the style back then."

"I liked them."

Boy, it had been a while since a young, beautiful girl talked about a surfing poster of his. But she's way too young, right? This would be robbing the cradle something fierce.

Right?

"Listen, Donald, take my card. If I can ever help you with getting in touch with Tyler or whatever, call me."

She handed Tremaine her card.

"Thanks, Heather."

"Aren't you going to give me *your* card?"

He handed Heather one of his cards, the same one he had given Tyler.

Heather said, "You know, we don't have to talk about Tyler. We could just have a drink or something."

Tremaine put on his sunglasses, some old gold wire rims, and heard himself say, "I think we could arrange that."

That robbing the cradle thing? Yeah, that went out the window.

Then, inexplicably, Tremaine said, "I'm probably twice your age, you know." It sounded unnatural, off, like a stock comment, like something you say just because you've heard it before.

She said, "So."

Sometimes the simplest logic was the best.

Tremaine said, "You make a good point."

She smiled and said, "I can see myself in the reflection of your glasses. I look funny," she added.

Tremaine thought, I can think of another word for how you look.

"Well, bye, Donald. It was nice to meet you."

"It was nice to meet you, too," Tremaine said.

And it was nice. Yes, very nice.

She walked away. Toward the entrance of Think Big. Her blonde hair falling to the top of her tight, but not too tight, black pants. Tremaine, sitting in his Cutlass, idling, said out loud to no one, almost involuntarily "She's special." Then he cranked up the Cutlass and pulled out of the parking lot.

Tremaine got home, straightened up the trailer, walked Lyle, thought things over. Later, he grabbed his longboard and drove down to the surf break nearest his house, just down the hill, a great little Malibu break. It was the evening glass-off. Waves weren't big, but the ocean was smooth, calm. The sun was a big orange ball slipping behind the horizon and the air was warm but not hot. Tremaine was alone out there. He'd see cars go by on the PCH and a person or two on the beach, but he was alone, just him and the waves, just him and his thoughts.

And he loved it.

He picked up a wave, rode it right, toward the shore. He glided up and down, up and down, not pulling any serious moves, just doing a little soul surfing, and searching.

Tyler Wilkes, he thought. A poseur, an asshole, probably a liar. Probably aware that his investments are shady. But a murderer? Who knows? You don't have to be cunning and convincing and impressive to kill someone. Quite the opposite, most of the time. A power–hungry, jealous drug addict could kill someone, might kill someone. But why, exactly? Was it just to get more business, to take out the other big shot in town? Did he have any other kind of relationship with Roger Gale, business or otherwise? According to phone records they never even spoke. Not once. Tremaine thought, I got him a little confused, though. He's not sure what I'm after. I'll use that to get what I need. Eventually . . .

And what about Roger Gale's late nights? The cops looked into his running around. Sawyer mentioned it. Tyler, too. Was there anything there other than a hard worker and an eccentric? That might be for Evelyn Gale to answer tomorrow, if he could get her to talk.

Tremaine, back at the trailer, having a beer, giving Lyle a pet. Roger Gale, Tremaine thought—who is this guy? What was he doing that nobody seems to know about or want to talk about? What got him killed?

Tremaine fell asleep right there on his couch in the main room, tired from lots of nights out. The one with his old friend Lopez, the one in a Honda Accord with his new friend Laurie Donnelly. Tired. Like dog, like owner.

CHAPTER 14

Tremaine pulled the Cutlass up to Evelyn Gale's palatial house in Bel Air. He thought, again, about getting into advertising. Then he remembered that Evelyn Gale had money, too, had money before her Roger Gale days, so advertising didn't necessarily buy the house.

He got out and looked at the fortress before him. Huge and beautiful. But, like a lot of the houses in Bel Air, it was isolated. Hidden by walls of greenery and shrubbery, a perfect lot, big and beautiful and manicured, but no sense of community. And no ocean nearby. At least at my place, Tremaine thought, you could see the ocean. Yes, you could also see some fast food joints and a Dumpster or two, but, whatever, you could indeed see the ocean.

He rang the doorbell. He heard some dogs barking—

not open-the-door-and-I'll-kill-you barks, just augment-ing-the-doorbell barks. The door swung open and there was Evelyn Gale, flanked by two brown curly-haired dogs looking at Tremaine skeptically. Tremaine looked at Evelyn. Elegant, beautiful. Thin and perfectly dressed. Classic-looking clothes and a gold necklace fashioned to look like a rope. Tighten it up and tie it into a knot and it could be a noose, a golden noose.

Introductions, and then she led him inside. Tremaine bent down and gave a proper hello to the two dogs.

"Portuguese water dogs," Tremaine said. "I love these things."

"That's Clio and Addy."

These were the names of advertising awards, Tremaine had learned. "After the awards," Tremaine said.

"Yes. They were given to us by my son, Phillip."

Phillip Cook. Tremaine had an appointment to talk to him.

"He named them," Evelyn said. Then, "Shall we sit out-side?"

Shall? Funny word, Tremaine thought. Who uses "shall"? People who live in Bel Air? Moses?

Tremaine followed Evelyn Gale through the house. Beau-tifully done. Wood and white everywhere. Big windows and doors, sunken rooms, the place impeccably designed to feel cozy despite its size, and open and warm despite the obvious wealth that buttressed it. Tremaine looked at the pictures that sat on end tables and hung on walls. These told a slightly different story. A little more pride, a little less dignity. Lots of Roger still up. Some with the two of them, some with friends, some with celebrities. But only dignified

A-listers. Movie stars with a political bent. Tremaine sure as hell didn't see Evelyn and Roger standing with Lou Diamond Phillips or Webster or the bass player from Foghat.

There were even some photos with presidents. Tremaine looked at a picture with Roger and Evelyn Gale standing next to a smiling Bill Clinton. He wanted to ask if it was real, but his private-eye skills told him it was.

It occurred to Tremaine that Roger's semi-celebrity status mattered to Evelyn. And he was the perfect kind of semi-celebrity. He wasn't a matinee idol, he was a businessman with a creative side. People at the L.A. Country Club could respect him, not be thrown by the fact that others knew of him by name and sight. Because the people who did know who he was weren't mall rats in Oklahoma. They were other smart business and advertising people. He was like a famous CEO. Like Jack Welch or Sam Walton. That kind of fame is what Evelyn liked, was *proud of*.

Outside, there was a garden and a sprawling lawn. Because the house was atop a hill, you could see down into the grounds of other Bel Air estates, estates that sat lower than Evelyn's on the hill. There was a quiet up in these hills. The other houses Tremaine could see almost looked like photographs. Still and small down below. Evelyn guided Tremaine to a table underneath an umbrella. A pitcher of iced tea waited for them.

She said, "This isn't easy for me to talk about. I was close to putting it behind me. Not his death, obviously, but the constant thinking about who is responsible."

She said it with that impatient edge, the one Tremaine had already heard on the phone.

"I understand. Thank you for talking to me," he said.

"My husband loved surfing. He's smiling somewhere knowing that you're on this case."

She was paying him a compliment, but there was some condescension there, too. She couldn't hide it, and even if she could, she couldn't hide it from Tremaine.

Sitting there, under the umbrella, Tyler Wilkes's comment rang in Tremaine's head: *Ask his wife, he used to cheat on her. . . .* Tremaine took a sip of his tea, thinking, I bet this woman wouldn't admit it if there was infidelity. No, she was too proud. That would be exposing a scar, a scar she didn't make but someone else did. No control.

Tremaine said, "Jack Sawyer told me that there was no way anyone at Gale/Parker killed your husband. Do you agree?"

"Yes, I do. In fact, I don't think anyone in the industry killed him."

"Why?"

"Advertising is a serious business. These companies live and die by what accounts they have. But have you gone into any of these agencies?"

"A couple."

"These people aren't dangerous. The older people dress slick and the younger ones dress hip, but these are normal people with jobs. And aside from a few people like Roger, most people are only half-committed. You've got to be committed to kill. But most of the writers in advertising want to be novelists. The art directors want to be artists. The account people want to be rich. And it's not like the movies or even Wall Street, where there's a shot at getting rich overnight. It takes years of work and determination and luck. Years. People pointed the finger at Tyler Wilkes.

What would he get out of it? Roger being dead doesn't mean he would get any more accounts. He still has to win them. I mean, really. What good would killing my husband do Tyler Wilkes?"

"The cops thought he might be obsessed with your husband, jealous to the point of obsession."

"Maybe. Tyler certainly isn't respected, and I'm sure that makes him crazy. But if he was obsessed, all the investigating in the world isn't going to help you or anyone else. You can't follow clues when someone has killed someone else because of a mental illness. There's no rhyme or reason to it."

"And in this case, there's no evidence either."

They sipped their tea. Tremaine thought, iced tea, it's good, I don't drink it often enough. But it's kind of a pain in the ass to make . . .

Tremaine said, "Do you have any theories, Evelyn?"

"Yes," she said. "I think it was a random accident of some kind. My husband was in the wrong place at the wrong time and somebody killed him and then deposited him at the agency to confuse people. It certainly would be easy to figure out who he was and where he worked. I just don't know why anyone would want to kill him. He didn't owe anyone money, he wasn't into drugs, he didn't have some life I didn't know about."

She was so sure of this. Tremaine said, "You mean he didn't have affairs?"

"Yes, that's what I mean. And I know that's why you're here, to ask me that. Everyone else did. And no, my husband did not have affairs. He came home every night. Every night, unless he was out of town. The employees at

Gale/Parker said he had crazy hours and they'd see him having a drink somewhere late at night. Well, guess what? He'd just left work and was winding down before he came home. And he'd probably just called me."

Tremaine thought, well, there was at least one night he didn't come home. Laurie Donnelly had told him that. And, man, this woman was defensive. And strong. She definitely wouldn't have liked the way an affair would have made *her* look. She was protective of herself and her husband and that was understandable, but this was more than that. Evelyn Gale needed to look good in the eyes of others. And she needed to be right.

"Roger and I," she said, "were married later in life. We didn't have any kids, which some people use to stay together. We didn't need that. We had a wonderful relationship. A loving, intellectual relationship. We loved to talk about books and movies and plays and business. We loved each other. He didn't run around. He didn't."

Tremaine sat for a moment, took another sip of his tea, and said, "Let's get back to Tyler Wilkes."

"Okay," she said. Her demeanor a little more relaxed now, she didn't need to stand quite as tall on this subject.

Tremaine said, "Why do you think he was questioned so extensively? Sure, he copied your husband when he built his new agency. He openly revered the guy, was openly jealous of him. But the two never talked. There are no phone records, nothing. For all intents and purposes, they had no relationship."

"I'll tell you why, Mr. Tremaine. They had nothing else. That's why I don't know if you or anyone else can solve this case. Nobody had any real motive. And if Tyler

Wilkes did it, nobody could catch him in a lie or force him to say something he didn't want to say."

"Nobody yet," Tremaine said.

Evelyn didn't respond; she just sipped her tea and looked down the hill at the other estates. Tremaine turned and looked, too. You could see lots of them, just sitting there, still and small in the distance.

CHAPTER 15

Tremaine pulled the Cutlass onto Rialto in Venice. He was going to Nina's, this time with an invitation. There was still some light left in the sky, he was getting a better look at Nina's block. He'd been down this street a million times before, but only now was he looking at it through the filter of knowing someone, of working for someone, of being intrigued by someone, who lived here.

Tremaine parked between a beat-up '71 VW Beetle and brand-new silver Maserati.

Tremaine knocked on Nina's door. It opened.

"Donald, thanks for coming by," Nina said as she ushered him in.

Tremaine realized now more than ever how pretty Nina was. Looking more casual than the first few times they had met, standing there in jeans and a T-shirt, but somehow looking even better.

"Can I get you a beer?" she said.

"Yes."

Tremaine had that feeling you get when someone invites you to their house, that good feeling, that feeling where the chemistry is just a little better, a little warmer than when you see someone in a neutral place. One person has reached out to the other and the other has accepted. Tremaine was glad to be there. He could even detect a little spark that she was glad that he was there. Not in a romantic sense, just in the way that says, we could be friends, it's good to see you, have a seat, have a beer, let's catch up.

Tremaine filled Nina in, sort of. Moving forward with Tyler Wilkes, with Evelyn Gale, just giving her brushstrokes, no details really. There weren't any yet. The speculation? That was only for Tremaine at this point. Nonetheless, he knew it was good to give a progress report, even if he hadn't yet made much progress.

Yeah, that's why he was over here. Not because he kind of missed her. Not because she was the type of woman his wife had been, the type that he wasn't able to make it work with. Smart, sexy, deep. Hey, she'd invited him. After he'd called and said let's get together.

But who's counting?

Tremaine took a swig of his beer and looked around her house. This time he could take it in, he wasn't rushing, wasn't guided by the fact that she might come home any minute and say, What the fuck are you doing here?

He looked at all the books, really able to see her collection now. Man, there were some good ones, ones you wouldn't necessarily expect to see on the same shelf. Robert Pirsig and Charles Bukowski. Toni Morrison and John D. MacDonald.

"You've got some good books in here," Tremaine said. *"Ham on Rye.* Bukowski. One of my all time favorites."

"Me too," she said. "He was a brute, but he had a heart."

"I love the scene where Chinaski is walking down the street with his face covered in gauze because he'd had his bad skin worked on."

"Yeah," she said. "And at that moment he felt better than ever, because he didn't have to face the world."

"And he felt so good that he lit up a smoke and strutted down the street, gauze and all."

They both laughed, enjoying that memory, that image.

Nina said, "He could be so vulnerable and so tough at the same time. It's a good combination."

"Yeah. And he's funny. He says stuff that's so bleak, but it's somehow hilarious. I always wondered how he did that."

"Found that tone."

"Right."

They stood there with their beers. Silent, for a moment. Wonder what's on her mind?

He said, "Did you always want to be a teacher?"

"Yeah. I haven't been at it too long, but I like it a lot. Lately, though, I've been concentrating on my book."

"How's it coming?"

"Slowly. But steadily enough."

Tremaine wanted to say, "I've read some of it, it rocks."

But he knew that would probably get him fired. So he said, "It's about your divorce . . ."

"Nope. It's about an ex-surfer who's now a P.I."

"You should consult with me. I might be able to help."

Then she said, "Yeah, it's about my divorce. But it's really about any divorce. I think. I hope."

"Like I said, you should consult with me."

"I've got myself for that one."

"Right . . ."

They had another drink and chatted more about her book and some of the other books she had on the shelf and she asked Tremaine about being a P.I. and he told her some tales from the job.

Then he said, "So, what's Darryl like?"

Nina, looking at her bookshelf, yanked her head around and said, with some terror in her eyes, "How'd you know about Darryl?"

"Because he's right here. I read his tag."

Darryl had entered silently, had slinked across the floor, and had quietly, deftly hopped up on a stool next to Tremaine. He was sitting, almost posing, looking right at Nina.

"Oh, Darryl's great. Does what he pleases, all the time."

"Darryl?"

"This little girl on my block back in Connecticut named him. He was just a kitten. Sean and I, Sean's my ex, got him from a neighbor, and we were walking home, and this little girl rode up on her bike and said, 'You should name him Darryl.' That's all she said. So we did."

Darryl looked at Tremaine with those magical, wild,

beautiful cat eyes. And then one of Darryl's eyes, just one of them, slowly closed and opened. It was a slow, strange, cat wink, that said to Tremaine, I know you, man, you've been here before. And then Darryl sprung down from the stool and zipped out the open sliding glass door, just as Tremaine had.

Tremaine left Nina's feeling good, looking forward to his next report with her, even if he didn't have anything to say.

Driving away from Nina's, Tremaine thought about their conversation, particularly the divorce part. Thought about the passage he'd read of her book and how much he liked it, knew it. He pulled out a smoke and lit it up. Man, it's brave for Nina to pull out the memories from her divorce and turn them into something. He wanted to read more. Maybe he needed to read more. Tremaine knew the pain of divorce, how it hurt to think about it at all, even for a second. And how, even though he'd never be back with Susan, some of him still loved her, and always would.

He dropped down onto the PCH, the sky black now. He couldn't help it; he was going over the things that led to his split. He remembered, first, when he and Susan met, how it felt so right. And then as time passed, how he began to slowly shut down, almost like a dying machine. He couldn't control it. She was always there for him, beautiful, bright, loving, everything. But he couldn't do it. He couldn't function as one of two. And so he, almost in a predetermined way, began to destroy it. He thought about how eventually he just turned off, trapped in a permanent state of ambivalence. He remembered how Susan had said that his inability to love her all the way was a result of the incident during his surfing days, the incident they never talked about. And Tremaine thought now as he did then that she was right. And it made him sick to think about it, how she'd said she'd do anything to help him get over it, how she'd questioned why he didn't want to try. Questioned why he seemed to want the solitary life she had pulled him out of. And how she'd eventually began to accuse him of simply being afraid, of fearing the intimacy she'd offered him.

Bingo. Susan, hitting the target dead center. But, Tremaine thought now, as he had then, he just couldn't see not doing what he did. Leaving. He remembered, it was crystal clear, how he'd left her, standing there, beautiful and willing to keep trying. He knew, then, now, always, that he was better off alone.

Yeah, Tremaine thought, pulling into the trailer park transfixed on the wretched memory of his divorce, Nina's brave to dredge that up. But she'll get something out of it. And other people will, too.

Me, probably.

CHAPTER 16

Tremaine woke up, 7:00 A.M., feeling good, feeling rested, lying in his bed in the back of the trailer. The first thought that popped into his head: Who killed Roger Gale and why? The second thought that popped into his head: Where's my L.A. *Times*? I'm going to crucify that goddamn Jumble. And he did. He sat there at his desk, coffee not ready yet, but that's okay, he didn't need its help, not this morning. The words were: OSSUE, PUREP, YATHAP, and KIPTEC. The riddle was *What the timber boss took to work. His "_ _ _ _ _ _ _."*

In less than a minute, he turned OSSUE into SOUSE, PUREP into UPPER, YATHAP into APATHY, and KIPTEC into PICKET. Five seconds later, he turned PRHOPEC into CHOPPER. *What the timber boss took to work. His "chopper."*

Tremaine looked at the stopwatch: fifty-five seconds. Not bad. Not bad at all. Mind was sharp, ready to figure some shit out. After that, he walked the bulldog, hit the waves, hopped in the Cutlass. He had a meeting with Phillip Cook at the prestigious L.A. Country Club.

Donald Tremaine had never been to the Los Angeles Country Club, but he knew at the very least he was dressed appropriately because he had called and asked and said he was a guest of Phillip Cook's and inquired as to what he should wear to have lunch at the Grill by the golf course. Collared shirt, short sleeves were fine, and pants, no jeans. He could swing that. He would even throw on a blue blazer for good measure.

He'd put on some khakis, grabbed a short-sleeved dark blue sport shirt, slid into the blazer, and now he was on Wilshire, finishing a smoke in the Cutlass, just about to enter the gates to the club.

His phone rang. He looked at it, at the caller ID. Nina, it said.

"Hi, Nina," Tremaine said.

"Hi, Donald," she said.

Donald. He liked that.

Nina was laughing, not guffawing, just laughing, when she said, "I forgot to tell you something about Phillip. Are you already at the club?"

"Just about to enter," Tremaine said.

"Good, I caught you in time. Phillip has a glass eye."

Tremaine laughed.

"A glass eye?" Tremaine said. "I've never seen one in person before. That's very Sammy Davis of him."

"Yeah, it's absurd. I thought you should know before

you met him so it wouldn't freak you out. Not that it would. I mean, I'm sure you can handle yourself."

"Thanks for telling me."

"Well, I know you have to go."

"Yeah, I'll keep you posted."

Neither one wanted to hang up, but neither one really had anything else to add, either.

Nina said, "Okay, talk to you soon, Donald."

"Yep," he said. And he would talk to her soon. Because he'd call her.

The guy at the gate gave Tremaine a little look as he pressed the button to let the Cutlass enter the grounds.

"Park anywhere you want," the guard told him. That's when he gave Tremaine the look. The look that said, you probably aren't going to see any other Cutlasses in the lot. Especially ones with surf racks and a HANG LOOSE sticker on the back windshield. There was no condescension in the look, though. It was more, right on, I like your style, sky blue Cutlass and all. Glad to see a guy driving a heap like that has a reason to be at the prestigious L.A.C.C. Tremaine thought, that's why he told me to park anywhere. Probably wants me to pull up close to the club so all the members will have to walk by and see my blue beauty. I'll do just that, then. Yeah, that guard has probably taken plenty of shit from the members here . . .

Tremaine said, "Thank you" to the guard and cruised through the gate, thinking, it's a shame today's the day my fan belt decided to scream bloody murder. Sounds like a choking squirrel underneath my hood.

110

Tremaine got out of the Cutlass, straightened his shirt and blazer, and headed over to the sidewalk that brought him around to the back of the clubhouse, where you entered the Grill. The back entrance faced two sprawling golf courses to the west. Tremaine looked around. Beautiful. Magical, even. A giant stretch of lush, green land right smack in the middle of Wilshire Boulevard, in the middle of Los Angeles.

Fairways stretched out in all directions. There were thick trees and streams and perfectly manicured flowers everywhere. How many times, Tremaine wondered, had he driven down Wilshire Boulevard and not even considered what was behind that wall of foliage. That wall of trees that was hiding, at least from a purely aesthetic point of view, an inner-city sprawl of real estate rivaled by no other in Los Angeles. Just based on the location of this joint, right in the heart of town, between Beverly Hills and Westwood, this *enormous* stretch, it simply reeked of money.

Tremaine knew about L.A.C.C., a little bit anyway. No entertainment folks; that's what Nina and Jack Sawyer had said. This was old money, white money, WASP money. As he strolled down the sidewalk, around to a big back patio flanked on one side by an enormous putting green, he looked at the people sitting underneath the umbrellas. And boy, did they look at him. They eyed him.

Mostly older men, Tremaine noticed. Older white men with those perma-scowls on their faces. White hair, parted on the side, pink, saggy faces, khaki pants, and Brooks Brothers shirts. Not many smiles around these parts. Place was peaceful, though. No cell phones. No loud groups convened together. Some women; not many, though. The occasional trio of female golfers would stroll by, tan faces and conservative haircuts.

As nice as the place was, certainly the most prestigious golf club in town, it was understated indeed. There was no flash. It was simple. And that simplicity gave it style and grace.

Tremaine entered the Grill to see groups of men at tables eating club sandwiches and drinking drinks and playing cards. This place, too, was very simple. Some card tables, some chairs, a bar with one bartender. Big windows everywhere looking out to the courses. But in terms of decoration, it was no more than you would see in a club in a small town in Middle America. Some game tables over in the corner. Paper napkins. No flash. This was the way the members liked it. Any kind of ostentation was show-offy. Tacky. Too much decoration said, "We've got money." These people weren't like that. The simpler the better. But, boy, did they have money.

Tremaine strolled through the Grill. Yes, there were some stares. He looked perfectly presentable, but the old-school surfer 'stache certainly threw off some of the geezers in the room. Passing by one table, a man who looked to be somewhere around a hundred just blatantly stared at Tremaine, his mouth hanging open in confusion.

"Howdy," Tremaine said.

"Who?" the old man grunted back.

Tremaine moved on. He thought to himself, that guy might die later. Then, standing in the middle of the room, sort of looking around for Phillip Cook, Tremaine heard, "You must be Donald Tremaine."

Tremaine looked down and to his left to see a man sitting at one of the square lunch tables. Tremaine had inadvertently found Phillip Cook. He was practically on top of him.

"Yes, I'm Donald Tremaine."

"Phillip Cook," he said as he stood up, extending a hand for Tremaine to shake.

Tremaine shook Phillip's hand, then sat down at the table and ordered a Diet Coke from a passing waiter. "Yes, sir," the waiter said.

"Thank you for agreeing to meet me here," Phillip Cook said, now seated as well. Tremaine looked for Phillip's glass eye. It wasn't hard to find, as Tremaine was face to face with a man whose left eye simply did not move. It just stared straight ahead, like a doll's. Tremaine thinking, that would be a good device for a P.I. A glass eye to confuse and fluster people you interviewed. Close your good eye and just stare at them with the glass one, freak them out. But then I couldn't see, he thought . . .

"My pleasure," Tremaine said. "I've always wanted to see the Club."

Tremaine studied Phillip Cook. He almost couldn't believe the guy was wearing a blazer with a crest and an ascot. Combined with his black hair with a part on the side that looked like a white line down his head and his glass eye, he fit the mold of a consummate country club gentleman. Or a villain in a James Bond movie.

"It's interesting that you're investigating this case more than a year after the murder."

Man, it was tough to tell this guy's angle with that glass eye.

"I'm a P.I. I investigate old cases all the time."

"Nina hired you, right? That's what mother said."

Mother? Another one of those words only these people used. Mother? Shall?

Phillip continued, "So, how can I help?"

Tremaine thought, this guy needs a big white Persian cat in his lap. So he could stroke it maniacally, giggle, and plot the destruction of the free world.

Tremaine said, "Your mother was nice enough to talk to me about Roger."

Phillip said, "You know, he wasn't my father; he was my mother's *second* husband."

"I know," Tremaine said, and thought, he's got that defensive air, just like his mom. What the hell do these people have to be defensive about? They have the world by the balls.

Tremaine continued. "Well, I'm looking into the case and, as you know, the cops never identified an official suspect. There's the guy who some people suspected . . ."

"Tyler Wilkes."

"Yeah, Tyler Wilkes. But he's not why I wanted to talk to you," Tremaine said. Then, with no obvious implication, "Did you like Roger Gale, Phillip?"

"I liked him because my mother liked him. He made her happy, so I liked him."

"But, regardless of your mother, did you like him? As a person?"

"You know what? I did. You couldn't not like him. Everybody at his agency liked him, everyone here at the Club liked him. I resisted his charms at first because I didn't think anyone could replace my father. But Roger was sensitive to that, and although we were never best friends, I liked him. I did."

"Lots of people said Roger Gale's life caused him to work insane hours and things like that, come home late."

"I don't think he was having affairs," Phillip said, getting right to it. "No one would do that to my mother."

"You sure?" Tremaine said.

"Yes. And I'm not alone in my contention, either," Phillip said. "Bill Peterson said the same thing."

Tremaine looked at Phillip.

Phillip said quickly, "Bill Peterson was one of the detectives who looked into this thing in the first place. He said the same thing. That they looked into the affair angle and there was just nothing there."

Phillip Cook was getting irritated.

Tremaine said, "Bill Peterson—he's the cop who moved to Atlanta?"

"Yes, that's right. How did you know that?"

"I have a friend on the force."

"So, you've talked to the detectives who looked into the case?"

"No, I haven't. But I know some of them by name. Bill Peterson, Larry DeSouza."

Phillip Cook's good eye began to shift a little. It scanned the room while the other eye just stared straight ahead.

Now this guy's like a lizard, Tremaine thought. A well-dressed lizard who can move just one eye at a time. Thinking, I gotta get me one of those glass eyes. Tremaine pictured a lizard sitting on a rock in the desert wearing a crested blazer and an ascot. Concentrate, Tremaine, concentrate.

Phillip said, "Do you plan on talking to the detectives who investigated the murder?"

Tremaine answered immediately, "No. Why would I? They filed what they found. Talking to them isn't going to make any new evidence appear." But, he thought, I might, probably will.

Phillip nodded, appearing to be a little relieved. He took a dainty sip of his sparkling water and said, "What do you do in a case like this where there isn't much to go on?"

"Start talking to people. Maybe I can find something that the cops couldn't."

"I doubt it," Phillip said, that upper-crust cynicism rearing its ugly head again.

"I don't," Tremaine said.

Then Tremaine said, "Are you upset that I'm investigating this case because the wounds have almost healed or because of something else?"

Phillip shifted in his seat, narrowed his eyes at Tremaine, and said, "During the investigation, the police and everybody else started asking people if Roger was having affairs because he kept these crazy hours and he would come home late. In the end, all it did was insult us. It made people, like the people in this very club, think things that weren't true. And we don't like that kind of attention. The detectives, they don't mind asking everyone, implying to everyone, that Roger ran around because they don't have to live with it. My mother does. Even though it's not true, they all stirred the pot so much that people started to believe it. It's insulting and beneath us to have to defend ourselves against a rumor. Now, obviously, I and my mother want the murder solved, but not if it's going to create a series of entirely ridiculous assumptions about the behavior of my mother's former husband. Maybe his murder was an accident. Somebody gave him an accidental blow to the head, then to cover up the mess, they suffocated him. I don't know. But I do know that he wasn't murdered on account of his doing wrong by my mother."

Tremaine nodded, paused, and said, "Thank you for answering my questions, Phillip. You've been very helpful."

Phillip Cook, appreciating Tremaine's manners and calming down a bit, said, "Would you like a club sandwich before you go?"

"Yes, actually."

CHAPTER 17

Tremaine pulled into the trailer park at dusk. He went inside, grabbed a beer, and then snuck over to the kitchen table, where he kept Lyle's leash. Then he quickly opened the drawer and pulled out the leash, making all sorts of noise, the leash jangling and jingling. Tremaine thinking, this familiar noise will certainly make Lyle sing with joy!

He didn't move. Tremaine shook the leash, rattled it around, banged it on the kitchen counter. Lyle didn't budge.

Tremaine walked over to Lyle, leash in hand, and said, "Who's a good boy? Who's the best little guy around?"

Lyle barely moved, except for the steady rise and fall of his stomach, as asleep as a creature can be.

"Who's my beautiful little bulldog? Who's the cutest of the cutest? Who's the king of the octogenarians?"

Lyle farted. Tremaine picked him up, rousing him out of his slumber. Lyle looked at him and growled a bit. Nobody likes to be woken up in the middle of a deep sleep. Tremaine took a healthy gulp of his Bud, put it down, then hooked up Lyle's leash and headed out the trailer door.

Tremaine and Lyle strolled around, enjoying the Malibu evening. Tremaine mulling everything over, maybe even thinking about Nina Aldeen a little here and there.

Marvin Kearns exploded out of his trailer door and said, "Mr. Tremaine, I may have made an error in judgment."

Tremaine turned around to see Marvin standing there in a black karate uniform, complete with the black shoes with the thin, red rubber soles.

Tremaine was going to ask about the outfit—must have an audition for a ninja movie—but instead, he said, "Marvin, what's up?"

"Hello, Lyle," Marvin said. "Always, ALWAYS acknowledge the presence of a canine. Especially one with the staying power of one Lyle Tremaine."

"You hear that, Lyle? He's paying you a compliment."

Marvin said, "There was a man here earlier today driving a silver Ford Crown Victoria. Probably a '99, maybe a 2000. Do you know anyone who fits that description?"

"Not offhand. Did you talk to him?" Tremaine said, interested.

"I did. I was finishing a run, and I saw him driving around the lot. He looked lost. I noticed he was looking at your trailer, so I approached him to see if I could be of assistance. He told me he was your old friend from childhood, and then asked me if your trailer was indeed your trailer. I said it was. Then he said he was going to surprise you, so don't say anything. I agreed. This was before I suspected he may have been TOTALLY FULL OF SHIT! I apologize for providing him with that information. I should have known better, considering your occupation."

"Marvin, it's okay. You didn't tell them anything he hadn't already found out in the phone book."

"Let me tell you what else transpired, how I came to determine he was not telling me the truth."

"We'll go to my place," Tremaine said.

They quickly walked Lyle, then went into Tremaine's trailer, sat down, and popped fresh beers.

Tremaine looked across his table at the human bowling ball dressed as a ninja.

Marvin said, taking a sip, "A truly large libation."

"Indeed."

"So, I happened to use your former nickname, Insane, in conversation with the gentleman in the Crown Vic," Marvin said. "And he had no idea WHAT THE FUCK I WAS TALKING ABOUT! And he had already told me he grew up with you. He would know your nickname, regardless of whether or not you like the name."

"That was smart, Marvin."

"Is this part of the case you got from the beautiful woman, the one I'm happy to help with should you need assistance?"

"Yeah. This is related. A guy I talked to the other day is now checking *me* out. That's my guess."

Tremaine thinking, Tyler Wilkes wants to know what I know or what I want to know.

"Well," Marvin said, "once I said 'Insane,' and he clearly indicated to me he didn't know what I meant, the conversation became very forced. He rolled up his window and drove off. I will say, to his credit, he was driving a superior machine."

"Can you tell me what he looked liked?"

"Can I tell you what he looked liked!" Marvin said. "Indeed. Thin, probably five-nine, bad skin, and dark hair. Young-looking."

Tremaine nodded and said, "Listen, Marvin, don't sweat talking to that guy. This could end up helping me."

Tremaine held up his beer and he and Marvin toasted.

"Largeness," Marvin said.

Tremaine cooked himself a half-chicken with some asparagus and thought about what he had so far. He was going to play with Tyler Wilkes's head a little, that was for sure, but he had to set it up a little more. Get Tyler a little more unsure of what's going on, then surprise him. And the guy Tyler no doubt sent to look into him? Probably a young private eye in his silver Crown Vic trying to look and feel official. Tremaine thought, I'll use him to help get Tyler worried, or more worried. And then maybe Tyler will tell me something about Roger Gale.

But right now, what was on Tremaine's mind was Phillip Cook and Evelyn Gale. Tremaine understood that the murder was painful for them, something that they wanted behind them. Their emotions were not unique in that regard.

But, Tremaine thought, why were they so insistent that Roger Gale didn't have an affair? Why do they care that much? And why did Phillip Cook make such a point of saying that Bill Peterson had determined there wasn't an affair? That felt forced, like a kid on a playground giving his alibi. Like, I didn't steal Jimmy's lunch money, just ask Billy. Billy being the best friend of the accused.

But, more so, it seemed like a slip of the tongue. Tremaine remembered how just after Phillip said it he kind of paused and looked at him. Maybe Phillip said it before he got a chance to think about whether he wanted to make such a presentation out of who could back him up.

Maybe Bill Peterson knew something.

Phillip sure as hell didn't want Tremaine talking to Peterson; he made that obvious. He came right out and asked him whether he was going to talk to the police. Tremaine could see, even in his goddamn glass eye, some worry.

So, next step, talk to Bill Peterson. Tremaine got online, looked for a plane ticket, a plane ticket to Atlanta. Got one, and a hotel, and a rental car, all with points off his plastic. No money spent. He'd tell Nina later she didn't need to know that a hunch was sending him thousands of miles away.

Yeah, that was the next step. Tremaine was going to visit Bill Peterson in person. The cop who'd moved, who had personally guaranteed Phillip Cook there was no infidelity. Tremaine knew he had to go to Atlanta. He couldn't just call because if Bill Peterson was going to tell him anything interesting, it would have to be face to face. If he just dialed him up, Peterson would either avoid him or just simply say, nope, everything he knew, Tremaine could find in the good old police report.

Tremaine threw his dishes in the sink, drank a beer while he cleaned them. Now his mind went somewhere else in the case. To the person who gave him the business in the first place. Nina, Nina Aldeen. Man, those sad, pretty eyes. He thought, wonder what she's doing over there in her cool Venice house with all the books. She's probably writing her own book, back there in her office, by the back deck. Tremaine, done with the dishes, stood there for a minute, the warm water running over his hands.

CHAPTER 18

The next morning, even before walking Lyle, Tremaine dialed up the Atlanta Police Department and asked for Bill Peterson, knowing he wouldn't get him. When Tremaine got kicked back to the receptionist, he said, "So's Bill around? I mean, is he on vacation or anything?"

And the receptionist said, in a Southern accent, "Oh, he's around. He just got back from a two-week vacation about a month ago, so he'll be around for a good while before he leaves again."

"Thank you," Tremaine said.

He hung up the phone, good, he wouldn't have to cancel his trip. Then Tremaine called Marvin Kearns and asked him to look after Lyle for a couple days. Marvin said, of course, and that was that. Marvin had the key to Tremaine's trailer and Lyle liked Marvin—as much as Lyle could like anyone.

In the car on the way to LAX, Tremaine saw a conspicuous silver Crown Vic in his rearview.

"Perfect," he said. And he meant it.

At the airport, Tremaine parked the Cutlass in Short Term, outside in plain view, so the guy in the Crown Vic would be sure to know exactly where Tremaine's car was. And could pick Tremaine up easily upon his return from Atlanta.

On the flight, wedged in between two rather large human beings—fucking frequent flier seat, Tremaine got out his L.A. *Times*, his pencil, and his stopwatch.

Quickly, in fifty-three seconds, he turned IXAMM into MAXIM, YAFLE into LEAFY, LIFTLE into FILLET, FLABEL into BEFALL, then finally, XLFITEF into LEFT in a FIX. *When the mechanic got sick, his boss was left in a fix.*

Done with that, he turned his attention to a picture of Bill Peterson, a picture Lopez had given him. Bald, hair on the sides like Terry Bradshaw, mustache, looked to be about fifty. Tremaine studied the picture, Bill Peterson in his LAPD uniform, his official photo.

The big guy to the left of Tremaine began looking at the photo as well and said to Tremaine, "Who's that?"

Tremaine looked at the guy and said, "It's a guy named Bill Peterson."

The man said, "Oh."

Tremaine picked up his rental at the Atlanta airport, a Geo Prizm. Not a particularly masculine car, but what are you going to do? It was free, for Chrissakes. He'd made his reservation at a Day's Inn downtown, near the police headquarters. He got directions from the people at Avis. Peachtree Boulevard to Peachtree Place to Peachtree Drive to Peachtree Court. Or something like that.

Tremaine found the hotel and checked into his room. A dark little styleless, charmless room. But clean. And quiet. And not a bad view. Downtown looked pretty cool—very metropolitan, lots of interesting-looking buildings, even a circular skyscraper. The feel of the city enhanced by dusk falling over the sky.

It was almost seven already, Tremaine losing three hours by flying east. Tonight he'd just relax, watch a little tube, and mull over the case. Then tomorrow he'd go down to the station and see if he could arrange for thirty minutes of face time with Bill Peterson.

He clicked on *SportsCenter*, then cracked open his complimentary copy of the *Atlanta Journal-Constitution*. He read the front section, then sports, then the arts. Pretty good paper.

Later, he ordered a cheeseburger and two beers from room service and just enjoyed the little private sanctuary that is an out-of-town hotel room.

The next morning, bright and early, Tremaine went downtown to the headquarters of the Atlanta police. He walked right into the building, looked at the computerized listing in the lobby of department employees, found Bill Peterson's name, then hopped on an elevator to the fourth floor. Not so much as a look from the security guards.

There was a receptionist's desk on the fourth floor. At it was maybe the same woman with the Southern accent that he'd talked to. Tremaine approached her and said, "Hi, I'm Donald Tremaine. I don't have an appointment, but I'm a friend of a friend of Bill Peterson's and I'd like to say hello."

"Let me call Bill, see if he's back there."

"Thank you," Tremaine said.

Tremaine sat down in the little waiting area and picked up an old, a really old, *People* magazine. He helped himself to some water in a Styrofoam cup. A couple minutes later, he heard, "Can I help you?"

Tremaine looked up, Bill Peterson stood in front of him in a brown suit with a vest. Must be hot when he's outside. Tremaine had an idea how he was going to handle this, but he wasn't sure if Peterson would take the bait. We'll see.

"Bill, my name's Donald Tremaine. I'm a private investigator."

Peterson, playing the role of the cop, just looked at Tremaine. He was stone-faced. Not upset, not anything. He was just waiting for Tremaine to continue, so Tremaine did.

"I'm investigating a case you worked on, the murder of an advertising guy named Roger Gale."

Peterson spoke. "Are you here from L.A.?"

A great cop question—direct, with some implications. But Peterson seemed a little surprised. He couldn't quite keep his cop stare. He looked, just in that instant, rumpled as opposed to worn. Not quite the veteran cop. He looked worried.

Tremaine continued. "Yes, I'm here from L.A. I'm actually a friend of one of your old coworkers on the force."

"Who?"

"John Lopez."

"Good cop," Peterson said.

Tremaine knew his next comment would calm Peterson down, if he bought it. "Listen," Tremaine said. "This is a tough case. I'm sure you remember, there's no . . . what's the word I'm looking for . . . *evidence*."

Peterson smiled, but he wasn't totally calm. Not yet.

Tremaine said, "I'm here because I heard you were good. I wanted to bounce some of my theories off you, see what you think. I'm working on conjecture here, and I need a sounding board, but I need a good sounding board, someone who not only knows the case but knows what they're talking about."

"You came all the way here to ask me if I think you're on the right track?"

"There's a steak dinner in it for you. Ruth's Chris."

Peterson said, "I remember the case well; it's a tough one. If you want me to tell you what I think, well, I'm happy to help a fellow investigator, private or otherwise."

Praise, Tremaine thought—nobody ever gets sick of it. Well, that was that, he had Peterson coming to dinner. And he was indeed going to tell him some of his ideas.

Ruth's Chris, Buckhead, big red booth in the heart of the joint. Bustling, but not really that loud. But not too quiet either. Just right, nice for his purpose, and a nice feel in general. Nothing like a nice restaurant to get a cop talking. That's what Tremaine was thinking, half-joking to himself. They both had a couple beers and Tremaine assumed they would engage in some small talk, life in L.A., life in Atlanta, the Dodgers, the Braves, whatever. Tremaine realized quickly, however, that he was principally going to do a lot of listening. Bill Peterson being one of those guys who's not afraid to talk about himself. The beer helping him, even though he didn't need any help.

"Atlanta's a nice town, but I gotta admit, I'm a little lonely," Peterson said.

Tremaine nodded.

"I took the job because I had a friend down here. The captain, actually. I knew he was planning on leaving the force. He didn't tell anyone else that, but I knew. Anyway, after he did leave, man, getting to know a new town takes time. I'm bored as shit. Maybe even depressed."

Tremaine thought, tell it to Dr. Phil, but he listened politely. Thankfully the steaks arrived and Bill Peterson began to dig in, forgetting for a moment about his social situation in Atlanta. Now he was eating as opposed to talking.

Peterson started talking again, this time about something Tremaine was interested in. "So, what's new with the Roger Gale case?" he said. "Why are you looking into it? Who hired you?"

"Family member," Tremaine said, a little surprised to hear his own voice. "Niece."

"The one from Connecticut."

"She lives in L.A. now."

"We never talked to her," Peterson said. "She was thousands of miles away, married and all, living her life."

Peterson took a big bite of his steak and said, still chewing, "So what's up? What did you want to bounce off me?"

"I'm working a few angles," Tremaine said.

"The other ad guy and the possibility that Gale was running around?" Peterson said.

"Right," Tremaine said, "and one other thing, the thing I wanted to hear your thoughts on."

Tremaine looked right at Peterson now and saw Peterson register his stare, think about it a little.

"What is it?" Peterson said.

"I've been thinking about you," Tremaine said. "About your involvement in everything."

Peterson was listening carefully.

"You had an offer here in Atlanta that you took right after the Roger Gale thing went cold. You knew you were leaving."

"Yeah," Peterson said.

"Well, I talked to Phillip Cook the other day, and he mentioned you. He mentioned you in a way that I found unusual."

"So, he mentioned me. So what? I worked on the case, why wouldn't he mention me?"

"Phillip Cook and his mother are desperate to prove to everyone in the world that Roger Gale didn't have affairs. Gale wouldn't do that to Evelyn, embarrass her like that. When Phillip brought your name up, it was almost like he had a relationship with you, like he knew you as more than a cop. And then, when I indicated I might talk to you, he didn't like that. But I got to thinking, maybe you and Phillip had some kind of agreement. That no matter what you knew, you were going to say what Phillip wanted you to say."

"Tremaine, this case is tough. There's nothing to go on. I understand your frustration. But you're creating something out of nothing here. The guy mentioned my name—so what. Read the report—get Lopez to give it to you. Everything I know is in there."

"Everything you wrote is in there. But is everything you know in there? Detectives don't make much money, Peterson. Everyone knows that. Say you found something and Phillip paid you to keep quiet. You were leaving anyway—out of sight, out of mind. You were the perfect guy to do it. And Lopez told me you were a good cop, no one would suspect you, you just took a better-paying job in a different city. A lot of cops would do that."

Peterson downed his beer. Tremaine flagged a waiter, who came over. An old man who looked like a butler.

"Let's do a shot," Tremaine said to Peterson.

No objection from Peterson.

"Two shots—Maker's, please," Tremaine said.

They waited, not talking now, for the booze to arrive. Peterson had his head down, making his way through the remainder of his steak. Eating the fat. Tremaine just sat still, watching him. Peterson in this moment looked like an animal to Tremaine. Head down, eating away.

The shots arrived. Peterson put his fork down, and he and Tremaine threw back the bourbon.

Tremaine looked at Peterson and said, calmly, "I'm not going to sell you out, Peterson. If you tell me something, it will never come back to bite you in the ass. Never. But if I don't leave this restaurant with something, something you know that I don't, I'm going to drop the Roger Gale case and investigate you."

"Are you threatening me, Tremaine? Are you threatening a cop?"

"Yes."

"I don't know shit. You came all this way and I don't know shit."

"Bullshit," Tremaine said.

"Pay the bill, Tremaine."

"Peterson, tell me what you know, and go back to your life. Don't tell me, and I'll find out about you if I have to rip out Phillip's glass eye and feed it to him."

Peterson laughed, the comment had caught him off guard. He'd evidently forgotten about that bizarre glass eye for the moment. He looked at Tremaine.

Tremaine said, "I'm not going to fuck with you, Peterson, no matter what you tell me. As long as you tell me."

Peterson slumped in his chair. Then, calmly, the veteran cop back for the moment, he said, "You got me, Tremaine. If I don't tell you, you're going to look into me. I don't want you looking into me. So I'm going to tell you."

Peterson paused, took a breath, and said, "I took a payoff from Phillip Cook to keep something out of the report."

Tremaine looked at Bill Peterson, not changing his expression, not expressing any satisfaction that he'd been right. He just looked at the guy.

"The only reason I took the money is because I found out, personally, that the information I had did not have anything to do with Roger Gale's murder. They were separate things."

"So what's the point in omitting it?"

Bill Peterson said, "Phillip Cook came to me with some information, something from Roger Gale's past. He gave it to me, I didn't find it through the evidence, he gave it to me. Said he'd give me the tip if I'd talk to him first about whatever I found out. So I investigated the thing he told me about, and I came to the conclusion that it had nothing to do with the murder. Then he asked me to make sure it didn't make it into the file or become public information. I said 'I can't do that.' "

Peterson shifted his eyes down toward the table. "Then he offered me the money."

Tremaine listened.

Peterson continued, "I'm not a bad cop, Tremaine. Ask Lopez. But we don't make squat."

Tremaine said, "What did you find out?"

"That Roger Gale had had an affair."

Tremaine listened.

Peterson said, "We thought that might be the case—obviously, that's Detective Work 101—but we couldn't find anything. Then, Phillip Cook told me about this woman. Told me that about a year *prior* to his murder, Gale's wife, Evelyn, had confronted him about some of his late nights, not coming home, whatever. She was suspicious and pissed off. She even told him that she was going to hire a P.I. to find out what he was up to. He denied everything, she hired a detective. Sure enough, he was seeing a woman on the side. So Evelyn busts him, and he stops. Well, Phillip Cook told me who the woman was, the woman who the P.I. had caught him with, so I could see if there was any connection to his murder. Phillip wanted to keep Gale's affair quiet, but he wanted to know if this woman might be involved with the killing. So I contacted her. She was a really nice lady. Probably not the brightest bulb on the tree, but really pretty and nice. Worked as the general manager of a bunch of gyms in L.A. L.A. Fitness or something. You following me?"

Tremaine nodded and ordered a couple more beers for the two of them.

Peterson continued. "So I met with her. She hadn't seen Roger Gale in over a year, hadn't talked to him since he'd called off the affair. She was just a cute girl who managed some gyms. When they were together, there were no promises from Roger Gale about leaving his wife or any of that shit. She wasn't in love with him, they had just boned a couple times. I looked into her. She was rational. She had found out Roger Gale was dead when she read it in the paper. There were no phone calls, nothing. She had no connection to him anymore. None, for sure. So I left it at that. If Roger Gale's affairs were what caused him to be killed, it was by somebody else, somebody that we never found. This girl didn't have anything to do with it. I'm positive."

"Does Evelyn know Phillip told you about the affair?"

"Yes."

Tremaine said, "What's the girl's name?"

Bill Peterson said, "I knew you were going to ask me that."

"I'm not going to sell you out, Peterson. I already know enough to get you into serious shit."

Peterson said, "You're just going to talk to her about this? Not Phillip, not anybody else?"

"You have my word."

"Her name's Wendy Leahy. I got her number, too."

Tremaine dropped Peterson off at his two-bedroom townhouse in Dunwoody. Peterson, now drunk and more talkative than ever, yapped the whole way back about life in

Atlanta. Tremaine did his best to pay attention while Peterson went through the entire Atlanta Braves lineup, their batting averages, their chances of being traded. Peterson, now with a little buzz, saying stuff like, "Goddamn Bobby Cox. Walks like a goddamn penguin. Goddamn."

Now in the little rented Geo all by his lonesome, Tremaine thought about what he had learned. Evelyn and Phillip knew about this affair, in their minds, the only one Roger Gale had ever had, and they'd had it looked into. Peterson assured them it wasn't connected to the murder. So, when the cops were snooping around at the time of the murder, Evelyn and Phillip really resented the affairs accusations, because, to them, he had had only that one, and no one knew about it. This one affair was the reason Evelyn and Phillip were so sure the murder wasn't about an affair. *So quit embarrassing Mother*, Tremaine could almost hear Phillip saying.

Tremaine got back to his hotel, pretty tired now, buzzed, and full, too. He cranked the AC and just enjoyed the quiet hum of the machine. After a few minutes, he clicked off the light. The flight back to L.A. would come early.

CHAPTER 19

On the way back from LAX, Tremaine heading home to say hey to Lyle and check his mail, regular and electronic, he noticed in his rearview mirror, in the distance, the silver Crown Vic.

"All right, you're back. Let's go look at some stuff," Tremaine said aloud.

Tremaine, now on the 405, put his blinker on well before he had to get off, giving the Crown Vic time to prepare. Sure enough, the car followed, way back there, a tiny image in the rearview.

Tremaine took the Venice Boulevard exit, then headed west out to the beach.

Next, he drove into Marina del Rey and hung a left on Maxella. The Crown Vic mimicked his moves. Tremaine took Maxella to Glencoe, then went left on Glencoe to a warehouse district full of machine and glass repair shops. Tremaine had gotten one of his surfboards repaired in this district a number of weeks ago, so he was familiar with the goings-on of the neighborhood. Just after he passed Gene's Glass, the block opened up to a large lot, the frame of a new building going up.

In the front of the building, there were a number of cement trucks bearing the name L.A. Stone in large, red letters on the side. Tremaine pulled the Cutlass off the road directly across from the construction site and the trucks. Two minutes after he pulled over, the Crown Vic slid by, then stopped at the stop sign about a hundred yards past Tremaine. Tremaine thought, I'll wait for him to go around the block before I do anything.

But the Crown Vic didn't round the block. It did go right at the sign, but it didn't show up behind him. Instead, Tremaine spotted it two blocks ahead, now facing him as it pulled into the driveway of a small office building. The Crown Vic settled into park, the passenger side window of the car facing Tremaine. Tremaine knew, whoever this master of investigation was, he was watching.

Tremaine looked in his glove and pulled out an old camera, not even digital, with no film in it. He got out of his car, held the camera to his eye, and pointed it at the cement trucks. Might as well be wearing a goddamn sign. After pretending to take a series of pictures, he got back in the Cutlass, cranked her up, and left.

The Crown Vic was not in his sights as Tremaine made his way back to Malibu. No, the guy in the Crown Vic had done his work for the day.

Home. Tremaine walked in his trailer, barely able to contain his excitement over seeing Lyle. Tremaine shot in the door, smiling from ear to ear, and said, "Hey, Lyle, I'm home!" Lyle didn't move. Tremaine felt like an old housewife whose husband had long ago stopped seeing her as anything other than the woman who lived in the house. Tremaine hung his head a bit and grabbed Lyle's leash. The noise of the leash didn't seem to register, either.

After managing to walk Lyle, Tremaine checked his mail, his e-mail, and his phone messages. Then he headed back out into the park, over to good old Marvin Kearns's trailer. He had to thank him for watching Lyle and, for the first time ever, he was going to ask him for some help on a case.

Tremaine knocked a couple times, but no Marvin. Was he jumping from trailer roof to trailer roof in character as a ninja? Nope, he just wasn't home. Damn, have to catch him next time.

CHAPTER 20

That night, at the Lobster, a restaurant right by the Santa Monica Pier that overlooked the Pacific, Nina said, "I like this place. It has a nice feel."

Tremaine nodded.

Nina said, "You really didn't have to take me out to fill me in."

"I like to take my clients out. It's good for business."

True, Tremaine did take clients out from time to time. Especially ones like Nina Aldeen.

"So Roger had an affair."

"Yes," Tremaine said.

"You're sure?"

"I got the information from a pretty good source."

"Who?"

"I can't tell you that. Part of the deal with the source for parting with the information."

Nina smiled and said, "I understand. I'm not paying you to tell me everything. Just the one thing I want to know."

Tremaine thought, this one's a cool customer, respecting him, respecting his job. He looked at her, seeing and feeling now a real familiarity.

But it was different, too, her appearance, now that he was getting to know her. Nina's face was beginning to change in a way, in the way that once you get to know someone they actually look a little different, even though it's all the same parts stuck together in exactly the same way.

Tremaine sipped his beer and Nina sipped her wine, and they weren't exactly looking at each other, they were just relaxing, there was a comfort between them now, the Pacific on one side through the glass, the lively restaurant on the other.

This kind of feels like a date, Tremaine thought. Wonder if she feels that way?

"What about Tyler Wilkes?" she said.

"I don't know what Tyler Wilkes is up to. He's not a good guy, I know that much. I'm confusing him right now. Getting him paranoid. And then I'm going to use his paranoia to find out what he knows."

"How are you going to do that?"

"I'll tell you later."

She smiled again. "I won't forget," she said.

"Neither will I."

They ordered lobster—they *were* at the Lobster—and when their orders were in, Tremaine said, "I've been thinking about your book. It's a brave subject."

"Thank you."

"You're welcome."

"I mean," she said. "Not so much for the compliment, but for acknowledging that the subject matter is kind of a tough one to deal with."

"Like I said before, I know from personal experience."

She went on. "It's one of the few things in life I've ever done that my whole heart is into. I'm facing my fears, in a way. Just getting it all out and analyzing it. And as painful as it is, I know it's the right thing to do because I can feel it in my heart. That sounds like a Hallmark card. What I mean to say is, I can feel it in my gut."

Tremaine nodded. He knew what she meant, he knew that feeling.

"When I talked to John Lopez about hiring you, that's what he said about you," she said.

"What's that?"

"That you did things from your gut. That you didn't always have a reason other than that."

"Sometimes that's the best reason."

A moment of silence, then Tremaine said, "So, no smart-ass remarks about me from Lopez?"

"Oh, there were a few."

"Can you remember any?"

"He might have said something about your trailer."

"What about it?"

"Something like, 'If your car breaks down, you can always drive your house.'"

Tremaine laughed and said, "It's a trailer, not an RV. Not a bad joke though. I'll have to get him back for that."

"Hey, don't tell him your source. You wouldn't tell me yours."

"Fair enough."

They ate, delicious. They dropped the case talk and got back to books, and, more specifically, her book. Tremaine liked hearing about it, the poetry she put into telling her story. Then, out in the parking lot, Tremaine found himself saying, "Want to take a walk on the beach? Walk off dinner? Tell me more about your book?"

"Yeah," Nina said. "I've lived in L.A. for a while now and I've never taken a walk on the beach at night."

Tremaine had Nina follow him to a spot off the Pacific Coast Highway about halfway between the Lobster in Santa Monica and his trailer park. She pulled her Volvo behind his Cutlass, off the main road onto a little dirt road between the PCH and the ocean. She got out of her car, he got out of his, and they walked toward each other. The ocean was loud but not too loud, the waves crashing into the sand.

"This is a great little spot. How'd you find it?" she said.

"Only the surfers know about it."

"Someday you'll have to tell me all about the tour. What it's really like."

"Yeah, maybe someday. It'll probably bore you, though, hearing about the size of waves or just how perfect the sets were on a certain day. It's like when golfers talk about shots. It's only interesting to other golfers. And sometimes not even them."

"What if I started surfing? Would you tell me then?"

"It's possible."

"I might hold you to it."

They took off their shoes and left them by the car. Tremaine guided her toward the shore, motioning which way to head down the beach. For a minute or two they strolled in silence, all they heard were the waves pounding the sand. And each, independently, not talking about it, watched the big mass of water suck the waves back in after they crashed.

Then Nina said, "You know, when it comes to divorce, everyone's story is different and the same in a way, too."

"Yep," Tremaine said.

"Because no matter what the circumstances, you learn just as much about yourself as you do the other person."

Did Tremaine agree? Had he been there? Yeah. But he didn't say it, he just listened.

"Sean and I, we both brought baggage to the relationship. But when you're in the middle of it, you blame the other person, like their baggage is causing all the problems. Then one day, if you really look hard, you see your stuff is just as much a problem as their stuff. You're looking at the other person, but you're seeing yourself."

"You've got to put that in your book. Just like that."

"It's in there, baby. It's in there."

Silence between them again, just the waves. Tremaine saw himself in his marriage, that vivid and painful image in his head again. Tremaine, walking down the beach with Nina but seeing himself driving away from his ex's house for the last time, never to return.

Nina said, "What I find amazing, about breakups, marriage . . . is that no matter how much it hurts, no matter how much you have to go through to get over it, you always, eventually, want to try again. That hope remains, even if it's way deep down inside."

Again, Tremaine didn't respond. He just listened.

They walked a little more, their cars were out of sight now. Nice night, nice temperature, but probably time to head back.

Nina said, "I should probably go."

"Yeah," Tremaine said.

"I had a wonderful night. Thank you for dinner."

"It was my pleasure."

As they turned around, they faced each other. Nina looked like an image to Tremaine now, the moon making her glow, almost. A silhouette. Like a ghost on the beach. A beautiful ghost on the beach. That hint of sadness in her eyes was there, but Tremaine thought he saw something else this time. Something else hopping around in there. But he wasn't quite sure what it was. He knew what he wanted it to be, but he wasn't quite sure what it actually was.

They got back to their cars and stood in front of them putting on their shoes and getting out their keys.

From the beach, from the side that they hadn't walked down, they heard, "Yo."

Nina and Tremaine turned around to see three men, looked to be in their mid-twenties, approaching. One

Latino guy, two white guys. Gangbanger types. Tank tops, lots of tats, giant jeans. They were all sporting smug looks, and Tremaine could tell from their glassy eyes and the smell that they'd been drinking.

Tremaine said, "Can I help you gentlemen?"

The three guys laughed.

Then one of the white guys started to talk. It was the one who'd said "Yo."

The guy said, "What the fuck you two doing up in this beach?"

This was a white guy trying to sound like a black guy.

Nina moved behind Tremaine when she heard the profanity, the threatening language.

"We just came out here for a little walk," Tremaine said. He could feel some adrenaline beginning to pump through his veins.

"Yeah, it's a nice-ass beach. But we ain't here to talk about the beach. We here because we want your wallet and that bitch's purse. So why don't you just give it to us."

The other two guys stood just behind the talkative one. These two looked at Tremaine and Nina and sported cocky, smug expressions.

"I'm afraid, gentlemen," Tremaine said, "that that's not going to happen."

The white spokesman who talked like he was black looked down at the ground and laughed. A mocking, smart-ass laugh.

"Why don't you quit calling us 'gentlemen.' That tone, I hear it, showing us disrespect." Then he reached in his pocket and pulled out a knife. Looked to Tremaine like a knife used in the armed forces. Pretty small blade, thin black handle, easy to conceal. And sharp. Then he picked his head up, looking at Tremaine now, and said, "And give me your fuckin' wallet."

He was holding the knife up, showing it off, tilting it to the side a bit. Posing.

Tremaine started walking toward him.

Nina said, "Donald."

"You better back the fuck up, 'less you wanna get cut."

Tremaine looked right at the guy and kept walking. Steadily, a beeline. He was about two feet in front of the guy, when the guy pulled back the knife, in position to take a swipe at Tremaine. Tremaine, still moving forward, cocked back his fist and drove it in the guy's nose. A piercing crack, followed by gushing blood. As the guy raised both of his hands to hold his ruined nose, the knife fell out of his hand. It fell at the feet of the two other guys. Tremaine made no motion to pick it up or kick it away.

Instead, he said to the two guys, "You want it, pick it up. Go ahead."

Neither one of them moved.

The white guy with the blood on his face removed his hands and looked at his two buddies. He said, "Let's go get the boys and come back and kill this bitch."

He turned to Tremaine, who could see the tears in his eyes, and said, "You dead. We'll be back."

Tremaine said, "No, you won't. And you should know, the way you're talking, you sound like an idiot."

The guys turned around and strutted, quickly, into the blackness, down the beach where they'd come from. The knife shined and sparkled a bit, catching some of the moonlight. It was right on the ground where the guy dropped it. Tremaine picked it up, opened his car door, and threw it on the floorboard in front of the passenger-side seat.

He turned to Nina and said, "Sorry about that. This little stretch is usually very peaceful."

CHAPTER 21

Wendy Leahy said, yeah, sure, I'll talk to you, when Tremaine called her and asked if she had some time to talk about Roger Gale. She obviously didn't know her affair had been kept out of the police report, that it was a secret to many. She was perfectly open about it, willing to discuss it. She said she didn't have a ton of time, but that he could come by the gym and they could talk at her desk. This woman, Wendy, acted very composed, not fazed at all about discussing the affair. Practice, maybe.

Tremaine arrived at L.A. Shape—that was the name of the gym, Peterson had gotten it wrong—at about noon. The place was packed. People running and lifting and sweating and grunting all over the place. Only in L.A., he thought. Tuesday mid-morning and a full house. Where did all these people work? In Los Angeles, the ebb and flow of people in public was just different. Most towns, Monday through Friday had a different feel from the weekend. Not really the case in L.A. You could go to the movies or to the mall or to wherever right smack dab in the middle of the workweek, in the middle of the day, and there would be people everywhere. And not just vagrants or octogenarians or teenagers ditching school. Twenty- and thirty-somethings who looked like they made money. What the hell did they all do? They couldn't all be successful actors or writers or directors. There was a mystery Tremaine would never solve.

Tremaine went to the desk at the gym where everyone showed their identification. The desk that determined whether or not you could enter the hallowed grounds of L.A. Shape.

"May I help you?" the woman behind the desk chirped.

"I have an appointment with Wendy Leahy."

"Do you know where her office is?"

"No."

Somehow, the woman made the directions very complicated when, in reality, all she needed to say was, "Go down the hallway right over there behind the bench presses and look for her name on the door."

Instead, she rambled, thinking out loud, verbalizing every way possible to get to Wendy's office. In the end, using his best P.I. skills, Tremaine deciphered what she had said and began making his way though the gym.

He spotted the hallway the receptionist had referred to. As he walked by one of the bench presses, he looked down at an enormous, red-faced man pushing up the bar, which was loaded with weights. There was another large man standing over him, spotting. The man lifting the weights was grunting and even spitting. Tremaine could see the veins in his head, filled with blood, looking ready to burst.

The spotter was talking to the lifter, saying, "Do it. Come on. You're a stud. Push it harder."

The lifter let out an enormous grunt and managed to get the weight up and back on to the bar that supported it. He stood up off the bench and faced the spotter. They bumped chests and let out a simultaneous grunt.

Tremaine, passing the two on his way to the hallway, said, "Excuse me, gentlemen."

He found Wendy's door and knocked. From inside, he heard, "Come on in."

Tremaine entered her office. She stood up to greet him.

"Hello, I'm Donald Tremaine."

"Wendy Leahy."

They both sat down.

"I was surprised when you called. I haven't talked about Roger Gale in so long."

"You didn't sound surprised," Tremaine said.

"Well, I was. I talk on the phone so much for work, I'm kind of on autopilot when I'm on the phone. That's probably why I didn't sound surprised. I probably sounded like I always sound."

Tremaine nodded.

"Anyway, I'm happy to talk about it, to help or whatever."

"Great. Thank you," Tremaine said.

Tremaine studied Wendy. She was pretty but not sexy. Just attractive, and put together well, and—the word kept coming into his head—friendly.

Wendy said, "After you called, Bill Peterson called and told me you were coming. I told him you had already called. He said, that's okay, he just wanted to tell me not to worry. You know, I hadn't talked to Bill since he questioned me before. But he was nice then, and he was nice when he called. He said I could trust you and I should feel comfortable telling you everything I told him."

"That was nice of Bill."

"Yeah, he's nice."

Switching the subject, Tremaine said, "So, how'd you meet Roger Gale?"

Quickly, she said, "I met him here at the gym. At the time I was just managing this one. Now I manage four of them in L.A. But he came in for a membership and I gave him a tour and a spiel and all that stuff."

Tremaine thought about how he'd phrase this next question. Yes, Wendy had agreed to talk specifically about her relationship with Roger Gale. But it was always tricky to ask about an affair because the question itself implied wrongdoing. You know, when did you start doing that horrible thing . . .

Wendy solved his problem for him, saying, "After Roger signed up, he left, then, about twenty minutes later, he came back in and asked me if I wanted to have dinner that night. I confess, I had looked at his finger during the tour. No ring. It wasn't until a little later that I found out he was married. Anyway, when he asked me out to dinner, I didn't hesitate. He was older than most of the guys I usually go out with, but he was so smart and funny. That was obvious immediately."

"How many times did you go out?"

"Six. The sixth being the time he told me he had to call it off."

"What would you two do?"

"Go to dinner, or bars, once, a movie."

"And the intimate part?"

Tremaine had to ask, even if it was just to see whether or not she'd answer. Or how she'd answer.

She said, "We went to my place a couple times. It's embarrassing, but it was so long ago. You know, I hadn't talked to him in over a year when I read that he'd been killed."

"So, basically, you had a very brief affair, which he called off."

"Yes, and I was upset because I liked Roger. He was so smart, always telling me about all the campaigns he was working on. But, see, he told me he was married after our first date. So, from the very beginning, a part of me was reluctant. I didn't want to be involved with a married man. So, when he called if off, I was kind of relieved."

"When Bill Peterson first questioned you about the case, were you scared?"

"Yes and no. Roger's wife knew about the affair. That wasn't a secret. But I got scared because I thought, what do they want with me? I haven't talked to Roger in over a year. Then Bill Peterson came to me and he looked at my cell phone bills and home phone records and e-mails, and he talked to my boyfriend who lived with me, and he realized that I hadn't seen Roger or even talked to him in ages. And that was it. I will say this though, it was weird."

"Weird?"

"Yeah, weird that I was being questioned about a murder. I mean, a *murder*."

"Is it weird now?"

"No, not really. I guess I'm more used to it. And I'm happy to help because I'm just as confused about it as the next person. I can't imagine anyone wanting to kill Roger Gale."

"Yeah, seems a lot of people feel that way."

Tremaine looked at Wendy for a second, at her face, her expression. Nice, but a little blank. Then he stood up, which may have surprised Wendy. Like she might not have been expecting the questioning to end. "Thank you," Tremaine said.

Wendy said, "You're welcome." Then she said, "Is that it?"

"Yeah," Tremaine said. "That's it."

CHAPTER 22

Tremaine was driving along, thinking, thinking first about Wendy Leahy and now about how, just exactly how, he could screw with Tyler Wilkes's head.

To his delight, Tremaine looked in his rearview, and a few cars back, there was his new buddy, the guy in the Crown Vic. The P.I. looking into the P.I.

Weird. The Crown Vic appearing just like that, just as he was thinking about it. Well, Tremaine thought, perfect time to get started on Plan Fuck-With-Tyler.

Tremaine put on the brakes, worked some automobile magic, and ended up right next to the Crown Vic at a stoplight.

He reached across the Cutlass's seat and rolled down the passenger-side window. He then motioned to the guy in the Crown Vic. The young guy with the dark hair and the bad skin, just as Marvin had described.

The guy looked surprised, did the "who-me" face, and powered down his window.

Tremaine said, "Hey, could I talk to you for a sec?"

The guy said, "What do you need, some directions?"

Tremaine thought, clever, playing dumb. And boy did Marvin describe him well.

"No, I don't need directions. I want to talk to you. I want to ask you why you're following me."

This question stunned the young guy with the bad skin.

"What?" the guy said.

"You heard me."

The light turned green, and the guy in the Crown Vic pulled away fast. Tremaine got behind him and followed him. The guy turned right into a neighborhood, a nice little section of Mar Vista. The guy was trying his best to lose Tremaine, breaking out his finest moves—last-minute turns, gunning it through red lights and stops signs—the classics.

This guy must have spent some serious time watching reruns of *T.J. Hooker* and *Matt Houston*.

Tremaine saw the Crown Vic go right down a side street, but he wanted the guy to think he'd lost him. So Tremaine conspicuously and quickly drove straight past the turn the Crown Vic had taken. Tremaine didn't even look down the street, just drove, fast, and straight ahead. Gunning it.

Tremaine pulled into a driveway two stop signs down from the street where the Crown Vic had turned. He tucked the Cutlass behind a camper and waited. He got out of his car and stood, looking through the front windows of the camper, at the street the Crown Vic had taken and he had not. Five minutes later, the Crown Vic pulled out from the very road it had gone down. It went left, away from where Tremaine was hiding. He gave it some time, got in the Cutlass, and pulled back on the road, following the Crown Vic. Now, the silver sedan was in his sights, up there about half a mile in front of him.

Tremaine stayed back, nice and careful, following the Crown Vic as it pulled onto National, then ducked into some back roads, then onto Barrington. Tremaine watched, keeping lots of cars between them, as the car pulled over into a little dirt lot that flanked a big park.

The park consisted of a big green field that was split up into some softball fields, some soccer fields, and a picnic area. Tremaine could see it now from where he was parked, on a side street three blocks away from the dirt lot and the park and the Crown Vic.

He watched the young guy get out of his car and walk over to one of the picnic tables and sit down. Tremaine took the keys out of the Cutlass. Then he reached down to the passenger-side floorboard and grabbed the knife that had been pulled on him and Nina the other night at the beach.

Tremaine got out of the car.

He walked the three blocks, quickly and quietly, and now he was on the grass of the park, nearing the picnic table where the guy was sitting. The guy's back was to Tremaine, who was moving slowly now, being careful and silent, like a cat. Like Darryl. Tremaine watched the guy pull out his phone and start dialing.

The light noise of the park, soccer players, softball players, Frisbee throwers, allowed Tremaine to get closer, closer, closer, right behind him now, without the guy hearing him.

Just as the guy finished dialing, Tremaine, standing directly behind him, raised the knife high in the air and slammed it down into the picnic table, right in front of the guy.

The guy jerked—startled—and dropped his phone.

Tremaine grabbed the cell and looked at the number the phone was calling: Tyler Wilkes. Tremaine ended the call and turned off the phone.

Tremaine walked around the picnic table and sat down across from the guy. The guy looked at Tremaine, then moved his eyes to the knife that was between them, standing straight up, blade an inch deep in the table. The guy looked, in this moment, like a scared animal, very wary of even moving and very aware of his every movement.

"How long you been a P.I.?" Tremaine said.

The young guy with the dark hair and the bad skin didn't answer.

Tremaine said, "Come on. I know you've been following me. You came to my trailer park, to the airport, you watched me take pictures of the L.A. Stone trucks . . . How long you been a P.I.?"

"Not long."

"You work on your own or for a firm?"

"Firm."

"I was a simple tailing job, so you got the gig?"

"Yeah."

"I'm going to make your job easy for you."

157

The young guy didn't say anything. He was still a little scared, a little caught off guard. But he motioned with his eyes for Tremaine to continue.

Tremaine said, "Tyler Wilkes is in some serious trouble with some very serious people. A guy named Paul Spinelli, to be exact. Remember that name, Tyler will know who I'm talking about. Tyler wasn't sure exactly why I came to talk to him in the first place. He wasn't sure if I wanted to talk to him about a guy named Roger Gale or a cement company called L.A. Stone. You know about L.A. Stone; you watched me take pictures of the trucks. We've already discussed that. Right now, Tyler's probably convinced I'm looking into the cement company. Tell him he's wrong. Tell him I'm looking into both. And tell him not to talk to anyone about this until I contact him. I'll be contacting him soon."

Tremaine looked at the young guy, the young P.I., and said, "You get all that?"

"Yeah."

"Good."

Tremaine got up, leaving the young guy sitting at the picnic table looking blankly at his surroundings. At a softball game, a soccer game, a knife standing straight up.

Tremaine went home and looked up the offices for L.A. Stone. He found them, in Culver City, near all the furniture stores, between Venice and Washington. Then he searched around online for a picture of Paul Spinelli. Found that, too.

The next day, Tremaine drove to the front of the L.A. Stone building. At one o'clock sharp, he watched Paul Spinelli exit the building flanked by two men. The two men, to Tremaine's astonishment, were actually wearing designer sweat suits. Not Spinelli, though, not the Shark. The Shark wore a suit. Wonder if it's a shark-skin suit? The Shark in a shark-skin suit. Tremaine stayed in his car for an hour and a half, until Spinelli and the two men returned to the building.

Tremaine drove home.

The next day, at five till one, Tremaine pulled the Cutlass into the exact same spot it had been in the day before, right in front of the L.A. Stone offices.

At one, Spinelli and the same two men exited the building. Tremaine watched them and said aloud, "Good. The Shark is like me. Likes to have lunch at the same time every day."

Tremaine drove home.

CHAPTER 23

Tremaine knocked on Marvin Kearns's door. This time, he was home, Tremaine could hear him in there. Marvin opened the trailer door and Tremaine said, "I need a favor."

"Enter, Mr. Tremaine," Marvin said.

Tremaine entered Marvin's trailer and, as always, marveled at the walls festooned with Bruce Lee posters.

"Have a seat, my friend," Marvin said. Tremaine did. "Let me say in advance that it will be my pleasure to assist the great Donald Tremaine in whatever endeavor you request that I indulge in. Ever since you pulled me out of the ocean that day, my death imminent, MY DEATH IMMINENT, I have felt like I owed you one. It will be my pleasure to return the gesture."

Tremaine had taken Marvin surfing one winter day when the waves were big and the ocean was a little angry. Marvin, a decent surfer, had been pulled over the falls and was really struggling. Leash: snapped. Board: nowhere in sight. Tremaine grabbed him, pulled a cramp out of his calf, and swam him to safety. Marvin constantly told Tremaine he owed him one. Things Marvin enjoyed, like taking care of Lyle, didn't count. Marvin wanted to really return the gesture. Tremaine didn't feel like Marvin owed him anything. But even if he had, he wouldn't need to use that favor now, because this was about a case, and he knew Marvin would want to help. This request was pretty big, though—so, Tremaine figured, two birds with one stone.

Tremaine said, "This is actually about a case, Marvin."

"Superior," he said.

"You've often offered to help me."

"I have."

"But this is a big favor, so this takes care of the one you owe me, too."

"I'm listening."

"You're an actor, right?"

"I am."

"I want to hire you to do a gig, an acting gig."

"Done."

The next day, Tremaine told Marvin he was going to pick him up around noon for his acting gig. Marvin didn't know who he was going to perform for, didn't ask. But Tremaine told him anyway, a man by the name of Tyler Wilkes and a man by the name of Paul Spinelli.

Tremaine had things to do before picking up Marvin. He wanted to talk to Wendy Leahy again. So he grabbed the L.A. *Times*, got in the Cutlass, and drove down to L.A. Shape, and parked outside the building. It was only 8:45, he was going to wait until nine to go in.

During about two of the fifteen minutes he spent waiting—he didn't have his stopwatch for an exact time—he did the Jumble. KLABN to BLANK, CHEEN to HENCE, BIVEAL to VIABLE, and HUPSTY to typhus, then finally, ANEEVLYH to HEAVENLY. *Camping under the stars can be this: heavenly.*

During the other thirteen minutes, he thought about what he was going to say to Wendy Leahy. About how he had come to the conclusion that he *needed* to talk to her again.

During his time as a private investigator, Tremaine had discovered something that he believed to be true. This was: Sometimes your subconscious makes decisions for you. Sometimes, when you're thinking about something really hard, your subconscious begins to take the information that you've compiled and make conclusions on its own. It begins to connect A to B, and B to C, and C to D, then D back to A, and so on and so forth. Then it deposits the information it has collected into your conscious mind. It gives you a little gift. Out of nowhere. An idea pops into your head. Just like that. Boom. Hey, where'd that come from?

Tremaine believed it was very important to examine these gifts and to treat them with the utmost respect. To listen to them. He believed your subconscious mind was just as valid, if not more, than your conscious mind. It's alive, it's relevant, and, Tremaine had come to learn with regard to the field of private investigation, it's right a lot of the time.

Sometimes he listened to his subconscious doing something as simple and stupid as the Daily Jumble. He wouldn't *try* to solve the puzzle; he'd just look at it, and, just like that, the unscrambled word would appear. Like magic, almost. Who figured it out? The conscious Donald Tremaine didn't. He was barely even thinking about it.

Other times, Tremaine's subconscious told him more important things, things that pertained to his professional life. It was, indeed, his subconscious that told him to come talk to Wendy Leahy. It gave him an idea he wanted to share with her.

At nine, Tremaine called Wendy, and she, open as ever, had told him to come on over. This time, being an old pro, Tremaine just walked by the receptionist, through the gym, past a grunting man or two, and down the hallway where her office was. Sure enough, the place was packed. Don't these people have jobs?

Wendy Leahy greeted Tremaine with a smile. She said, "So, what's up? I'm telling you, there's not much else to say, unless you want the bedroom details." She giggled at her own comment, flirting in a way with the P.I. standing in front of her.

"No, I don't want the bedroom details," Tremaine said. "I just have a question for you."

Wendy Leahy gave him a look like, okay, go ahead.

Tremaine said, "You didn't have an affair with Roger Gale, did you?"

Wendy Leahy stared at Tremaine. She didn't speak for

what seemed like an eternity, but was probably closer to ten seconds. She fidgeted behind her desk, and then said, "It depends on your definition of 'affair.' What I told you happened, happened."

"Wendy, the man is dead, and you're not going to get into any kind of trouble for what you tell me. It stays here. Remember, if you're protecting him, you're not just protecting a guy who's dead. You're protecting a guy who was murdered. Somebody out there took another person's life. And if I'm going to find out who did it, I need to know the truth."

She didn't respond.

Then Tremaine said something he didn't want to say. He said, "You're not a suspect."

This of course made her feel like she was one. Instilled a little fear in her. Her eyes opened a bit, changing her face, the way it looked. Tremaine was almost amazed at how the brain's reaction to something could alter one's physical appearance.

"It's hot in here," she said. "Can we go out into the courtyard?"

Tremaine and Wendy Leahy sat in a pretty, tree-lined courtyard that was between the building L.A. Shape was in and the parking deck next door.

Wendy said, "Roger Gale did come to look at the gym and I did have an immediate fondness for him. And we did become friends, sort of."

"What do you mean?"

"I mean I got to know him a little when he asked me to do him the favor."

Tremaine waited for her to go on.

"He told me his wife suspected him of having an affair. I guess he worked late a lot and sometimes even spent the night at the office. Then he told me that he wasn't having an affair, but that his wife wouldn't let it die, and had even hired a private investigator to follow him around. He said his plan was just to pretend that he was having an affair, get caught, then promise to stop, just to get it over with. Just to get the notion out of his wife's head. He kept saying his wife was obsessed, and that he couldn't convince her that she was wrong. He'd given up trying. So, he was going to admit guilt to something he wasn't guilty of."

"To make her think she'd caught him. And inspired him to end it," Tremaine said.

"Yeah."

"What did he offer you for going along with it?"

"Five thousand dollars."

She looked at Tremaine with guilt in her eyes. She said, "I was broke, it seemed pretty harmless."

"And when you found out he was murdered?"

"I talked to my brother—we're really close—and he said, well, to change the story now would seem crazy. You know, tell the cops that Roger had paid me five thousand dollars to *say* we had an affair? It would sound nuts. Who knows who Roger had told that we'd actually had one? We figured it would be better just to stick with the original story. That the affair was real. Because, you know, if the cops couldn't solve the case, then suddenly I'm this woman with a crazy story who Roger had given a bunch of money to. You know?"

"You figured it was between you and Roger, and since no one else but Roger knew the real truth, it would be better to let sleeping dogs lie."

"Like I said, I didn't know who he had told or whatever. I just figured he paid me to say one thing, so, once he was dead, I just stuck with the original plan. I figured that would keep me out of it. Keep me from looking suspicious. Just admit to the affair. People have affairs all the time. That way it wouldn't look like I was involved in some other thing. Because I wasn't. Truth is, I didn't know Roger Gale from Adam. Plus, the five thousand he'd given me was long gone."

Tremaine looked at Wendy, her big, wide, honest face. The blonde hair and the blue eyes. Charmed by Roger Gale, she probably would have had a real affair with him. Then, out of nowhere, she was stuck in a situation she didn't know how to handle. So she just stuck with what would ruffle the least feathers.

Tremaine said, "Roger Gale never made a move on you?"

"Never."

Tremaine stood up and said, "Thank you, Wendy."

She stayed seated, looking up toward Tremaine. Her face began to redden a bit and her eyes filled up with the beginnings of tears. "Roger Gale seemed like a really nice guy. I was just trying to help him." Then she said, "How did you know our affair was made up?"

Tremaine thought about her question. Was it that her answers just seemed so thought out? *We had six dates and on the sixth we ended it.* Was it that she and Roger Gale just didn't seem to go together?

Tremaine answered her question. "I didn't."

Wendy looked at him, desperate almost, and said, "Am I going to get into trouble?" like a little kid.

"No, Wendy, you're not."

CHAPTER 24

It was noon. Tremaine was back at the trailer park, but not at his place—in front of Marvin's. It was time for Marvin to perform. The trailer door opened and Marvin Kearns came out, his bald head freshly shaved and glistening in the mid-morning sun. He was wearing black slacks with thick gray stripes running down the legs. The shoes, black and shiny. Up top, he wore a ribbed black tank top and a brown leather blazer. His eyes were covered by silver aviator-style sunglasses. His stocky build filled out the clothes nicely. He stood outside the car for a moment, almost posing, then got in.

Tremaine said, "You look perfect."

"I know," Marvin Kearns responded.

Tremaine dropped Marvin Kearns off in front of Paul Spinelli's office building, then headed over to Think Big Advertising, pulled into the lot, and got out his cell phone and began dialing.

Tremaine heard Drop-Dead Heather say, "Tyler Wilkes's office."

"Heather, this is Donald Tremaine."

"Donald, hi. I was just thinking about you the other night."

Tremaine thought about the parking lot that day and the way Heather looked when she struck her surfer pose. Tremaine stayed on point.

Tremaine said, "I wonder if you could pass on a message to Tyler for me."

"We were going to have a drink. You never called."

She was right, he had never called. He thought, losing focus for just a second, how could you forget to call this one? Get your shit together, Tremaine.

He said, "I didn't call, but I will."

"Good. Do you want me to put you on with Tyler? He's just sitting in his office."

"That's okay. Just tell him something for me."

"Okay."

"Tell him I'm out in the parking lot, and I want to talk to him for a minute."

Tremaine sat in his car watching the goings-on in the Think Big parking lot. That same look of employee, young, decked out in ironic clothing. He saw a guy, looked to be about thirty-five, wearing a *Dukes of Hazzard* T-shirt. He saw some Fonzie memorabilia hanging from the rearview of an Audi A4. One woman sported the Catholic high school girl look—pigtails and a plaid skirt. Tremaine could have used another second or two of her before she disappeared inside the building . . .

Then Tremaine saw Tyler Wilkes come out of the Think Big entrance. Some of his employees waved to him—he's the boss—but Tyler, Tremaine could tell by his body language, was nervous and in no mood for small talk. Tyler was looking around for Tremaine. Tremaine stuck his hand out the window of the Cutlass. Tyler spotted him and rushed over.

Tyler got to Tremaine's car, and Tremaine smiled and said, "Good afternoon, Tyler," through his opened window.

"What's this about?" Tyler said. He was frantic, even angry.

"This is about you, Tyler. Specifically, this is about your relationship with a man named Paul Spinelli. Do you know him?"

Tyler Wilkes looked at Tremaine and said, "Yes, I do. I'm in business with him. He has a cement company."

"Yes, he does." Tremaine said. And then continued, "Can I borrow an hour of your time?"

"Right now?" Tyler Wilkes said. The movements his face made suggested that right now wasn't an option.

"Yes, right now."

"I'm busy, Tremaine."

"Did the private eye, the one you hired to tail me, give you my message?"

Tyler didn't say anything. He just looked at Tremaine, worried.

Tremaine said, "I suggest you get in my car right now.

See, Paul Spinelli doesn't trust you anymore. He thinks you're the kind of guy who might get him into trouble. Who might *want* to get him into trouble. And when he thinks someone is out to get him in trouble, he gets angry. Very angry."

"Paul Spinelli does not think I'm out to get him in trouble. He's a cement man and I gave him some money."

"Get in the car, Tyler, and I'll prove it."

Tremaine and Tyler Wilkes drove down Lincoln Boulevard, then right on Washington toward Culver City.

"There are some smokes in the glove if you want one," Tremaine said.

Tyler Wilkes didn't go for one. Or respond.

"Well, if you're not going to have one, will you hand me one?"

Tyler Wilkes did as he was asked. Tremaine lit up.

Tremaine pulled down Chapin Street in Culver City, the street Paul Spinelli's office building was on. Tyler looked nervous. Tremaine thinking, the closer we get to the L.A. Stone offices, the closer my accusations are to becoming real to Tyler.

Tremaine and Tyler Wilkes sat in the parked Cutlass, sat right where Tremaine had sat those two days he'd come to watch Spinelli go to lunch.

Tremaine said, "I want you to watch something."

At one, Spinelli exited the building, his two lunch buddies in tow. Tremaine and Tyler, sitting in the Cutlass, watched Marvin Kearns, dressed like a tough guy, a mob guy, walk toward Spinelli and the two men. Tremaine and Tyler then watched Marvin reach the men and, with a big smile, shake hands with them. Marvin was introducing himself, but Tyler didn't know that.

Tremaine said, "That man, the bald one with the leather jacket, is one of Paul Spinelli's right-hand men."

"All right," Tyler Wilkes said.

Tremaine and Tyler watched Marvin hand Spinelli an envelope. In it was a gift certificate to a nearby restaurant, Herman's. Marvin was telling Spinelli that he worked for Herman, and that Herman wanted to reach out to a successful local businessman with a gift certificate to his restaurant. And that he'd be honored if Spinelli, a man of great stature, would accept the gift certificate and come by for an expensive dinner any time. Free of charge. Spinelli took the envelope, smiled wide, and put it in the inside pocket of his blazer.

In the Cutlass, Tremaine said to Wilkes, "That envelope he handed Spinelli? That was a report on you."

"On me? What do you mean, on me?" Wilkes said.

Tremaine pulled the Cutlass out of the spot and guided the car right, around the corner. Paul Spinelli's building was now out of sight.

Tremaine said, "You know how you couldn't tell what I was looking for when I first came in to your office?"

"Yeah."

"Well," Tremaine said as he steered the Cutlass down a long alley behind a warehouse, then right again to an area of Dumpsters closed in by high cement walls on three sides, "I work for Paul Spinelli. We were looking into you."

Just after Tremaine said this, Marvin Kearns appeared

from behind one of the cement walls. Tremaine and Tyler looked at him, stocky, bald, leather blazer over a tank top, mean-ass expression on his face.

Tremaine looked over and down. Tyler's hand was visibly shaking.

CHAPTER 25

The three of them, Tyler, Marvin, and Tremaine, were now standing in the area with the Dumpsters and the three cement walls. Marvin Kearns stood stone-silent with a stern look on his face, those big shades adding to the mystery. Tremaine began talking to Tyler Wilkes.

Tremaine said, "You're in trouble. Like I said, this man here is what you might call a very close associate to Paul Spinelli. Paul Spinelli thinks you're going to get him in trouble. That you're suspicious of him."

Tyler Wilkes's eyes were open wide now, sweat was forming on his forehead. Marvin moved closer to Tyler, just a little closer.

Tyler said, "What is this? I have no idea what Paul Spinelli is up to. All I did was invest in his company."

"Paul Spinelli hired me to look into you because he thought you were the type of person that might assume things that weren't true. Example: After I came and talked to you, you hired someone to follow me. You know why you hired someone to follow me?"

Tyler Wilkes couldn't speak. He tried, but nothing came out. So he just shook his head, no.

Tremaine said, "You did that because you think Paul Spinelli is up to something, don't you? Instead of being confident that you've made a sound investment in his company, you thought you had a reason to be suspicious. So I played right into your hands. As soon as you found out I took pictures of the cement trucks, you thought, I knew it! Spinelli's a bad guy. And Paul Spinelli can't live with that."

Tyler, stuttering, said, "I hired the P.I. so I could tell Spinelli about you."

Tremaine said, "I don't think so. And neither does Spinelli. You wouldn't have hired a P.I. if you didn't think Spinelli was up to something. And, like I said, Spinelli can't live with that."

After Tremaine said this, Marvin Kearns moved his blazer to the side and pulled out a gun. A black Browning Hi-Power 9mm. It wasn't loaded. But Tyler Wilkes didn't know this, would never know this.

At the sight of the gun, Tyler Wilkes gasped. He was breathing very hard. Marvin Kearns didn't point the gun at Tyler, but he moved even closer now and said quietly but with force, Marvin's first line in this performance, "What do you know about Paul Spinelli?"

Tyler could barely get his words out. A stain appeared on the front of his pants. The poor guy had wet himself.

"I don't know anything. I swear. I don't suspect him of anything. I never have, and I never will say a word to anyone about anything he does."

Marvin Kearns took another step closer to Tyler. Tyler fell to his knees and clutched his chest. Marvin pursed his lips. Despite the calm Marvin betrayed, you could feel the rage beneath his skin. A really good performance, Tremaine was thinking.

"Now is not the time to lie, Mr. Wilkes," Marvin said.

Mr. Wilkes. Marvin threw that one in on his own.

"I swear I don't know anything. I swear. Please . . . Please . . . Don't kill me," Tyler begged.

Tremaine and Marvin both knew now for sure that Tyler Wilkes was thoroughly convinced that this was a serious situation. The man thought he was going to get killed.

Next came the pivotal question.

Marvin said, "What do you know about the murder of Roger Gale?"

Tremaine tensed imperceptibly. Would Wilkes be able to put two and two together and discover that this had absolutely nothing to do with Paul Spinelli? That they were using his relationship to the Shark to get information on Roger Gale? That Tremaine kept Tyler thinking it *might* be about Roger Gale so Tyler wouldn't talk to Spinelli before he had a chance to put his plan into action? No way, the guy was on the ground, soaked in urine, begging for his life.

Tyler, on the ground, desperation ravaging his face, said, "Nothing. Nothing about Roger Gale. He was a rival in business. I had nothing to do with his murder. Oh, God. I'm seeing black spots."

Good, Tremaine thought.

Marvin clutched the gun, so Tyler would see him, and said, "I will repeat the question once. What do you know about the murder of Roger Gale?"

Tears welled up in Tyler's eyes. He struggled to breathe and said, "I don't know anything about the murder. I don't."

Tyler turned to Tremaine. "Please, tell him not to kill me. I don't know how or why Roger Gale was killed."

Tyler was on all fours, sweating, stammering, slobbering.

Tremaine said, "What do you know about Roger Gale? Anything. What do you know that I don't know?"

Tyler looked up at Tremaine. He had an almost puppy-dog expression in his eyes, on all fours like he was, next to some Dumpsters and bleak, gray cement walls. Thinking, for sure, what a terrible place to die.

"I used to follow him around," Tyler said.

With a motion of the hand, Tremaine gestured to Marvin to back off. Marvin backed up and put the gun away.

Tremaine looked at Tyler on the ground, looked right into Tyler's eyes, and said, "Follow him? What do you mean?"

"I got a little obsessed with the guy, all right? A lot obsessed, really. When you work in my business, certain people start to get worshipped, he was one of them. I started to idolize him, think about him all the time. I couldn't stop thinking about him. And then, I wanted to know what he did and where he was all the time."

Tyler began to get his breath back. He crawled over to one of the walls and rested his back against it, regaining his composure a bit.

"For a while," Tyler said, "he never went anywhere interesting. He'd go to work, then go home, just like the rest of the world."

Tyler had calmed down. Having been pressed to the edge of death, he was able to speak with clarity and honesty.

"But I followed him anyway. I'd sit there, outside his office. It was pathetic. Then once, on the weekend, I saw him drive out of his house alone and go downtown. And I tailed him, of course. He went to this karate studio. It was one of those studios that sits in, like, a strip mall. A strange little place. I was a couple blocks away, parked, but I saw him go in."

Tremaine said, "What, he was taking karate lessons?"

"That's what I thought. But when he walked in, he wasn't wearing a karate uniform. And there were no other students showing up. I guess he could have changed and showered in there, and taken a private lesson or something, but this place was a little dump. It seemed weird. So the next weekend, I went down to the studio by myself, just to check it out. I made sure to go at the same time he had gone. This time I parked in the strip mall. I walked in, and there was no one around. Then, this guy comes up to me, the owner I guess, and says, 'Can I help you?' I said, 'I hope so.' Then he said, 'Do you want a karate lesson?' And I said, 'No.' And he said, 'Then what do you want?' And I just looked at him. And he looked at me. Then he said, 'Do you have a card?' And I gave him one. And he called my office, talked to my assistant and didn't leave a message. I figured later he was checking to see if I was a cop. Then he said, 'The show's five hundred bucks.' I paid him and he took me into a room in the back. I sat down, the room was pretty nice, and there was a stage in front of the chair I was in. A few minutes later, a stripper walked in and started to dance, taking off her clothes, writhing around, the whole deal. And then . . . and then a man walked in. And . . . and he stripped, too. And . . . screwed her, fucked her, right there on the stage. And I watched. It was a live sex show."

Tremaine and Marvin were looking down at Tyler Wilkes. Tremaine, for the first time, fully believed something coming out of the mouth of this guy.

Tyler continued. "I quit following him after that. I'm not exactly sure why, but I quit. But I never told anyone. What's weirder, Roger Gale going to a sex show or me following him to a sex show?"

With Marvin Kearns in back, Tremaine drove Tyler Wilkes back to Think Big Advertising. The three rode the majority of the way in silence. Tremaine asked Tyler exactly where the karate place was and Tyler told him, but, mostly, the three men sat in silence. It was just the wind coming through the windows and the noise from the street. As Tremaine pulled into Think Big, he said, "Paul Spinelli never wants to hear about any of this. It didn't happen. Understand?"

Tyler Wilkes, calm now, said, "What do Paul Spinelli and Roger Gale have to do with each other?"

Nothing. Tremaine knew that. He looked at Tyler. He didn't answer his question, he just looked at him. Right at him.

Tyler held up his hands and said, "I don't know and I don't care and I'll never even think about it much less talk about it."

Tremaine nodded. Tyler got out of the car and slowly walked toward the entrance to his ad agency.

Tremaine and Marvin watched him and Marvin said, "Did you get the information you needed?"

"Yeah, that guy had nothing to do with Roger Gale's murder. He's no longer a suspect."

Marvin got in front, then Tremaine threw the Cutlass in drive, and headed back to the trailer park.

"Your performance was nothing short of stellar, by the way," Tremaine said.

"Thank you."

"And, just so you know, when Spinelli goes to redeem his gift certificate, he'll be treated well and told that Herman, who has long since sold his stake in the place, had to go back to New York to take care of his mother."

"An admirable thing to do."

"I thought so."

Tremaine reached in the glove for a smoke. Marvin said, "I think I'll join you in one."

"Every now and then they aren't so bad."

They dropped down to the PCH, smokes in their mouths, both enjoying the familiar, nostalgic feeling that they were headed back to Malibu.

"Oh, and Tyler Wilkes?" Tremaine said. "You have nothing to worry about. He'll never say a word to Paul Spinelli."

"I know," Marvin said, and he blew out a plume of smoke that, in an instant, got sucked out the open front window of the Cutlass.

CHAPTER 26

Tremaine was on his way down to the karate place. It was gray out, a rarity in L.A., a nice change. He was on Olympic, taking it all the way downtown, through Westwood, Beverly Hills, Hollywood, and Hancock Park. He was seeing myriad sections of the city and never going left or right. Just straight, due east, away from the beach.

He thought about what he knew. Was it more or was it less? Was the whole reason Roger Gale had pulled the Wendy Leahy ruse just to keep his wife from knowing about a stupid sex show? Tremaine knew, from the inception of his research on the guy, that Roger Gale had no problem going out of his way to mold the way people thought—about him, his company, his ideas. His work stint in a plant in Detroit proved that. But paying a woman to pretend she was having an affair with him? Would he go that far just to hide the fact that he liked to go watch people have sex? At the end of the day, that's not that big of a deal. Real-life porn, that's it. And it couldn't have been that hard to sneak downtown every so often. The guy, according to everyone he'd talked to, was always on the move. No one would notice. So why get Wendy Leahy involved? Why go to those lengths?

And why was his wife so convinced he was having an affair in the first place? Where was the intellectual, adult relationship Evelyn Gale had referred to? *We go to plays and talk about books and ideas* . . . Hiring a P.I. to follow around your husband? That's more like soap-opera love. Did Evelyn get paranoid just because of a trip or two downtown for a little live smut? Or was Gale doing something else, something even Tyler didn't know about?

Tremaine thought, that's the question. What was Roger Gale's motive for paying Wendy Leahy to help facilitate that illusion? Tremaine understood the psychology of it. Admit it, really admit it, and his wife would be off his back so he could do what he wanted. Go downtown at his leisure, whatever. But again, why go to those lengths? Why was it so important that his wife not know what he was up to?

Or maybe, maybe, it was just as it seemed. Roger Gale wanted freedom from his wife's suspicions, for whatever insignificant thing he was up to, so he got her off his back. In his own crazy style. The guy was a professional manipulator. That's what he did for a living. Better than anyone in the world. So he figured out a way to manipulate his wife's thinking, and he executed it. In an extremely high-concept way. And the five grand he gave to Wendy? That was nothing to Roger Gale. Yeah, Tremaine thought, maybe it was just another campaign for him. Another dramatic form of manipulation. And, in his stellar style, it worked.

Downtown L.A., some skyscrapers and a thriving business community during the week, but a world apart from Beverly Hills and Hollywood and Malibu and Santa Monica. No glitz, no flash, but a nobility that's palpable. Old buildings mixed in with the skyscrapers, locals crawling the streets who lived there, who worked there, who weren't a part of the stereotypical L.A. Tremaine liked it down here, resented that this part of the city played stepchild to the famous and fancy sections.

Tremaine weaved his way through the streets, looking at the shops and the buildings, soaking in this forgotten and unappreciated part of town. He got to Seventh Street and went left, west for a few blocks, back toward the beach. The buildings began to shrink around him, he was nearing the outskirts of downtown proper. And there was the little strip mall, right on the corner of Seventh and Coronado, right where Tyler said it was.

The strip mall took up the whole corner of the block. It was comprised of five or six random little establishments and the karate studio with its façade that said KARATE STUDIO, right there in the middle. There was a sushi joint in the corner space of the strip mall, and next to it sat a sad little store that sold nothing but lightbulbs. It was called Just Lightbulbs. There was also a barber shop, an old one, run-down, sad-looking. Flanking the karate studio, there was an aquarium and reptile place on the left, Underwater World, and a wig store on the right, Expert Wigs.

183

Tremaine thought, maybe I'll pick up an iguana for Lyle to pal around with. The bulldog and the lizard. He could ride around on Lyle's back. No, Lyle wouldn't like that . . .

Tremaine parked the Cutlass in the strip mall's little lot and sat in it thinking about what to do. He pulled out a Marlboro, lit it, smoked it. He looked at the karate studio. Bright lights, mirrors on the walls, but no action going on inside.

Tremaine got out of the Cutlass and walked in.

He stood inside, alone, looking around. It was pretty small, just one big room with wooden floors, mirrors everywhere, and bright, bright lights. There was a door in the back of the room that presumably led to a back section of the studio. Tremaine was staring at the door as it opened.

A black man in a karate uniform walked out of the back. "Can I help you?" he said.

It was the same thing he had said to Tyler, and to Roger Gale, probably, too. The man in front of Tremaine looked dangerous. Had a look in his eye, a glimmer, that Tremaine suspected he could use to be charming or mean as shit.

Tremaine smiled and said, "Man, is there a bathroom I could use here?"

"Only for students."

The two of them stood there looking at each other. Out of the corners of his eyes, Tremaine could see a million versions of himself and the black man in the ubiquitous mirrors.

"I'm in a jam," Tremaine said. "Too much coffee. Please. I just have to take a piss. I already tried the aquarium place next door, they said no."

The man laughed and said, "All right, man. I'll show you where it is."

He led Tremaine to the door he had come out of at the back of the studio. He opened it and led Tremaine in, following closely behind him. Once behind the door, Tremaine could see a hallway, a long hallway, with several doors on the right-hand side, maybe four, and two doors on the left. It was clean and kind of nice-looking. Freshly painted white walls, no dirt anywhere, and blond hardwood floors just like up-front.

The guy led Tremaine to the first door on the left, still standing close, right there, and said, "This is the bathroom."

Tremaine thought, he could have stayed up-front and said, "The bathroom's the first door on the left," and let me find it on my own. But he didn't. He led me back here personally. Maybe he didn't want me to go in the wrong door . . .

Tremaine went in the bathroom and the man stood outside, watching him as he went in.

The bathroom was also clean and nice. Tremaine made sure to actually use the bathroom, as he was sure the man was standing outside, right outside. After Tremaine flushed, but before he washed his hands, he heard, through the wall, what sounded like a woman laughing. Had to be coming from the other room on the left, adjacent to the bathroom, not any of the rooms on the right.

Tremaine washed his hands, dried them, then walked out of the bathroom, and there was the guy, waiting for him. Looking right at him, that glimmer holding firm in his eyes.

"You're a lifesaver," Tremaine said.

"Been there."

The guy motioned for Tremaine to lead the way out, back to the front of the studio, and Tremaine did, walking straight out, not even looking to the left at the four closed doors.

And there they were again, the two of them, standing face to face in the front of the studio, their reflections all over the place. Tremaine thought, how does this guy fit in to my puzzle? And then he thought, should I ask him about Tyler Wilkes, about Roger Gale? Tremaine looked at the guy. Intense, but calm. No, this one's not the person to ask.

Tremaine said, "Thanks. I really appreciate it."

The guy looked at him and nodded. Before heading for the door, Tremaine took one last look at the guy standing there, his black skin contrasting with the white cloth of the karate uniform. Tremaine looked in the man's glimmering eyes for just a moment, and, in that moment, he could see charm, suspicion, and evil.

CHAPTER 27

Tremaine left the strip mall and drove two miles west, back toward the beach. Then he turned the Cutlass right, back on Olympic now, then right again, back toward downtown, back toward the karate studio. But this time he approached it from the back side, north of Seventh Street, from behind the strip mall. He pulled the Cutlass into the alley behind the stores in the mall, where the employees of the aquarium store, the wig store, the karate studio, the sushi restaurant, and the barber shop parked. He then went left down an alley that ran perpendicular to the one he was on, did a U-turn, and tucked the Cutlass behind a four-foot brick wall, facing the alley behind the strip mall. He sat in the car and waited.

Dusk fell, then night. Six smokes and side one of the Allman Brothers *Live at Fillmore East*.

He watched various people from the various establishments head out into the alley and get in their cars and leave for the day. Mostly people he didn't recognize, and then one guy he did. The black guy from the karate studio. Tremaine watched the guy get in his car, a Corvette, a new one, and cruise down the alley, away from him. Then the Corvette went left, away from Seventh, and was gone.

Tremaine stayed put.

Moments later, Tremaine saw two people leave from the same door the black man had left. A young man and a young woman, an attractive young woman with blonde hair and some serious surgical augmentation. Tremaine could tell from where he was sitting and watching. And he wasn't that close. The two people got into separate cars. The man, a yellow VW Golf. The woman, a white Ford Explorer.

Tremaine was interested in the woman. He watched her drive down the alley, right past him. She hit Cornado and went left toward Seventh. Tremaine cranked up the Cutlass, pulled out from his little space by the brick wall, and followed her.

On Olympic now, headed west, Tremaine had the Ford Explorer in his sights, pretty far up there, lots of cars in between them, but he wasn't going to lose her. Fifteen minutes later, back in Hollywood, the Explorer went through the light at La Brea, so did the Cutlass.

Tremaine followed the Explorer right down a side street, then left, then right, then onto Wilshire. Tremaine thought, this is her home turf. The Explorer pulled into a metered parking space in front of some little shops and restaurants right there on Wilshire. Tremaine got lucky and found a spot three spaces up from the Explorer. Tremaine watched the woman get out of her car and walk into a Chinese Restaurant, not fancy, take-out style.

Tremaine got out of the Cutlass and stood next to it, waiting. Ten minutes later, he saw the woman exit the restaurant, a bag of Chinese food in one hand, the keys to her Explorer in the other.

Tremaine started walking toward the Explorer. The woman was next to the driver's side door as Tremaine was next to the passenger's side door. She clicked the unlock button on her keychain twice. She opened the back door on the driver's side and put the bag of Chinese food on the back seat of the Explorer. She shut the back door. Then she opened her door and got in. As she was about to put the keys in the ignition, Tremaine quickly opened the passenger's side door, got in, and shut the door.

The woman screamed. A wild and fearful look possessed her eyes.

Tremaine said, "Calm down. I'm a cop."

She looked at him, frozen. She had her keys in her right hand, and Tremaine could see there was a small bottle of mace on her keychain.

"Don't use that mace. Put your keys on the floor. Do it," he said. "Do it now."

She did.

The woman was porn-star attractive. Fake everything. An almost-orange tan, bright-white bleached teeth, and an absurd chest. And wild-eyed, crazy blue eyes that suggested a sexual confidence that was palpable, impossible to miss.

Tremaine said, "I know what you do, I know what your

boss does, and I want you to know this: I don't care. I don't give two shits."

She stared at him. She was scared, but she had an aggression about her. She'd been in sticky situations before. And she hadn't said a word since Tremaine had gotten in. The only sound she'd made was the initial scream.

Tremaine said, "I'm going to pull some pictures out of my pocket and show them to you. I want you to tell me if the people in the pictures have ever been to one of your shows. We are looking for these people. We do not care what you do at your studio. We are just looking for these people. If we cared what you did at your studio, you would be out of business and your boss would be in jail. You might be, too."

Tremaine pulled a picture out of his pocket. It was a picture of Tyler Wilkes. He showed it to the woman.

She said, calmly, "Yeah, he came in. I think a couple times. But he hasn't been in for a while."

Tremaine nodded. She wasn't lying, not yet, at least. Tremaine said, "Now, I'm going to show you someone else. I want you to tell me the same thing, if he's ever been to one of your shows."

Tremaine pulled out a picture of Roger Gale and showed it to the woman.

She looked at it, closely, and said, "I don't think so. I don't think I've ever seen him."

Tremaine thought, was she lying because she and the karate studio people were somehow involved with Roger Gale, or was she telling the truth?

Tremaine said, "Is it possible that you might not have seen him but someone else did?"

"It's possible, if he just came in once or something. But I doubt it. Most people are repeat customers. There are a couple other girls there, a couple other performers, but we're all there most days. And we can look in the room at our guests. Even when we're not performing. And we do. Look at our guests, I mean."

Tremaine said, "You've never seen this man? Don't lie to me."

"If you're a cop," she said, "why don't you shut us down? If it's so important that you find these guys, what difference does it make to you if you take us down in the process?"

"Like you said," Tremaine said, holding up the picture of Roger Gale. "Your customers come back. We want him to come back."

"I don't think he's ever come in."

"We didn't know that. Now we do."

"So now that you know that, are we going to get shut down?"

"Not if you keep your mouth shut."

"About what?" she said. "Our operation or you jumping in my car?"

"Both," Tremaine said. And he opened the door to the Explorer and got out.

CHAPTER 28

Tremaine was on the roof of his trailer in Malibu, a beautiful night to be on the roof of a trailer in Malibu. How did all of this stuff connect? His conscious mind wasn't helping him. Neither was his subconscious mind. He picked up Lyle and put him in his lap. Lyle, being agreeable tonight, not bickering over being moved.

"Who's telling me the truth, Lyle? And, Lyle, who's lying?"

Tyler Wilkes wasn't lying, not under the pressure they put him under. He saw Roger Gale go in that karate studio. Tremaine thought, maybe, just maybe, Roger Gale had gone in there just to use the bathroom, like I had pretended to do. Maybe Gale had just innocently gone into the studio, and Tyler Wilkes reaped the fruits of that accident and got himself a peep show or two. Or maybe Gale just went in once or twice for the experience, then never went back. And the girl had missed him.

Or was the girl in the Explorer lying? Was she protecting her boss, her pimp? That guy was tough, intense, Tremaine could see that, it was obvious. Maybe she would lie, even to a guy she thought was a cop, just to protect him. Tremaine thought, were they involved somehow with Roger Gale? But if Gale had gone in there and just seen a few shows, and the karate studio people weren't involved with him in any other way, why would she lie about it? She didn't lie about Tyler. She'd come right out and said, yeah, that guy's been in here a few times. But, but, was she cool enough under pressure to admit to having seen Tyler Wilkes, but not admit to having seen Roger Gale, if she had indeed seen Roger Gale?

Hmm, Tremaine thought, Lyle on his lap, the beautiful Malibu sky black and dotted with stars above his head. What do I know? What do I *really* know? That Roger Gale said he had an affair but he didn't. And that he'd gone into a karate studio in downtown Los Angeles and may or may not have seen a sex show. Tremaine sat there, silent, Lyle, a hot sleeping mound on his lap, breathing, up and down, up and down.

"What's going on here, Lyle?"

Lyle didn't answer.

Tremaine's cell rang, he looked at it, didn't recognize the number on the caller ID.

"Tremaine," he said.

"Donald, it's Heather," the voice said.

Heather? Oh, Drop Dead Heather. Tremaine thought,

shit, how is it possible that I keep forgetting to call this girl?

Heather said, "We had a deal."

Tremaine thought, I'm not making this mistake again, and said, "You're right. What are you doing right now?"

"Driving home from work."

Tremaine said, "Should we meet at Casa Del Mar, in Santa Monica? Half-hour or so?"

"Perfect," Heather said. "I can walk there from my apartment."

"See you soon."

And when Tremaine walked in to the big, sprawling hotel bar with big windows out to the beach, he did see Heather, immediately, standing at the bar, and he thought, man, Drop Dead Heather is truly the perfect name. She's a killer, an assassin, big white teeth smiling at him as he approached. He remembered her now approaching him that day in the parking lot. Walking toward him. The long blonde hair, the body . . . The body that defies physics. The body that made you say, out loud, "How'd they do that?" The body that was skinny in the right places and not skinny in the right places and was about to make Tremaine just run out the door, dive into the ocean, and end it all.

Tremaine could see others in the bar, men *and* women, thinking, who's the lucky guy? Who's the guy who gets to have a drink with the bombshell?

Tremaine said, "Heather, you're looking well."

"Thank you, Donald."

It was honestly hard for him to focus. If someone offered him a million bucks to add two and two, he might not be up to the challenge.

"What did you do to Tyler?" Heather said. "When he got back the other day, he seemed . . . scared."

"I just asked him some questions."

"Well, do that more often. He gave us the rest of the day off, and I went to the beach."

Heather stepped over to Tremaine and put her arm up against his and said, "See my tan?"

"Pretty good," Tremaine said. "But I might still have you beat."

She smiled at him, her eyes smiled, too, and she said, "You've had more years in the sun than me."

"I was afraid you might point that out."

They settled into two seats down at the corner of the bar. Tremaine looked around. Tremaine enjoyed a nice hotel bar. And Casa Del Mar was a good one. Big rugs, big chairs, and those big windows out to the beach. And locals came here, too, after work, to see people, wind down, chat a little, maybe do some Westside networking.

"By the way," Heather said, "what case are you working on? Can you tell me?"

Heather. She was cool. She respected the fact that maybe he didn't want to tell her, so, because of that, he would.

"I'm investigating the murder of Roger Gale."

"I remember when he was killed. I was just getting started in advertising. So, does Tyler . . ."

"He has nothing to do with it," Tremaine said. Then, with a grin, "But I still don't like him."

Heather returned the grin and said, "Me neither."

Tremaine bought them another round, then another,

then another. And then there was that Drop Dead Heather smile again, coming toward him. She leaned in as she said, "I looked you up online again. Why'd you quit surfing right after you won the title?"

Tremaine said, "It was time."

Despite her buzz, she didn't push him, she just said, "You know, you can buy that video, *Insane Tremaine*, online."

"That's a really dumb name."

"I like it," she said.

"I didn't do anything insane on that video. I was just trying to catch waves."

Heather got off her barstool and stood up in front of Tremaine. He looked at her, standing there in her work clothes, gray pants and a black oxford, unbuttoned a few buttons down. She moved a little closer to him and grabbed his hand. He couldn't help but look at her, check her out again. The blonde hair, the white teeth, the tan arm touching him.

"Let's go to my apartment."

"I'll race you there," he said.

They got to her apartment, a really nice place, tucked away on a quiet little street just blocks from the beach. Tremaine had almost forgotten that she was in her early twenties, then he saw the Monet print on the wall.

"I still have that from college. Don't make fun of me. I needed to fill up some wall space."

Heather, he thought. Just as I'm about to pin the foolish-little-girl rap on her, she comes up with something like that.

Then Heather did something that really surprised Tremaine. A genuine surprise, the kind that only comes around a couple times in a lifetime.

She said, "I want to show you something."

"Okay," he said.

"Stay right here."

She walked into the back bedroom, and then, moments later, came back out. She was wearing nothing but a black bra and black underwear.

Tremaine was having some trouble breathing. He said, "You look terrific."

She walked closer to him. She was now standing right in front of him.

"Question," Tremaine said.

"Yes," Heather said.

"Why are you making this so easy for me? Most guys . . . no, every guy on the face of the earth would give an arm and a leg—and then another arm and another leg—for this opportunity."

"I like you," she said. "I get so sick of guys drooling all over me that I never get to do anything like this. I'm repulsed—sometimes scared—most of the time. When someone comes along that actually plays it cool, I don't want to miss that opportunity. Because I really like doing stuff like this."

Tremaine thought, one of the reasons she thinks I'm playing it cool is because I genuinely forgot to call her because of the case. Then he told himself what Heather had told him once: "So."

Heather unclasped her bra, and Tremaine watched it fall

to the floor. Heather's big, white smile was gone, she was getting serious. She grabbed Tremaine's hands and placed them on her breasts.

Tremaine thought for a moment that he'd died and gone to heaven. But that actually came a little later.

CHAPTER 29

The next morning, Tremaine woke up in the trailer. He'd left Heather's in the night, a stupid smile plastered on his face for the entirety of the drive back to Malibu. He felt refreshed, the frustrations of the case eased a little. He knew what he had to do next, so he called Lopez and told him what he wanted, and where he wanted to meet, and how much he would buy him in order to get him there.

That evening, Tremaine pulled the Cutlass into the Chez Jay parking lot in Santa Monica. Tremaine looked around, didn't see Lopez's black Mustang, not here yet. He hopped out of his car and walked toward the entrance. Chez Jay, a spot both he and Lopez enjoyed. An old-school sailor bar right across from the beach. Lots of tradition, nice and dark. The kind of place where most nights you'd see regulars, but because of the atmosphere and the extra-cold beer and the juicy steaks, often you'd see a Michelle Pfeiffer or a Jeff Bridges tucked away in the corner.

Tremaine grabbed a table near the back, lucky, the place was packed. He ordered two bourbons and sat back and waited. Five minutes later, Lopez entered, a manila folder under his arm.

"Mr. Lopez!" Tremaine said as he stood up and handed John Lopez his bourbon.

"Tremaine, I'm getting lobster. I hope you know that."

"I didn't *know* that, but I figured it. That's what I do in my line of work. I figure stuff. You rarely know stuff."

Lopez tossed the manila envelope onto the table and sat down. "There you go," he said. "There are police reports in there for all of the murders in the greater Los Angeles area, a week before and a week after the murder of Roger Gale. There are some nice pictures in there, too."

"Thank you."

"Getting desperate, huh?"

"No comment."

"That Donald Tremaine magic eluding you?"

"There's not a whole lot of evidence in this one, John."

"Sometimes the guys down at the old station house do their jobs. And sometimes there's just not a lot of answers. As you know, Tremaine, there are lots and lots and lots of unsolved cases out there."

"Thanks for the history lesson, pal."

Lopez put the brakes on giving Tremaine shit. He said, "Just so you know, Peterson and those guys looked at the other murders in town around the time of the Roger Gale thing. Said none of 'em even gave them the slightest indication of anything."

Tremaine thought about Peterson, the bribe he took, the dinner they had in Atlanta. But he didn't mention it. He just said, "Like I said, there's not a whole lot of evidence."

Tremaine took Lopez through the case, where he was, the stuff he'd found out, omitting, of course, information he couldn't part with—the Peterson stuff, posing as a cop in the Explorer . . . Lopez listened, sympathized. Some intriguing stuff, sure, but most of it was vague and left the mind still questioning, grasping for connections.

When the waitress came around, Lopez said, "How's the lobster?"

The waitress responded, "Oh, it's real good."

Lopez said, "Actually, I don't care how it tastes. Just as long as it's expensive."

"It is," she said.

"I'll take it," he said.

The next day, up on top of the trailer, Tremaine examined some of the crime statistics and police reports Lopez had given him. In the year Roger Gale was murdered, there were more than five hundred murders in the greater Los Angeles area. Five hundred. Pathetic. During the two weeks surrounding Roger Gale's murder, there were sixteen, including his.

Tremaine thought, more than one a day. So, every day, somebody in L.A. wakes up for the last time . . .

Tremaine focused on the sixteen murders. Miraculously,

most of them had been solved. Closed cases. Four of them hadn't been, one of those being Gale's. Of the three other people who had been killed during this time, two of them had been killed on the same day as Roger Gale. The other person had been killed two days before Gale was.

The two people who had been killed on the same day as Gale were named Juanita Hernandez and Kelly Burch. The person killed two days prior to Gale was named Theodore Epps.

Tremaine studied these three murders. First, he looked at the information on Theodore Epps. Black, twenty-five years old. Murder took place in Compton, California. Shot to death, gang-related, drive-by.

Juanita Hernandez was stabbed to death in a crack house in Englewood, California. Tremaine didn't need to look much further to know that this case probably wasn't the most heavily investigated in LAPD history. The police report didn't list a single possible suspect. It just described the scene. Abandoned crack house, one local relative who refused to do a body identification. Dental records confirmed the woman's identity.

Tremaine looked at the third murder, Kelly Burch. This killing certainly didn't scream of a connection to Roger Gale, but this wasn't a gang murder and it didn't take place in a crack house, so, to Tremaine's eye, there was at least a little mystery to it, a little hope.

Burch was shot in her studio apartment in Hollywood. She was listed as twenty-eight, Caucasian, addicted to cocaine, no living parents, no job. Her sister, Angela Coyle, who lived in Indio, California, had come out to bury her. Tremaine looked at the report. According to police officers, this was probably a case of someone either not paying or betraying her dealers and getting killed for it. The cops, however, never found out for sure. Probably had to move on to another case, Tremaine thought.

Tremaine looked at the photo of Kelly Burch. Dead on her own kitchen floor, shot in the face. Tremaine tended to agree with the cops—probably a drug crime. Often those were macho killings. You fucked me, I'm going to blow your face off.

Tremaine never really got used to looking at crime photography. You could become desensitized, to be sure, but that was a trick the brain played. Because if you allowed yourself to stop and think about what you were looking at, it got you every time.

Tremaine, up on his roof in the sun, enjoying another beautiful day, but looking at a horrifying sight. Kelly Burch's picture. Whatever that girl had going, whatever hope she had, even if it was absolutely minute, it was gone now for good. Anyone she'd ever affected, a family member, a friend, a clerk at a grocery store, would never see her again. Ever. Looking at this picture in some perverse way made Tremaine realize why he'd taken the Roger Gale case in the first place, why he took any murder case.

Because someone was dead.

CHAPTER 30

Kelly Burch had lived on North Harper, in Hollywood. Tremaine took the Ten to La Cienega, then headed north for a couple miles into the flatlands of Hollywood. This wasn't the Hollywood of movie stars. It wasn't bad, it was okay, pretty nice even, but it was a far cry from the Hollywood people dreamed about. Not too many millionaire actresses walking designer Chihuahuas and driving electric cars that they didn't even like. No, this was the Hollywood where you lived before you made it. If you made it. Apartment living. And shops and modest restaurants and a sizable amount of angst in the air. Intensity. Lots of people walking around with heads full of dreams and ideas. And lots of traffic, too. Tremaine sat at the light at La Cienega and Beverly forever. But he didn't really mind. He hadn't been to this little stretch in a while. He could see the Hollywood Hills to the north, the Beverly Center Mall right to his left. He even snuck a glance over at Nude Nude Nude, a famous strip club right on La Cienega. He remembered a case he'd investigated a few years back that required him to visit that particular establishment a handful of times. But he hadn't enjoyed it at all, going in there and talking to all the strippers. Nope. It was just business. That's right, just business. Tremaine smiled as he drove by it. What was that one dancer's name? The one he interviewed a couple times? Rhonda? Tonya? Something like that. She was pretty. Couldn't spell her own name, but she was pretty. She could dance, too. Stay focused, Tremaine . . .

Tremaine got off La Cienega, weaved through some of the back streets, then onto North Harper. He found a spot right away. Out of his car now, he looked at the names listed on the panel at the front door of 347 N. Harper and, sure enough, he found Vicky Fong, the landlady from the police report. He rang the bell.

"Who is it?" a voice said from the buzzer box.

Tremaine said, "Is this Miss Fong?"

"Who is it?"

"I'm a private detective. I was hoping to talk to you about Kelly Burch."

The buzzer rang.

Tremaine entered the building—not a dump, but certainly not nice. He found Apartment 101 and, before he knew it, Vicky Fong appeared. About five-two, with a furrowed brow. Her black hair graying a little. She wore a little kimono dress.

She said, "Is someone finally looking into the case again?"

"Not really," he extended a hand. "My name is Donald Tremaine."

Her skeptical look turned into a smile and she said, "The old hippie surfer?"

Tremaine laughed. Hippie? Whatever. That year he won the world title paid off every now and then. "I don't think I was ever a hippie, but those years are a little foggy."

Vicky Fong laughed and said, "We used to watch you at the U.S. Open. I grew up in Huntington."

Tremaine politely thanked her for remembering him, then gave her the standard routine about his life after the waves. She invited him in.

Inside her neat, modest apartment, Tremaine sat down and began explaining himself. "I'm actually investigating another case. Another murder. A man by the name of Roger Gale. Do you know that name?"

"No. But what does he have to do with Kelly?"

"Nothing."

"So?"

"So, the case I'm on is a tough one. I've found out a lot about the man, Gale, but it's only made me more confused. Right now, I'm doing a little poking around with the murders that happened on, or near, the date of Gale's."

"You think they might be connected?"

"I don't know. But I'd love to ask you a few questions about your former tenant."

Vicky Fong made some coffee and continued to pepper Tremaine with questions about his surf days. When they both had a cup, and were both seated in the living room, they got to the matter at hand.

Tremaine said, "What was Kelly Burch like?"

"She was a drug addict. But don't let me get off on the wrong foot. I loved Kelly, she was a sweet girl. I felt sorry for her."

"Why?" Tremaine said.

"She was so beautiful, so beautiful, but she was sad. She had no family except one sister, who wasn't in her life." Then Vicky said, "She didn't live in this building. She lived above the garage in the back. I barely charged her rent."

"Can I see where she lived?"

Tremaine and Vicky walked out the front door, then around to the back of the apartment, where there were six garages. Over the last two, the building became two stories. Kelly Burch's old apartment.

"That's where she lived," Vicky said. "We rented out the room to her for five years. When she first got to town, she wanted to be an actress. But that never really went anywhere. After a while, she didn't go to any more auditions, she just went to the parties. And then she got into drugs. She was a sweet girl."

"Who lives there now?"

"No one. We were only taking four hundred a month from Kelly."

"So what's up there?"

"Storage for the other tenants. Do you want to see inside?"

There was nothing to what was formerly Kelly's apartment. Just one room, kitchen attached, hardwood floors, a bathroom, a shower and boxes and other things that belonged to the current tenants.

Vicky scanned the room and said, "This place is a mess. It needs to be cleaned up. It's a mess."

It actually doesn't look too bad, Tremaine thought, as storage rooms go. It certainly didn't have that utterly depressing feel like some can have. An old, beat-up bike here, a random tennis racquet there, broken strings, of course . . . Nope, it looked pretty organized, comprised of things that would be used again someday.

Not to Vicky Fong, though.

Tremaine said, "Do you have any theories as to why Kelly was killed?"

"You know, Mr. Tremaine, many times you only know the side of a person that they let you see. I did know Kelly did drugs, so that would be my only guess. But really, to me, Kelly was a sweet girl. Very beautiful. Dangerously beautiful. But she got into drugs, it was obvious. Started losing weight. I started seeing her less and less. I'd catch her in little lies. She had this old boyfriend from when she first moved out here, Evan, who kept an eye out for her, felt sorry for her. He came to me a couple times when he couldn't find her. Evan confirmed what I already thought. That Kelly was on drugs. And drugs, when you're addicted like that, lead to bad things."

Vicky scurried around the room, inspecting the boxes and other stored stuff, making sure she recognized everything. Making sure everything belonged to people who were paying rent.

"You mean like, prostitution, dealing, those kinds of bad things?" Tremaine asked.

"I don't know. I'm not the P.I.," she said.

Tremaine laughed. Clever was Miss Fong. He said, "But in general, that would be your guess—the drugs led to her getting killed? Maybe she got wrapped up in a world, maybe she owed somebody some money or something, maybe she stole something from the wrong person—then paid the ultimate price?"

"Yeah, that's about right. Who knows? I don't know about the drug world and all that. I know what I see on TV. And I know Kelly was missing her rent sometimes and looking bad. Thin. But still beautiful. Drugs make you make the wrong decisions. Who knows?"

Tremaine scanned the old apartment, the picture of the dead girl coming in and out of his vision. He walked over and stood at the spot where Kelly Burch died. Where she lay in the picture.

Tremaine said, "What about the old boyfriend, Evan?"

"Evan Mulligan. Really nice guy, kind of a jock type. They dated for years when she first got out here. When she was innocent. But Kelly was too much for Evan, too fast. I think he loved her, but eventually gave up. She was too fast for him. You should talk to him. He's a good guy. Maybe a little dense, kind of a jock type, like I said, but a good guy. But he wasn't Kelly's speed. He kept an eye out for her. He was devastated when Kelly was shot."

"Was he ever a suspect?"

"Oh, no. Heavens, no. He's just a regular guy. He was out of her day-to-day life. But he was the only one who knew Kelly's family—her sister. He tried to help the police, but they gave up on the case very quickly."

Tremaine nodded.

Vicky said, "Right before she and Evan broke up, he told me he thought something weird was going on. That she was acting strange. You know, disappearing for days and things like that. It hurt him to lose her. To see her become someone else. To go from this beautiful, innocent girl to this beautiful, tragic one. But boy, was she sexy. One of those people who was just born good-looking. Kinda like you, Mr. Tremaine."

Little Vicky Fong gave Tremaine a friendly wink.

Walking back to her apartment from the garage apartment, Vicky said something and Tremaine wondered why she hadn't said it before. "I have a box of some leftover personal items. Of Kelly's. Would you like to see it?"

It never ceased to amaze Tremaine the process by which people decided to dispense information. Why in the hell wouldn't she have said that earlier?

"Yes," he said. "I'd like to see it."

Vicky Fong dug around in her closet, back in her apartment now, and produced an old cardboard box about three times the size of a shoebox. On the top of the box, in Magic Marker, it said PERSONAL ITEMS.

It was initialed KB.

Tremaine said, "Why do you have this?"

"Nobody wanted it. The police looked through it for about five minutes. Kelly's sister didn't want it. So I kept it. I have no idea why."

"Kelly's sister, Angela Coyle?"

"Yeah, if you want to call her a sister. They had no relationship. I didn't even know Kelly had a sister until Angela came out to tell the police what to do with the body. Angela, she wanted nothing to do with any of it."

"What about Evan? He didn't want this stuff?"

"He's seen it. He looked through it, too, but said he didn't want it. He said it made him too sad. You know, because every little thing in there was a piece of Kelly."

Tremaine nodded. Vicky Fong handed him the box and said, "You can't take it, but you can look at it all you want. Why don't you go in the kitchen."

Tremaine sat at Vicky's little kitchen table and studied the contents of the box. His initial reaction was very similar to the cops'. Not a whole lot here.

Pictures of Kelly, of Kelly and her friends. Yeah, Kelly was stunning, like a femme fatale almost, you could see the tragedy in her beautiful eyes. And there were letters, a book or two, some personal items from childhood, an old newspaper clipping reviewing a performance of Kelly's in a small play in Santa Barbara. Amazing, Tremaine thought, how a little box of stuff, a small collection of items, could give such a personal glimpse into someone's life. Not necessarily a broad or even totally accurate look, but a personal one, to be sure. Reinforced by the sheer fact the little collection of things was meaningful enough to be kept in the first place.

Outside the kitchen, Vicky shuffled around, straightening things, making her already neat apartment that much neater. She said aloud, "I've got to straighten up that storage room. It's a mess."

Tremaine appeared outside the kitchen.

Vicky said, "Are you finished looking through the stuff?"

Tremaine said, "I'm going to go make a quick phone call, then I'll be right back. Okay?"

"Sure," Vicky said. "Take your time."

Tremaine walked out to his car and got in. He pulled out his cell phone and dialed up Lopez.

"Lopez," he said.

"Hey, it's Tremaine. Got a quick favor. You can just add it to my tab."

"Your tab's getting pretty long there, buddy."

"Yeah, well, I'm looking into the Kelly Burch case, so you could argue that I'm actually helping the LAPD. I'm doing you guys a favor."

"A valiant effort, Tremaine, but this is going to mean you buying me another steak. At this rate, you might just want to buy me a cow. Or a farm."

"You should take your act on the road."

Lopez laughed and said, "What's up?"

Tremaine said, "You at your computer?"

"Yeah."

"Look up a guy named Dean Latham."

Tremain spelled it out for him.

About twenty seconds later, Lopez said, "Got two of 'em."

"Just like that," Tremaine said.

"Modern technology strikes again. It looks like one of them probably isn't of too much interest."

"Dead?" Tremaine guessed.

"No, but close. He's ninety-seven. But if you do decide to talk to him, make sure to talk into his good ear."

Tremaine laughed. "What about the other one?"

"The other one's forty-five. Lives in the Hollywood Hills. And, looky here, he's got a criminal record."

"Drugs?" Tremaine guessed.

"No, public drunkenness, indecent exposure."

"Could be he took a leak on the side of the road and ran into a cop having a bad day, but, you never know—could also indicate the guy gets into trouble," Tremaine said.

"So, who is this guy?" Lopez asked.

"I don't know. I was looking through some of Kelly Burch's stuff and I came across the name."

And he had, on a card that was stuck in the middle of an old paperback, almost like a bookmark. It was like a business card, but it didn't have an address or a phone number, just a name.

Tremaine continued. "Could be nothing, but I thought I'd have you run a check while I was here at Kelly's old apartment. Just in case it generated something interesting."

"Well, the Latham here in the old computer seems to be pretty clean. Other than, like you said, possibly taking a whiz in public. You want his address and phone number?"

"Yeah," Tremaine said, "I do."

Tremaine walked back into Vicky Fong's apartment. Vicky was standing in her little living room in that way that people stand when they're waiting for someone to enter. Sort of an unnatural pose.

She said, "Did you find something in the box?"

"Probably not," Tremaine said. "Just a name I wanted

to check out while I was here. Guy named Dean Latham. Kelly kept his card. Have you ever heard of him?"

Vicky thought about it. "No," she said. "It doesn't ring a bell. But that doesn't surprise me. Kelly never dropped many names. She wasn't into specifics."

"Maybe Evan can help with that one. Could be nothing. Could have been an accident that the card was even in there. It was stuck in a book," Tremaine said.

"Yeah, ask Evan. If he can help, he will. But that name, Dean, doesn't ring a bell," Vicky said.

Vicky Fong walked Tremaine out to his car.

"Thank you for your help, Vicky."

"I never thought an old hippie surfer would be showing up at my door today."

There she goes again with the hippie thing, Tremaine thought, smiling as he opened the door to the Cutlass.

Vicky said, "How come they called you 'Insane Tremaine'?"

"That was the name of a surf video a company released. It showed me attempting to ride some pretty big waves. Waves I guess they thought I shouldn't have attempted in the first place. On the video I do a lot of falling."

"Well, when you went for the waves, did you think you could make them?"

"Yeah, I did."

"So what's so insane about that?"

"I don't know," Tremaine said.

CHAPTER 31

Finding Evan Mulligan was, in a word, easy. Vicky Fong had given Tremaine his address: 132 Courtney Street, L.A. It was a little green house, just above Sunset. Nice street, nice neighborhood.

It was getting dark now, Tremaine had spent almost two hours with Vicky Fong. He pulled the Cutlass into a spot, got out of his car, and walked up to Evan Mulligan's house. He rang the doorbell, the door opened, and there was Evan Mulligan. The guy he wanted to talk to, right in front of him, just like that.

Tremaine looked at Evan Mulligan, probably thirty-five, good shape, big even, brown hair, balding a little, blue eyes. He was dressed in running shoes, shorts, and a shirt drenched in sweat. Vicky had said he was a jock type. He sure looked like it now.

Evan said, "Yes?"

"My name is Donald Tremaine. I'm a private investigator. I wondered if I could talk to you for a minute."

Evan said, "Dude, I paid my taxes, and I've got all the receipts for my write-offs."

Tremaine smiled at his joke. "Actually I'm investigating a murder. Not specifically the murder of Kelly Burch, but I'm looking into the possibility of there being a connection between her murder and the murder I'm investigating."

Evan's expression changed. Tremaine could see by this change, in his eyes and in his body language, that this was a subject Evan took very seriously. No more jokes. Evan said, "Come on in."

Tremaine entered Evan's house. Pretty nice place. Definitely a guy's place. Beads hanging down in a couple of the doorways. Carpet, dark furniture. A basketball sitting in a chair. But a pretty nice house, probably worth upward of seven, eight hundred grand. Looked like two bedrooms, the front one that Tremaine could see had been converted into an office.

Evan said, "Let me change my shirt. I just went for a run. Have a seat."

From the back room, Evan said, "Wanna beer?"

"Beer would be great," Tremaine said.

Evan was now in the kitchen, in the back, and Tremaine could hear him open the fridge and clank a couple bottles together as he grabbed the beers. Evan reentered the main room, where Tremaine was still standing, and said, "Grab a seat, man."

Both of them were now seated in comfortable chairs in

the living room, having a beer. Tremaine watched Evan, now wearing a T-shirt that said FRESNO STATE SOCCER, take a big swig.

Tremaine said, "Did you play for Fresno State?"

"First two years. But then, dude, I tore my ACL. It was brutal."

"That's a great program. Ranked number one in what, '87?

"Dude, I can't believe you know that."

"Addicted to the sports page."

"Solid," Evan said, finishing his beer. " 'Nother?"

"Not yet," Tremaine said.

Evan got himself another beer, then sat back down and started the Kelly Burch dialogue for Tremaine, saying, "I have to admit, when you said you were a private detective, I had no idea what you wanted. And then you mentioned Kelly, and it, like, shocked me, hearing her name. It's been a while since I've talked about it with anyone. But I'm glad someone's looking into it, because at the time of the murder . . ."

Evan paused for a second, almost reconsidering what he was going to say. Then he said, "Well, I'm just glad someone's looking into it. I hope I can help. What's up?"

"You were Kelly's boyfriend for a time?"

"Yeah, when she first got to L.A. We met at a party. We dated for a few years, her first few years here. Dude, this girl, before she started with the drugs and all that . . . You know about the drugs?"

"Yes."

"Well, anyway, she was a ten. I mean, she was perfect. And sweet, too. Really sweet."

"What," Tremaine said, "after a while you couldn't take her lifestyle?"

"Yeah. I wanted to stay together at first. But then she started doing coke all the time, not calling me back and stuff. I'd catch her in lies. It was sad. The classic beautiful girl who comes to L.A. to be an actress and gets swept away by the scene. It's a cliché. But it happens. I've seen it firsthand."

"How long after you broke up was she killed?"

"Just over a year."

Tremaine said, carefully, "Were there other men in her life after you? I mean, anyone she had a relationship with, anyone I could talk to?"

"Nothing serious," Evan said. "I mean, let's face it, drugs lead to things—she was *with* other men, probably lots of them. But nothing serious."

It probably hurt Evan to admit this, but he had a maturity about the subject, a willingness to talk about it. He said, "She was approached all the time, everywhere she went. But she never got serious with anyone, at least she never mentioned it to me. You know, I don't think she could get serious with anyone. She was married to her habit."

Tremaine said, "Like I said, I'm actually not investigating Kelly's case directly. I'm investigating the murder of a man named Roger Gale and looking for a connection. Do you know that name, Roger Gale?"

Evan said, "Yeah, he was the big ad guy."

"Right," Tremaine said.

Evan, wearing an expression that was both surprised and confused, said, "Did he have something to do with Kelly?"

"Probably not. Except for the fact that they were murdered on the same day."

Shaking his head as if saddened all over again by the news, Evan said, "And probably lots of others in Los Angeles, too, right?"

"Just one," Tremaine said. "I checked that one out as well."

"Are you finding a connection between any of them?"

"Not yet," Tremaine said.

"Well," Evan said, suddenly showing some edge, "I don't think the police ever really had any interest in solving Kelly's murder. She had a drug problem and had no money, no family to speak of. I really don't think they gave a shit."

This must be what Evan had wanted to say before, when he cut himself off, Tremaine thought. Maybe he didn't want to appear too cynical right off the bat.

Tremaine said, "Unfortunately, you may be right." Then, "You mentioned the drugs. Do you think that's what led to Kelly's murder?"

"Probably," Evan said, more pensive now than irritated. "I think Kelly got way more into drugs and cocaine and crack than she ever let on, especially to me, because every time we talked, which was less and less after it got worse, I was always on her case about it. But you couldn't control Kelly. And then, maybe she did something that pissed off the wrong person and . . ." Evan paused. "They killed her."

Tremaine said, "I'm sorry to make you dredge this up. I appreciate your talking to me."

"It's okay. Like I said, it's nice to know someone is looking into it. Even if you're actually investigating another case."

Tremaine said, "Have you ever heard of a man named Dean Latham?"

"Dean Latham?"

"Yeah."

"No. I've never heard of him. Why do you ask?"

"It's a name that has come up in my investigation."

"Who is he?" Evan said.

"I don't know, actually. It's just a name I came across in looking at some of the information on Kelly's death. I managed to get access to the LAPD computers and police reports."

Tremaine didn't want to get into the fact that Vicky Fong had showed him the box of Kelly's personal stuff. He didn't want Evan to know this random P.I. got a glimpse into the very personal items of his dead girlfriend. So he threw out the police report bullshit and hoped Evan wouldn't question it any further. He didn't.

Evan said, "Well, I don't know Dean Latham. But if he had anything to do with Kelly's death, I hope you find him."

Tremaine said, "Finding him won't be hard. He lives right up the street, in the Hollywood Hills. Whether he had anything to do with Kelly's death, that's another story."

Evan got up. He had finished his second beer. He was holding the empty bottle gesturing to Tremaine. *Want another*?

Tremaine said no thanks, he needed to go. Tremaine had just wanted to meet Evan, put a face to the name, see if he could connect Roger Gale to Kelly, see if he knew Dean Latham.

"Man, a P.I. What a cool job," Evan said. "How do you become a P.I.?"

Evan was letting out his "guy's guy" side.

"You apply for a license," Tremaine said. "Then if you get one, you hope you can get some business."

Evan nodded and said, "Well, if you have any more questions, come back, call me, whatever."

Evan jotted his number down and handed it to Tremaine, who was standing now, just about ready to leave.

"Thanks," Tremaine said, meaning it. A number to call never hurt, especially in this case. Then Tremaine pointed to the front bedroom that was used as the office. "Do you work out of your house?"

"No. I work at a dot-com called Chainsaw. It's a company that rates other dot-coms. I've been there for five years. We're one of the few that survived the crash."

Evan knocked his hand on the table next to him. It was wood.

Tremaine made his way to the front door. As he opened the door, he said to Evan, "I really appreciate you talking to me without notice."

"Hey, no problem. I hope you find something."

"I'll keep you posted if I do."

It had been a long day. Tremaine got in his car, fished around in the glove for his smokes, only a few left, he'd have to get some more soon, then cruised back down La Cienega to the Ten, which he would take all the way back to his familiar Pacific Coast Highway.

In the car, headed home, he thought about everything he knew so far. The things he'd been able to discover had indeed continued to lead him into new directions, but how close to the truth, at the end of the day, was he? Not that close. He'd discovered some interesting things about

Roger Gale. But did the things he'd found all connect? Did they?

Tremaine took a deep breath as he got his first glimpse of the ocean, hitting the PCH from the Ten. It seemed from a cursory investigation into the other murders around the time of Roger Gale's that the only one that could possibly be connected to Gale's was Kelly Burch's, and there was literally no evidence of that.

Now that he was back at the beach, back home, a step back from the new developments, Tremaine felt more skeptical about a connection between the Kelly Burch case and the Roger Gale case. They seemed to be worlds apart. He wouldn't tell Nina about these new developments—that he had been, and was currently, investigating an entirely different case. Not yet. Wouldn't that imply, even if it was just a little, that he was running out of ideas?

But Tremaine knew not to ignore what he'd discovered. Not to ignore where the combination of his subconscious mind and his conscious mind had taken him. From Wendy Leahy to the karate studio to the murder of a beautiful young wannabe-actress named Kelly Burch. Keep going, Tremaine, keep looking. And he knew he would. Next, call this guy Dean Latham. See if he could swing by and say hello. Maybe Latham would shed a little light on things. You never know. Tremaine stamped out his smoke in his ashtray. Yeah, you never know.

CHAPTER 32

The next day, a Saturday, Tremaine got up, and instead of going for a surf, he went for a jog. Hit some old trails in the canyons of Malibu. It was a hot morning, which Tremaine liked. He ran for about an hour—it was hot, really hot—and was glad to be back at the base of the trails, at the Cutlass, parked and waiting to take him back to the trailer. He drove home, cooled off a bit, then grabbed the phone and dialed up Dean Latham, looking at his notes for the number.

A man answered, "Hello."

Tremaine got a little stroke of luck. Latham was home.

Tremaine said, "Dean?"

"Yeeees," Dean Latham said, a little irritated. Probably had caller ID and didn't recognize the number.

"My name is Donald Tremaine, I'm a private detective."

A beat of silence. Then Latham said, "Can I help you?"

"Maybe. I was wondering if I could talk to you for ten minutes or so, in person."

"What's this about, Mr. Tremaine?" Dean's voice now losing the irritation and gaining some worry. Latham reacting normally now. Like, *I didn't do anything . . .*

Tremaine said, "I'm investigating a murder. Two murders actually. And your name came up."

"What murders are you investigating?" Latham said.

"I'd like to tell you in person. Can I? It won't take long, Dean. Just a couple questions."

There was a pause, and then Latham said, "Yeah, sure. But not today, I'm busy. How 'bout tomorrow? Sunday."

"Tomorrow's fine," Tremaine said.

"Why don't you come by around four. Do you know where I live?"

"Yeah," Tremaine said. "Hollywood Hills. 2512 Lookout Mountain."

"How'd you know that?" Latham said. "I'm not listed."

"You've got a criminal record."

"Barely," Latham said.

"Barely counts, too," Tremaine said, and he hung up the phone.

Seeing Nina that afternoon was refreshing and, at this particular time, unexpected. Tremaine was sitting on top of his trailer, the completed Jumble (one minute, thirty-nine seconds) at his feet next to Lyle, when Nina pulled up.

She got out of the black Volvo, looked up at Tremaine, and said, simply, "Hi."

"Hello."

"What are you doing?"

"I'm trapped in the mind right now, mulling over the new and, as always with this case, mystifying developments."

Tremaine started to talk about the case. Nina politely interrupted him and said, "That's not why I came over."

"Oh," Tremaine said. "How can I help you, otherwise?"

"I want you to take me surfing."

"Really. Right now?"

"Right now. I told you I was going to try it and, well, here I am."

Tremaine thought, duty calls . . .

He stood up on the trailer and looked out into the ocean, checking out the conditions. A ways away, but he knew the big blue body of water well.

"Looks like about two to four. Shouldn't be too rough for a rookie."

Nina gave Tremaine a look—a look that said, quit while you're ahead, buddy. While you're barely, imperceptibly ahead.

Tremaine put Lyle inside, then grabbed two longboards out of the adjoining storage space he had next to his trailer. This would be nice—Nina, the waves, the water. A little break from the heavy thinking. Tremaine planned to skin it, no wetsuit, but as he was loading the boards, it occurred to him that Nina might need a wetsuit, might not have one. He paused for a moment and looked at his storage shed, thinking about whether he had one of his ex-wife's old suits tucked away in there somewhere.

"I brought my own," Nina said.

She held up her spring suit, a wetsuit with short sleeves and short legs, that she'd already gotten out of her car.

"You read my mind."

"I come prepared," she said.

Tremaine liked that.

They drove down to one of Tremaine's favorite spots, right down the road, parked the Cutlass, and stood on the beach looking at the waves.

Nina strapped her leash around her right ankle.

"Regular-foot, just like me," Tremaine said.

"Regular-foot?"

"Yeah. If your left foot is forward, it's called regular-foot. If your right foot is forward, it's called goofy-foot."

As Tremaine and Nina entered the water, now walking out to sea and gliding their boards on the water with their hands, Nina said, "Where does that come from, the term goofy-foot?"

"There's a lot of different theories. The one that most people believe is, there was an old drawing in a surfing magazine, might have been the early days of *Surfer*, and the cartoon character Goofy was riding a surfboard. Right foot forward. So people started calling people who rode right foot forward goofy-foot."

"Tremaine, you might be a good P.I., but you're a horrible liar."

Nina splashed him with some water. It was cold on Tremaine's bare skin.

"I'm serious," he said. "You think I could make something like that up?"

"Yes, I do."

They jumped on their boards and began paddling out to where the waves broke. Tremaine was impressed as Nina charged out, a beginner for sure but fearless of the waves breaking in front of her. And her form? Not bad, not bad at all.

They got out past the point of impact and sat on their boards, rising up, then down again, as waves rolled in. Nina was having a little trouble with her balance, but not too much.

"You must have surfed every day for a long time when you were trying to go pro."

"Yeah, I think about it now, it's hard to believe. I used to surf sometimes seven hours a day."

"And you went pro when you were young, right?"

"Yeah."

"So, no college?"

"No. My only education after high school was reading. I tried to read a book a week when I was on tour. Still do."

A wave headed toward them.

"There's your wave," Tremaine said.

Nina turned her board around and paddled hard. Impressive, Tremaine thought, as he watched Nina lower her head and go for the wave with everything she had.

She missed it, the wave rolling in toward shore without her.

"Almost," Tremaine said. "That one backed off a little, nearly impossible to catch."

Nina saw another wave and turned her board around, ready to charge ahead. The last wave of the set. Tremaine paddled over next to her, then hopped off his board, treading water. The wave was upon them and, as Nina paddled, Tremaine got behind her, and pushed the back of her board, giving her the thrust she needed to catch the wave. She screamed, but regained her composure, then pointed the nose of the board in the direction of the open face of the wave and tried to hop up. Close, but not quite.

"Almost!" Tremaine shouted, impressed, genuinely.

She paddled back out to where Tremaine sat on his board. He clapped as she neared him.

"Next time," she said, "I'm standing up, guaranteed."

"I believe it."

The wave came, about a three-foot face, and Nina, this time, caught it without Tremaine's help. And true to her word, she hopped up, standing up just long enough to stick out her tongue at Tremaine.

The rest of the session was utterly pleasant, that's what Tremaine thought, anyway. He gave Nina some pointers, and she accepted them with open ears, really wanting to learn as much as she could from the old pro.

As they walked in to the shore, trudging through the waist-deep water, Nina began aggressively splashing Tremaine with water. This was something she was an expert at.

Tremaine retaliated, picking Nina up and throwing her into oncoming whitewater. She squealed and pointed to her board, which was drifting off, now unattached. Tremaine, having to pay for his games, swam after it and, after some tangling with the whitewater, retrieved it.

Back in the Cutlass, Tremaine, enjoying the salt and the sun on his skin, drove back to the trailer, Nina next to him, silent and tired. There was a light breeze in the car and Tremaine looked over at Nina, the wind moving her wet hair just a little.

Nina said, "Why'd you quit the tour?"

He looked at her sideways, still driving, feeling pressure in his chest. Then he started talking.

"It was the year after I won the title. The tour was starting, in Australia. I was in love with a girl named Mandy Rice. I can't describe to you how I felt about her without sounding like a character in a bad romance novel."

Nina nodded.

"She wanted to come to Australia. She wanted to come watch the first event, watch me start the defense of my title."

There was that feeling again. Tremaine could feel it in his chest and feel heat behind his face. He started to sweat a little, moisture appearing on his forehead. But he didn't wipe it off, he just let it happen, let it ride.

Nina said, "You don't have to tell me."

Tremaine continued, "I told her she couldn't come. As much as I loved her, as much as it almost made me feel insane to be around her, I said no. I felt I had to go it alone. I had to be the guy who showed up alone, the gunslinger, to kick everybody's ass."

Nina's eyes widened. She knew there was more to the story.

"So I went. And on the first day of the competition, I got a call, from Mandy's mother. Mandy had gone to a 7 Eleven to get a pack of smokes. When she was leaving, some guys came in and held the place up. The guy behind the counter pulled a gun, the fuckers who came in to rob the place started firing, and Mandy got shot in the back. Shot in the spine."

Nina looked at Tremaine, sympathy and shock in her eyes.

"She was brought to the hospital—she went into a coma. I flew back immediately, but by the time I got to the hospital, she was gone. Dead. I never returned to the tour."

"Donald . . ."

Tremaine knew what she was going to say. It's not your fault, you were young, pursuing your dreams, things like this happen, it's not your fault. But no soothing remarks, no it's-not-your-fault-think-about-it-sentiments, nothing rational, could put an end to the three things Tremaine lived with.

Guilt. Pain. Fear.

Guilt for being selfish, for putting himself before someone he loved, for being macho, preening, while she was back home getting killed. Pain that comes with losing someone you loved, forever. And fear. Fear that if you get close again, you'll get stabbed in the gut twice as hard. Is that why he'd never gotten close enough to Susan? Of course.

He knew it was ironic—he had pushed Mandy away and *that's* when she got killed. So wouldn't it make sense to try to get close to someone so that wouldn't happen again?

Nah, life doesn't work that way. Just the opposite, in fact.

Tremaine said, meaning it, "It's all right Nina, you don't have to say anything."

Back at the Old Colony Trailer Park, Nina sat in her car, ready to leave.

She said, "Thanks for telling me that, Tremaine."

"I'll talk to you soon, Nina."

Nina said, "I came to you because I wanted to do something good. Is that why you became a P.I.? Because after Mandy, you wanted to do something good?"

Tremaine said, "I became a P.I. because I needed a job. After Mandy, I didn't do much for a while. Like, years. Finally, John Lopez came to me and started giving me work."

But he thought, *doing something good*, maybe that is why.

Nina said, "John had to know you could handle intense situations."

"Yeah, I guess. And he trusted me. That, for us, for me and John, is what life is all about. And because he's a friend, he knew doing something, anything, would help me. Anyway, I got into it, and here we are."

"Here we are," she said.

Then she said, "Come here."

"Where?"

"Here."

He leaned over and she kissed him on the cheek. "Thanks for taking me out. That was fun," she said.

Tremaine stood there, right where he was when she kissed him, and watched Nina Aldeen drive off, down the hill, toward the PCH.

CHAPTER 33

The next day, driving toward the Hollywood Hills, toward Dean Latham's, Tremaine, in his most optimistic daydreaming, was trying to envision situations in which this guy Dean Latham could fit into the Roger Gale case. Was this the desperate daydreaming of a frustrated P.I., or was Tremaine simply following the leads he had, never ignoring a clue, allowing the tiniest of leads to capture his attention? That's what good P.I.s did, right? That's what he'd always done. But it was a fine line. Chase too many bad leads and you're a fool.

Dean Latham, sure, he could have absolutely no relevance to anything Tremaine was interested in. But what if he was the key, the connection? Could it be that Roger Gale had a drug habit, and Dean Latham and Kelly Burch somehow played a part in that? Kelly being into drugs. Roger Gale being, at the very least, mysterious. The medical examiners didn't find anything in Roger Gale's blood during the autopsy, but maybe Roger Gale owed a drug debt from the past. Maybe he'd kicked but never paid off his suppliers. Or maybe Kelly Burch and Dean Latham were somehow connected to the karate place. The karate place where Gale may or may not have enjoyed a sex show.

Jesus, Tremaine thought, *who knows?* It could be anything or nothing. The more Tremaine thought about it, the closer he came to actually confronting Dean Latham, the less likely it seemed. His mind just kept going back to the most sensible possibility. The one that Lopez had ribbed him about. That he was chasing a bunk hunch.

Tremaine was cruising down Santa Monica, just looking around at the buzz of Hollywood on the weekend, when his cell phone rang. He didn't recognize the number but didn't worry about it, either. He just picked up the phone and said, "Tremaine."

"It's Vicky Fong."

"Hi, Vicky. What's up?"

"You know how I was saying I needed to clean up that storage room a little? The one where all the boxes were?"

"Yeah," Tremaine said. "But I gotta be honest, I didn't think it looked too bad."

"Oh, yes it did. But that's not why I'm calling."

Both Tremaine and Vicky knew that's not why she was calling, but neither one of them acknowledged that fact. It was a segue to something else, just a piece of innocuous conversation.

"I found something when I was cleaning up. I think you should come over and see."

"I'm actually near your apartment," Tremaine said. "I'll be right there."

Vicky was waiting for Tremaine, the door to her building already open when he pulled up. He got out of his car, walked into the building, then into her apartment.

Vicky stood in her living room anticipating his arrival, like before, but this time she held an envelope in her hand.

She said, "Hi, Donald."

"Hi, Vicky."

"I found this when I was straightening up. There was an old guitar case in there, I guess it was Kelly's. It's just been sitting in there and I thought it belonged to one of the other tenants, but I wanted to check. So, I opened it up and took out the guitar. And behind it was this envelope, just loose in there."

She handed it to Tremaine. Just like before with the box, he went in the adjoining kitchen and sat down at the table. He opened up the envelope and inside it there were two letters. Tremaine pulled them out, splayed them out on the table, and looked at them. Both typed. And both with the same signature, in blue pen, at the bottom.

I love you, Dean, they both were signed.

Tremaine read the letters.

After no more than two sentences, Tremaine realized they were what he figured they were: love letters to Kelly. They were intense, well written, and overtly sexual. Riddled, in fact, with references to sex, and the incredible, intense sex between the two of them. But there was a sweetness to the letters, too—Dean saying he truly loved her, that they'd be together one day, that he felt, looking at her across a table at a crowded restaurant, that he was alone on the planet, alone with just her.

Tremaine finished the letters and turned to Vicky, who was standing there, still and quiet. Tremaine said, "Dean Latham. I'm on my way to see him."

"Does this help you?" Vicky said.

"Yeah, it does," Tremaine said.

He didn't know quite how it helped, but he knew it did.

"Thank you, Vicky. Thank you for calling."

"You're welcome," Vicky said, standing there, still, like a little statue.

Tremaine pulled the Cutlass into the Country Store right there on Laurel Canyon, right near the road that would take him up to Dean Latham's. Tremaine went in—what a great little old-fashioned grocery store—bought himself a bottled water and replenished his smokes, thinking it might be nice to have a smoke on the way home and think things over. He got back in his car, and before he cranked her up, he put the love letters in his glove. He wasn't going to take them in to Dean's house with him. He wasn't going to show Dean what he had. No, this visit was just to feel things out.

Tremaine pulled out of the Country Store and headed up Laurel Canyon for a stoplight, then hung the Cutlass left onto Lookout Mountain, then up, up, up into the Hollywood Hills. Way up on the left was 2512, plenty of parking, too.

There was a tall fence surrounding Latham's yard, but

the gate wasn't locked, so Tremaine opened it and went in. Inside, there was a big yard with a garden. The house was a small, cottage-type house toward the back of the lot. This wasn't the home of a rich man. But it was a nice, well kept house tucked deep in the famous Hollywood Hills, a neighborhood many people loved and most people associated with high-quality, hip living. Houses, bungalows, even mansions, all tucked away amid the trees and the hills. It was like living on a mini-mountain, right in L.A. Tremaine looked around the yard, nice, but, Tremaine thought, too land-locked for me, you're looking at an hour minimum before you're in the ocean . . .

There were three steps up to the front door, but before Tremaine got there, it swung open and there was Dean Latham. About five-ten, short dark hair, but a hip cut, glasses, and a little heavy, a little out of shape. Probably forty-five.

Tremaine studied Latham. Just standing there on his front stoop wearing a silk robe over his pants and shirt, holding in his right hand a drink, looked like booze.

Jesus, Tremaine thought, guy's in his pajamas.

"Donald Tremaine," Latham said.

Tremaine nodded.

"You're the surfer."

Tremaine nodded again.

"I'm a movie producer. My company, my *former* company, wanted to do a surfing movie years ago, so we all did a little research on surfers. I remember your name."

Tremaine gave the obligatory polite smile. Then Latham said, "Come in."

As they walked in, Latham said, "Sorry about the mess."

But it wasn't too bad, Tremaine noticed. Vicky Fong might think it was a mess, but it was really just a little disheveled. The house was dark—dark walls, dark furniture. There was a lot of Japanese art on the walls, mixed with big sprawling movie posters all over the place. Mostly old movies—Bogart pictures. Cary Grant pictures. Billy Wilder films. It was an odd combination, Japanese art and Hollywood posters . . .

"Do you still produce movies?" Tremaine said.

"Are you implying that I'm washed up?" Latham said with a wry grin.

"You said your 'former company.' I think *you* implied it."

Latham plopped down on a big couch, let out a big exaggerated breath and took a sip of his drink. "I really don't produce anymore. It's been years since I've had a deal with any studio. But in this business, you're only one script away."

Latham stared straight ahead for a minute, like he was thinking about his career, his former career, then said to Tremaine, "Can I get you a drink?"

"No, thanks," Tremaine said.

Latham looked at Tremaine and said, "So, what do you want to know?"

"Are you married?" Tremaine said, wondering if there might be a spouse around.

"Used to be. Divorced. Twice. No kids." Then Latham said, "So, who got killed?"

Tremaine looked at Dean Latham. There was a kind of confidence to this bizarre man. He sported the robe and the cocktail. Kind of relished talking about his present failures, as if to suggest he used to be a big shot. Probably had some dough and was content to sit up here in his house and drink booze and watch movies. Yeah, this guy had some stories, this guy's seen some late nights. But was he a bad guy? Couldn't tell yet. Not from simple chit-chat.

Tremaine said, "Two people got killed. I want to ask you about both of them. One of them went by the name of Kelly Burch. Do you know anybody by that name?"

Dean Latham took a sip of his drink and then contorted his face as if to show Tremaine he was really thinking and then said, "No. Who was she?"

"She was an out-of-work actress who lived not too far from here."

"So why are you asking me about her?"

"Kelly Burch was in contact with a man named Dean Latham."

"Hmm," Latham said. "Wasn't me."

"You've never heard the name Kelly Burch?" Tremaine asked.

"Like I said, no," Dean said, this time quickly. "Who was the other person?"

"The other person was a man named Roger Gale."

"The ad guy?"

"That's right.

"I remember reading about his murder. They never caught the guy who killed him?"

"No, they never arrested anyone. Guy or girl."

"Is there a connection between Roger Gale and the girl?"

"Kelly Burch," Tremaine said.

"Right," Latham said.

"I don't know," Tremaine said. "Did you ever meet Roger Gale?"

"No. Read about him. Even before he was killed. But never met him. That's an interesting thing about this town. You would think that there would be more communication between the ad business and show business. But there isn't. Two industries, both dedicated in many ways to pop culture. But not much interaction. I remember reading about Roger Gale and thinking, there's a guy with a big brain full of ideas. And I remember wondering whether he cared about Hollywood."

"But you never met him?"

"No. I would have liked to."

Tremaine studied Dean Latham. The guy seemed calm, almost interested in keeping the conversation going. No nerves. Maybe some loneliness, though. Might be one of those guys who tries to keep the telemarketers on the line. Tremaine looked around the room the two of them sat in. Lots of pictures of people, friends and family probably, but not many pictures of Dean Latham, not many pictures of himself. Unusual, Tremaine thought, most of these Hollywood guys like to have their likeness all over the place.

"Not many pictures of you around here."

"No," Latham said. "They depress me. I'm not one of those people who likes to have a photo library of all that was."

"Live in the moment."

"Right."

Tremaine informed Dean Latham of the week that both Roger Gale and Kelly Burch were killed. And then he asked him if he could remember what he was doing that week, what he was up to.

Again Latham gave a dramatic pause and said, "That was a long time ago—but not that long ago—and if I'm not mistaken, I was in Seattle visiting my mother. I went and stayed with her for a couple weeks, she was sick."

Tremaine, usually, would have stopped this particular line of questioning here. He wouldn't normally have badgered the guy. He would have just looked at him and thought about his answer a bit. But he really felt like pressing this guy. He wasn't going to get the letters and confront him, that might scare him and cause him to really clam up. But, subconsciously, Tremaine might not admit this, he was trying to force this lead, this Dean Latham lead, into being something. *Come on, baby, be something that helps me.*

So Tremaine pushed him and said, "I don't suppose you can prove that—that you were out of town." Tremaine was a little surprised at his accusatory tone. A little ashamed that he showed a small glimmer of frustration.

Latham said, "I could probably dig up the tickets. I'm a frequent flier freak. Want me to look?"

"No," Tremaine said, he didn't want Latham getting too nervous, too concerned about him. "If you find them, call me." Tremaine handed Latham his card and stood up. "Thank you for your time, Dean. I appreciate it."

"I hope I was helpful. I don't feel like I really provided you with anything."

Tremaine walked over to the door and turned around. He said, "You were helpful, Dean. Just talking to me, that was helpful." Tremaine paused and said, "By the way, what movies have you produced?"

Tremaine could see Dean Latham's face contort a bit to betray some pleasure. Like, finally, you asked . . .

"The most famous one is *Turnaround*."

Tremaine nodded and smiled and said, "Good flick," then said, "Thanks again for your time," and left.

CHAPTER 34

Tremaine got home at about seven. He sat in the Cutlass, the sun was low now, it was barely light out. He didn't get out, he just sat there, thinking. Thinking, why is this guy Dean Latham lying? Why is Latham, like the stripper from the karate place, playing dumb when it comes to people I'm pretty damn certain they've had contact with? The stripper with Roger Gale, Latham with Kelly Burch. Are all these people intertwined in some grand conspiracy? What is it? What am I missing?

Tremaine sat still in his car. It was quiet. His cell phone rang, startling him.

Without looking at the incoming number, Tremaine said, "Hello."

"Yeah, Donald, it's Dean Latham."

Tremaine shifted in his seat.

"Dean, what's up?"

"I found my old plane tickets. I was right. I was in Seattle that week."

Tremaine didn't answer right away.

"Did you hear me?" Latham said. "Did we break up?"

"We didn't break up. I heard you."

"Well, do you want to see the tickets? Do you want to come back by?"

"Not tonight," Tremaine said. "I tell you what, if I need to see them, I'll give you a buzz."

"All right then."

"Thanks for the call, Dean."

"No problem. Hey, *Turnaround*'s gonna be on TNT next month. You should check it out."

"I'll try," Tremaine said.

He clicked off the call.

Tremaine went inside the trailer thinking about this eccentric former movie producer Dean Latham. Now the guy's calling him with proof that he was out of town at the time of both murders. It seemed a little convenient, his calling right after Tremaine left, suddenly having found the tickets. Was this some gamesmanship, Latham trying to play the innocent? Or maybe, Tremaine thought, Latham knew Kelly but didn't kill Kelly.

Tremaine sat down at his desk and got online to IMDb. com, the Internet Movie Database. You could find everyone's credits who'd ever had anything to do with a movie, from stars to writers to directors to extras. Tremaine looked up Dean Latham, producer.

There were his credits.

Hasn't done anything for a while. Tremaine scanned all of them, all the movies Latham had produced. There was *Turnaround*, and three other movies Tremaine had never heard of: *Big Boy*, *Aliens in America*, and *Faster*.

Then Tremaine looked up Kelly Burch, the failed, dead actress. There were two Kelly Burches listed. Tremaine clicked on the first one, an actress from the 1920s, and evidently a pretty successful one. Not a star, but a character actress, a substantial list of credits, old black-and-white movies, some of which Tremaine had seen and liked. She'd made it, this Kelly Burch, one of the lucky ones. Then he clicked on the other Kelly Burch. Not much information, no picture, not even a date of birth—or date of death—and only one credit to her name, as an extra in a movie that came out four years ago called *Continental Drift*. This was probably the Kelly Burch who had been murdered. This was probably the Kelly Burch Tremaine was interested in. But this information, an extra in *Continental Drift*, didn't help him.

Hmm, Tremaine thought. Hmm.

He got some Maker's out of the cabinet, got some rocks out of the fridge, poured himself a bourbon on ice. He put on Derek and the Dominoes, *The Layla Sessions*, and sat down in a big leather chair next to his desk.

The hot booze and the ice, it was an amazing combination. He sat in the chair, refilling as necessary, listening to Eric assault his ax. Then he lay down on his bed, staring up at the ceiling. He closed his eyes and went into the blackness.

Next morning, the first person Tremaine called was a woman named Sally Kasmin. Sally was an old client and a sort of friend. She was a senior development executive at Paramount Pictures. She'd hired Tremaine some time back because people in her office suspected that someone was breaking in to get an advanced look at some of their projects. Their suspicions were correct; Tremaine caught a couple hired guns from a rival studio in the act, and that was that. The people who hired them went to prison. Did twelve months in a white-collar lock-up.

Sally was beautiful and single. Tremaine had never slept with her. Shame about that. Was that why they were still friends?

"Sally Kasmin's office," her chipper assistant said.

"Donald Tremaine calling for Sally."

A few seconds later: "To what do I owe the pleasure?"

"Sally, how are you?"

"I'm good, Tremaine, I'm good. It's been a while, but you know, I was just thinking about you the other day."

"Were you in the shower?"

Sally laughed that Sally laugh. It was loud—it was amazing. She probably thought his little quip was funny, but her laugh made him feel like it was *really* funny. She was good, this one.

"I need a favor," Tremaine said.

"Anything, babe."

"I need to find out if an actress was in or was an extra in one or more of the following movies."

"Okay, what are they?"

"*Turnaround*, *Big Boy*, *Aliens in America*, and *Faster*."

"Sure, *Turnaround* was pretty big. Who's the actress?"

"Her name is Kelly Burch. That's Kelly with a y."

"Is this about Neil Franks? He directed *Turnaround*."

"No. I'll tell you later what it's about."

"No, you won't."

"You're right. So, when will I hear about Kelly?"

"End of day, maybe."

"Can I take you out for a drink to say thanks?"

"I don't see why not."

"I know this great little place called my trailer."

Sally laughed that Sally laugh.

The next call was to Indio, California, information. Indio was a desert town about twenty-five miles east of Palm Springs. But it didn't have the vibe of Palm Springs—the pink sweat suits, the Rolls-Royces, the enormous glasses. It had its nice parts, but much of this small desert community consisted of unglamorous houses on bleak, sun-pelted streets. A town where it was so goddamn hot much of the time that you could only stand, mouth agape, and try not to melt. Or go inside, zip up the blinds, and sit in the AC. If you had AC. And the people, they were different from the Palm Springs crowd, too. They were sun-beaten, crazy almost, roaming the hot streets in a zombie state.

"What city and state please?"

"Indio, California."

"Name."

"Angela Coyle."

Kelly Burch's sister.

Tremaine got the number. And the address. He got in his car and headed straight east on the Ten.

On I–10, Tremaine cruised through West L.A., through downtown—wonder what that bad ass karate guy is up to—then through the little towns that border downtown proper on the east side, then into the brown, bleak desert. As he got past the clusters of towns outside the city limits, the landscape started to open up, and it was beautiful in its stark, monochromatic way.

Hot as shit, though, really incredibly hot, but stark and apocalyptic and interesting.

Palm Springs was about two hours, Indio about two and a half. But Tremaine was already at the windmills, about a half-hour west of Palm Springs; he was making good time. It had been seventy minutes at the most. Windmills everywhere, an enormous stretch of them. Tremaine drove down the singular stretch of freeway, the Ten, that ribbon of black through the tan desert. And windmills everywhere. Everywhere. Massive, modern, white windmills as far as he could see. Spinning all at different paces, and just massive, huge. When the road would get close to one, it was almost unbelievable how big the blades were, spinning round and round. Round and round. The desert wind propelling them.

If you weren't careful—and Tremaine wasn't being careful right at this minute—you could freak out. Yeah, looking out on that brown landscape, with the rock formations and the sun high in the sky and the big, freakishly large windmills spinning and spinning, round and round, hypnotizing you, making you almost hallucinate, your senses not used to this surreal vision.

Holy shit—he was on the wrong side of the road.

Tremaine lit a smoke, the windmills now in his rearview, thank God. Still spinning though. Even tiny in the rearview, they could take you to that hallucinatory place.

Now he was passing though Palm Springs, the desert giving way to some greenery, some palm trees—granted, all brought there and planted, but it was a nice change after those wild-ass windmills.

For a long time, Tremaine didn't understand the allure of Palm Springs. Didn't understand the appeal of roasting in the sun all day, then going to high-end chain restaurants with a bunch of middle-aged to old red-faced rich people who were swilling booze, wearing shorts and weird golf shirts, talking golf and about tennis and golf and real estate. And golf.

He didn't understand that you'd go to some places and, in hundred-and-fifteen-degree heat, there were tables and chairs *outside* with devices set up that sprayed you down with very fine water pellets to cool you off so you wouldn't pass out. Like elephants at the zoo getting hosed down in the summer.

That's how these people lived. It was so hot you'd have to be sprayed with water constantly just to sit somewhere. And then, ridiculously, the only thing anyone talked about was how hot it was. Tremaine would always say to these people, "I have an idea about how to deal with this heat."

And they'd say, "Yeah, how?"

And he'd say, "Go the fuck inside."

But over time, Tremaine got it. Got the appeal of the desert lifestyle. It was decadent, it was about pleasure and camaraderie. There was something otherworldly out here with the brown land and the cacti and the rocks and the roadrunners. Sitting in the heat by the pool getting wasted all day. It was like you were on another planet—it was different and the culture demanded that you luxuriate. So people did.

It's almost like the heat slowed people down, got them in a more relaxed mood, got them to let go.

And then eventually you just bought in. Bought a thin, light blue terrycloth jumpsuit, got way too sunburned, bought some enormous glasses, went to big, loud, expensive restaurants, and just got tanked.

If you had dough, that is. If you didn't, this desert life just kind of made you nuts.

Palm Springs was in his rearview now. And the glamour was in his rearview, too. He was now in Indio, in a sad little section of this desert town where people got wasted, sure, but it was in their basements, working their meth labs, or sitting on a street corner somewhere huffing gasoline.

Tremaine called Angela Coyle. She answered.

"Hello."

"Hi, Angela?"

"Who's this?"

This woman was rough, Tremaine could hear it. This wasn't Eveyln Gale, not even close.

"My name is Donald Tremaine. I'm a private investigator."

"What do you want?"

Really defensive. But not with an aristocratic edge. With a poor edge, a defensiveness born out of something real, not born out of what people would think at the club.

"I was hoping to talk to you about your sister, Kelly, just for a few minutes."

"Nothing to say. She's dead."

Man, this lady was harsh.

"Five minutes, Angela. I'm in Indio. Can I come by?"

Tremaine pulled down her street. A side street off the main drag through town. Treeless, pelted by heat, bleak. Her house sat too close to the road, was institution gray and looked paper-thin. Tremaine could picture it rolling and bouncing in the wind across the countryside like some massive tumbleweed.

Tremaine got out of his car as Angela Coyle opened her door. She was thin and blonde, and he could see Kelly in her face, somewhere down in there. Her skin was scratched. Tremaine had seen that look before and had always wondered, how does that happen? How does someone get a big scratch on her face? Did Angela have an angry-ass cat?

Angela didn't invite Tremaine in. She motioned for him to sit on the chair on the little deck outside her front door.

"What, are you investigating Kelly's murder?" Angela said.

"Yeah, I am. I'm wondering if it's tied to another thing I'm looking into, the murder of a guy named Roger Gale."

The expression on Angela's face couldn't have been blanker. No way. Tremaine looked at the scratch, followed it from one end to the other.

"I don't know nothing about Kelly's death. Alls I know is she thought she was better than everyone, and went out to Hollywood and became a druggie. It runs in our family."

"What, the drugs?"

"Yeah."

This honest admission from Angela endeared her to Tremaine. He felt for her in this moment.

Tremaine said, "Did you know anything about her life around the time of her death? Like, did you know her boyfriend at all, Evan?"

"Nope. She never called me. We really didn't speak. We weren't friends."

Tremaine could see some pain come over her face. Emotional pain, not physical pain like the scratch. He knew that look, said she loved her sister anyway.

"How 'bout a guy named Dean Latham? Did you ever hear that name?"

Something else registered on her face.

"Why do you care, anyway?" Angela said.

"I can't say I was personally affected by Kelly's death. I didn't know her. But what I can tell you is, I care about justice. I care that people like you, and people like the woman who hired me to look into all this stuff in the first place, get to the truth. Because what's really happening here, what I really do this for, is I don't like it when people get fucked over. And that's what happens when someone kills someone else and nobody does anything about it. Somebody is getting fucked. Like it just doesn't matter somehow that they're dead. So, that's why I care."

Angela said, "Hold on a second."

She walked inside and shut the front door behind her. About a minute later she came back out holding a picture, and said, "This was in Kelly's stuff. Cops looked at it, they didn't want it."

Before she showed Tremaine the front of the picture, she showed him the back of the picture. Written on it in a pink ballpoint pen was *With the one and only Dean Latham.*

"That's Kelly's handwriting," Angela said.

Tremaine turned the picture over and looked at the front. Kelly—beautiful, sexual—on the left, Dean on the right. They were at a black-tie party, and from the looks of the picture, it was a fun one. They were arm in arm, laughing hysterically. Kelly looking right at the camera, almost flirting with it, her big eyes saying *look at me.* Dean had his head tilted back, in the throes of an exaggerated laugh. Like Burt Reynolds on the *Carson* show, head tilted back, letting out that high-pitched laugh. Tremaine looked at the picture, looked at Kelly on the left, looked at Dean on the right. Dean with shoulder-length black hair and black Elvis Costello–style glasses. It was an odd way to look at Dean's face, seeing mostly his chin. He had that black hair, though, longer here but still the hip look, and he had the glasses, too, just a different style. It was enough.

"Can I have this picture?" Tremaine said.

"No. It's all I have. It's literally the only picture I have of her."

"I may need it to prove a point to someone. To Dean."

"No, I don't know you. What if I never see the picture again? Then I'll never be able to see Kelly again."

Tremaine's cell rang. He recognized the number.

"Tremaine," he said.

"Hey, it's Sally."

"Hey."

"So, Kelly Burch?"

"Yeah."

"She was an extra in *Aliens in America.*"

"You're the best, Sally. Thank you."

Tremaine clicked off the phone.

He looked at Angela, at that face with the scratch, and said, "Thank you for seeing me. As it turns out, I don't need the picture."

CHAPTER 35

Tremaine got back to L.A., tired from driving through the desert heat, thinking, Dean Latham is lying and I need to make him admit it. Not when he's ready to admit it, no, right now. Tremaine didn't take the Ten back to Malibu, he took it to La Cienega, wound his way through Hollywood, then up the canyon back to Latham's.

Sitting outside Latham's now, man, wrecked from the heat. Beat. Beat from the heat.

Tremaine thinking, the letters, the picture, and the movie *Aliens in America*. The movie was the confusing element. Surely Latham's smart enough to know I could find out that he had produced a movie that Kelly Burch was in. But he's never heard of her? Is Latham dumb? Could that be it? Does he think I'm dumb?

Could it have slipped his mind that Kelly's credits would be accessible? Could he have been sitting up here with his memories, in his former producer's throne, four drinks in, thinking that extras don't get credits?

Still sitting in his car, Tremaine thinking, this case is bizarre, this case is bullshit. Roger Gale had an affair, but he didn't. He went into the karate place, but he didn't. Dean Latham produced a movie Kelly was in and wrote her love letters, and took a picture with her, but he doesn't know her. Bullshit. And he doesn't even have the sense to at least admit that he knows her, even if he didn't kill her.

Man, Tremaine was hot. From the desert, from the case.

Tremaine, opening his door, clenching his jaw, saying to himself, let's see how Latham handles a little pressure.

Tremaine, through the front gate, at Latham's door, knocking.

Latham opened the door.

"I thought you were going to call me," Latham said.

"I lied," Tremaine said. "Just like you."

Tremaine walked in Latham's house.

Latham said, "What are you talking about? You want to see the tickets?"

"Shut up, Latham, I know you knew Kelly Burch."

Tremaine took a tone with Latham, gave him a look. Telling Latham with his eyes, I'm gonna fuck you up, man.

"I've never heard of her," Latham said. "Not until you said her name."

"I know you knew her."

"Tremaine, I've never heard of her."

255

"She was an extra in *Aliens in America*."

Dean looked at Tremaine, hung his head, shook it, and said, "So were about a thousand other desperate people in this town."

"The girl had love letters with your name on them, she was in one of your movies, she was stunning. You knew her. You were in love with her."

Tremaine was in Latham's face. Trying to press a confession out of him, making Latham think he was about to blow his top. But he really wasn't going to blow his top, right? This was a bluff. The frustrations of getting nowhere weren't affecting him, making him angry.

Right?

"What? I didn't know her," Latham said. "And I sure as hell wasn't in love with her. If she had love letters, they weren't from me. She *might* have loved me, like from afar or something, but I didn't even know her. I've never heard of her. And when she was killed, I was out of town. I'll show you the tickets."

Tremaine didn't know what he was going to do with Latham's confession once he got it, but he was going to get it. He ramped up the insanity in his eyes.

"Bullshit," Tremaine said. "Admit it, admit you knew her."

Tremaine walked toward Latham, stood right in front of him. "Admit it, Latham. Right now. Or you will wish you had."

After laying down the threat, Tremaine felt less and less like he was bluffing. His act was colliding with his true feelings. His act was allowing his true frustrations to come out. He was realizing that maybe he didn't know shit.

Maybe even if he did pull the truth out of Latham, what was he doing threatening some washed-up producer about a case he wasn't even on? But Tremaine wasn't stopping now, nope, too late.

Latham said, "I don't know who the fuck you think you are or what you think you know. But if you don't get out of my house, I'm going to call the cops. Then I'm going to call my lawyer."

"I'm sure they'd all like the information I have," Tremaine said.

"They can have it," Latham said.

"Tell me what you know, Latham."

Tremaine inched closer to Latham.

Latham picked up his cordless, "Tremaine, get the fuck out of my house or I call the cops."

Tremaine grabbed the phone away from him and said, "I don't buy your bluff, Latham."

And did he buy his own bluff? Or was he about to do something violent with that phone? He sure had the feeling, the adrenaline shot, the one he'd always had sliding down the face of a monster wave.

Tremaine held the phone in his hand. "The fucking girl was in one of your movies, Latham. Any idiot could have found that out."

Latham said, "I never went on the set of that movie. I got a producer's credit and was banned from the set. It happens all the time. I had nothing to do with the movie. Much less the goddamn extras."

Tremaine could see himself striking Latham. The bluff was fading, going away—gone?

He was about to do it.

He said, "Tell me you knew her or I'm going to put this phone through your head."

"Hold on a second," Latham said.

Latham reached in his pocket and pulled out some plane tickets.

Tremaine grabbed them, looked at them. They were old. They looked real. They indicated that Latham was in Seattle at the time of the killings. Tremaine was confused now—still mad, but about what? The case, the fact that Latham had some proof? Doesn't mean Latham didn't know Kelly, but it was evidence. It was something real to support what he was saying. Tremaine knew he could find out if Latham knew Kelly, one way or another, on his own. But he'd never have *this* chance again. To make him say something he didn't want to. But Tremaine now had lost a bit of his bluff. The tickets had taken some wind out of his sails. And his chance of pulling something out of Latham was almost over. Was almost dead. Like Kelly Burch and Roger Gale.

"Plane tickets are easy to fake," Tremaine said.

"Those aren't fake. You could call my mom and ask her, if she weren't dead. Call the airline, whatever."

Tremaine stepped closer to Latham.

Latham backed up, backed up more, until he was against the wall, next to the door in the front room. Tremaine was in his face, his eyes inches from Latham's eyes. Tremaine held the phone up to strike Latham, but his rage was dying, as was his bluff. Maybe Latham knew it.

Tremaine said, "I don't care if you were out of town when she was killed. Admit that you knew her, Latham. Tell me about your relationship to Kelly Burch."

Latham looked at Tremaine and said, "You're in my house and you're threatening me. Get the fuck out."

Tremaine grabbed Latham by the throat. One last try. Tremaine wanting to follow through on the bluff—and it was a bluff now. The real rage that had crept in was damn near gone. But the bluff? Tremaine knew this shit wasn't working. He squeezed, hard, simultaneously pushing Latham against the wall, pinning him against the wall.

Tremaine stared at Latham. He couldn't read his expression, he couldn't. Tremaine let go and backed up. Latham stood against the wall. Tremaine looked at him, tried to pull something out of Latham's face. Nothing.

He took his eyes away from Latham and looked at the plane tickets he'd thrown on the floor. He leaned down, grabbed them. Then, he looked over toward the kitchen and saw the cradle for the cordless phone. Tremaine walked over to it, placed the phone in its cradle and placed the tickets on the kitchen table.

Tremaine walked back, looked down at the floor again, where the tickets had been before he'd picked them up. Then, he looked at Latham, standing against the wall, but no longer pinned against it. Latham tilted his head, furrowed his brow a bit, a mixture of confusion and defiance in his face.

Tremaine walked out the door.

CHAPTER 36

Tremaine got home. Exhausted. Confused. Angry. Now was the time, Tremaine knew, that he was going to have to let go and think. Think, Tremaine, think. What are you missing? Of all the pieces of the puzzle, which two or three or four fit together?

Tremaine had to close his eyes and look at the clues, examine the people, the circumstances, the subtle nuances of everything he'd learned this far, and do everything in his power to take the separate little strings of this case and tie them together. What was he missing? What the fuck was he missing? On the ground, in the trailer doing pushups, mulling it over in his head. Who, of all the people he'd met, had a good reason to kill Roger Gale? This wasn't a random crime. It wasn't. Thirty pushups, forty pushups, fifty pushups, sixty pushups, they didn't hurt, he couldn't even feel them. This wasn't a goddamn random crime. He looked at Lyle as he went up and down, up and down. Thinking: Is there anything here? Is there any goddamn connection between any of the things I've found out?

He paced around the trailer, popping beers, listening to some old Bob Dylan, *Blonde on Blonde*—*I want you, I want you, I want you soooo bad*. He considered everything. Everything. Everything he knew, everyone he'd talked to. He thought about all the people who knew Roger Gale and then he thought about the crazy tangent he'd just been on. Kelly Burch, Vicky Fong, Dean Latham. Dean Latham? Was he kidding himself to even consider chasing down another, possibly unrelated—probably unrelated—cold case in the first place?

He went up on the roof of his trailer. A beautiful Southern California night. The stars out, the ocean a black, nearly invisible force in the distance.

Who were the people in this case who mattered? Roger's widow and his stepson were cryptic, but ultimately they seemed to just be protecting their feeble image of themselves as perfect. As people with money and reputations and no skeletons in the closet. Yeah, right—we've all got 'em. And we all try to hide 'em. But if the stepson would bend the law to protect his mother's reputation, what else would he do? That glass eye, that shifty manner. Maybe the business with paying off Bill Peterson was a ruse to keep cops and detectives away. You know, he paid off a cop to protect his mom, but he definitely didn't *kill* his stepdad. Or did he?

And Wendy Leahy? Okay, she lied, she lied a couple

times. So? She was a nice girl who ran a gym who got offered five large by a charismatic Roger Gale and took it. So sue her.

Tyler Wilkes? The guy's a joke. Hires another P.I. on a paranoid, implanted fear that he was gonna somehow end up in trouble for doing business with Paul Spinelli. And the karate studio? The sex show? What was Roger Gale doing there? Did he see a show? Did he not see a show? Did some sex performer have the poise to tell Tremaine that Roger Gale had never come in when in fact he actually had? Did these sex-show people connect to Roger Gale's death or to Kelly Burch or to Dean Latham or to anything? Anything at all?

Who killed Roger Gale and why?

The one murder that might have had any connection at all was Kelly Burch's. But wasn't that a friggin' shot in the dark? So what if they got murdered on the same day. So what.

Tremaine lay down on his back and looked up at the sky. A disconnected thought popped in his head. Even in the midst of this whirlwind of analysis, he thought to himself, it'd be nice to solve this one, even if it was just to impress Nina . . .

He looked at the sky, at the stars, the white dots among the blackness. He envisioned each star to be an element in the case. He started drawing imaginary lines between them to form figures in his head, like constellations. Everything, from the moment Nina appeared at his trailer until now, moved around in his brain as he looked at the vast California sky and the stars.

He drifted off to sleep.

At about three in the morning, he woke up. Thinking: Where the hell am I? Then he went down the ladder, went inside, and went to bed.

He woke up again at about 5:00 A.M. His mind, before having a chance to process anything else, went directly to the case. He walked into the kitchen, made a pot of coffee, and stood there, watching the pot slowly fill up with dark brown liquid. Drip. Drip. Drip. Just standing there in his little kitchen at the crack of dawn, watching the coffee but focusing on the case. And then his mind—almost out of nowhere—went to Dean Latham.

And that's when it happened.

He realized that the man he'd talked to, the movie producer, Dean Latham, was not the Dean Latham in the picture with Kelly Burch.

That robe-wearing washed-up movie producer was innocent. He had told Tremaine the truth. He'd never met Kelly Burch and he'd never met Roger Gale. Tremaine owed him an apology, and he'd give him one.

Dean Latham, the movie producer, did, however, share his name with the man in the picture, the man with the long black hair and the glasses, Kelly Burch's lover.

But it was by sheer coincidence. The Dean Latham in the picture was a different Dean Latham. The Dean Latham Tremaine had met had absolutely nothing to do with the case.

Yes, Tremaine thought, the Dean Latham in the picture was someone else. Someone who was, without question, entirely vital to the case he'd been struggling with.

Tremaine got a feeling in his stomach, his subconscious mind connecting with his conscious mind. His logical attack on the case colliding with his instincts.

And he realized that the girl from the karate studio, the sex performer, hadn't lied to him either. She'd never seen Roger Gale before. That was the truth. In fact, Tremaine realized, Roger Gale had never even been to the karate studio. No, Tyler Wilkes was mistaken. Tyler thought he'd seen Roger Gale go in the karate studio, but he was wrong. Roger Gale had gone somewhere else.

Tremaine focused on the name Dean Latham, examining it closely. Then, staring at the name in his mind, the letters in Dean Latham's name began to float independently of each other. Tremaine's eyes were pointed at random things on his kitchen counter, but what he saw was the name Dean Latham etched in his imagination. The letters danced around and began to take different positions. Began to re-order themselves to form something new. Tremaine letting his mind go, letting it work on its own, as he'd done so many times working that silly Jumble word game.

Tremaine thought about the words, the name, Dean Latham. The letters began laying themselves down into new creations.

First he saw: DEAN LATHAM.

And then he saw: DEA LANTHAM.

And then he saw: THE LAD MANA.

And then he saw something else, something that made him shake his head and even smile. And he grabbed a pencil and a piece of paper and he wrote what he saw down. Tremaine knew, as he wrote it, the identity of the man in the picture with Kelly Burch, the man who had written her love letters. A man who had gone to great lengths to disguise his appearance. A man who hadn't gone to a karate studio but had gone next door to a wig store, Expert Wigs, to buy himself a long black wig. That way, disguised, he could be *across a table at a crowded restaurant* with Kelly Burch, the beautiful young girl he loved. Yes, the man in the picture had even changed his name so when he was with her he could completely become someone else. But he hadn't chosen just any name. No. He'd made the perfect name using only the letters of a title that described him to a tee. He'd left a clue. Of course he had, he was too creative and clever not to.

This is what Donald Tremaine wrote down out of the letters in the name Dean Latham: THE L.A. AD MAN.

CHAPTER 37

Tremaine got in the Cutlass instantly.

He called Jack Sawyer as he drove toward Gale/Parker.

"You up, Jack?"

"What do you mean? I'm old, I wake up at three in the morning."

It was just 6:00 A.M., but Jack Sawyer, the Salty Dog, was alive and kicking, thankfully. Tremaine asked him if he could meet him at Gale/Parker not in an hour, not in a half hour, but as soon as possible, right now, preferably. Sawyer, the good man that he was, said, "absolutely."

At the steps leading to the Gale/Parker reception area, open for business, as always, Tremaine stood there waiting for Sawyer. He saw Sawyer pulling in, looking alive in his pickup at this early hour.

As Sawyer approached, he said, "You P.I.s keep funny hours. Luckily, so do old advertising farts."

"Thank you for doing this."

"It's okay. They're gonna think I'm in the office early to work. Never hurts. Even at this stage in my career."

"I'll tell you what I need as we walk in."

They got inside, got to Sawyer's office, and Tremaine told Sawyer what he'd discovered. Kelly Burch, the secret affair, the love letters, the disguise, the double life that Roger Gale had been living. Then Tremaine said to Sawyer, "I know I'm not wrong, but this case is insane. Nothing is as it seems. I needed to bounce this off someone who knew Roger well. Who knew what he was capable of. And what I'm wondering is, now that I've told you what I found, does it connect to anything you know about Roger?"

Sawyer took a long pause and then said, "We had a big, crazy costume party here at the agency once. I've got some pictures of it. I think you'd be interested in seeing some of them."

Jack Sawyer went into a filing cabinet in his office and produced a photograph from the costume party. And there was Sawyer dressed as a clown, standing next to Roger Gale dressed not as a recognizable character but as someone else. A guy with long black hair and big black glasses.

Sawyer said, "Roger came to this party, not wearing a costume-party costume. He just came as someone else. That was his costume. And nobody recognized him for a while. It was typical Roger, playing with people's minds."

Tremaine looked at the picture from the costume party. It was the same guy who was in the picture Angela Coyle had shown him.

Sawyer said, "This help you out?"

"I was sure. Now I'm positive." Then Tremaine said, "When Roger Gale was with the girl, Kelly, he went by a different name, too. He called himself Dean Latham. Not just a random choice. Gale used the letters in the moniker 'The L.A. Ad Man' to come up with, to create, Dean Latham."

Sawyer nodded, but his face betrayed confusion, this onslaught of bizarre information hitting him at such an early hour.

"Read these letters he wrote to her," Tremaine said.

Tremaine produced the letters, handed them to Sawyer. Sawyer read them, then just kind of stared for a moment and said, "Wow. There's a lot in there. Love, lust—obsession, maybe."

"Yeah," Tremaine said. "And Gale couldn't tell Kelly how he felt when he was Roger Gale, ad exec, L.A. Country Club man-about-town. So he became someone else when he was around her and told her his deepest feelings."

"You think she knew who he really was?"

"I don't know," Tremaine said. "I'm sure she knew he wore the wig. If the sex was as great as he says in the letters, I'm sure she yanked on his hair a time or two."

Sawyer managed a laugh.

Tremaine said, "I don't think she cared who he really was. She was a drug addict, maybe he paid for her blow. But I'll tell you this. She probably knew him as well as anyone. The guy sure as hell went out of his way to keep people in the dark."

Sawyer looked at the letters, at the picture, then at Tremaine.

Tremaine said, "You read those letters . . . Those were real feelings from a part of Roger Gale that he never showed anyone else. In the end, the guy who wrote them . . . That's Dean Latham, not Roger Gale. Same body, different guy."

Sawyer said, "In the ad business, we call that body copy."

Gallows humor. Tremaine knew he liked this guy.

CHAPTER 38

After leaving Gale/Parker, still in his car, Tremaine called John Lopez. If he'd needed his help before, he'd definitely need it now. Luckily, Lopez answered. And listened. Listened as Tremaine told him his theory and his plan. This was when the bullshitting between them was over, and Lopez didn't make any of the jokes that were par for the course. No, he just listened and, in the end, agreed to Tremaine's request.

Then Tremaine made another call. This one he pulled his car over for. No distractions. The midmorning traffic was in full swing—it was almost nine now—so Tremaine ducked into a random parking lot in Marina del Rey that serviced some small businesses. He sat in his car facing a 20/20 Video, a nail salon, and Rubio's Fish Tacos.

He pulled out the little piece of paper Evan Mulligan had given him, the one with his number on it, and dialed him up. Tremaine sat in his car, concentrating on the matter at hand but looking at an old poster in the window of 20/20 Video for *Blade II*. Tremaine was in a stare-down with a Mohawk-sporting Wesley Snipes vampire when Evan said, "This is Evan." The standard at-work hello.

"It's Donald Tremaine," Tremaine said.

There was no immediate response from Evan. But then, just before the silence became an awkward silence, Evan said, "Sure, the P.I. I didn't expect you to call. So quickly, anyway."

Tremaine said, "I was hoping to talk to you a little more." Tremaine, measuring very carefully his words. Making sure not to say too little, not to say too much.

"Um, okay. What about?"

"About Dean Latham."

"Dean Latham? The guy you asked me about? I told you, I don't know him."

This is where Tremaine had to be careful, had to make sure that what he said had the right result. Tremaine said, "Dean Latham was having an affair with your former girl-friend, Kelly."

What Tremaine got in response was another pause. Now Evan exhibited a little edge, just a slight one, but it was there, as he said, "Okay. So? Are you calling to tell me I was wrong about her not being involved with someone? Dude, I was just telling you what I thought."

"Listen, Evan, will you meet me to discuss this further? I want to tell you a few things, but I think we should meet in person."

"Listen, I don't know Dean Latham, and if you're sure Kelly was having an affair with him, then maybe you should look into him. But if you have questions for me, can't you just ask me now?"

"This is about more than Dean Latham," Tremaine said, at this point choosing his words with total precision, choosing them so they'd have just the right effect on Evan Mulligan. He said, "This is about how Dean Latham's affair with Kelly led to her murder. I want to talk to you before I talk to the police, before I talk to anyone."

"Why?"

"Because you can help me determine if I'm right."

"Right about what?"

"Right about who killed her."

"Where do you want to meet?"

"Wherever you want."

Evan paused. Then he said, the edge in his voice gone now, "Why don't I come to you. I don't want any more memories of my girlfriend's murder to be in my house."

Tremaine said, "Do you know where Crystal Point is, in Malibu?"

"The public beach?"

"Yeah," Tremaine said. "Why don't we meet there. There's a couple benches, and they light up the sitting area at night. You can leave your memories there."

"What time?" Evan said.

Tremaine hung up the phone, the *Blade II* poster still stared at him. The hustle and bustle around Rubio's and the surrounding shops seemed liked a cartoon, everybody going on about their day, while he sat in a hot 1971 Oldsmobile Cutlass contemplating a case where he hadn't had much help all along from the little things most detectives, private or otherwise, called facts.

Tremaine pulled out of the little parking lot, seeing the signs for 20/20 Video and Rubio's Fish Tacos and the nail salon getting smaller and smaller in his rearview as he headed back to his trailer park, back home.

That night, as Tremaine drove to Crystal Point to meet Evan, he smoked a cig and tried to shut out the thoughts in his head. He knew now was the time to trust himself. As he'd done so many times on the big waves back in the day. Trust yourself, Tremaine. It might seem crazy, what you're about to do, but trust yourself, your mind is made up. Trust yourself.

Yeah, just enjoy the night air and drive, he told himself. He looked out at the PCH, caught glimpses of familiar settings, noticed a Ford Mustang in his rearview. But the encroaching thoughts, the what-ifs, he tried to keep out of his mind. The work it took to shut it all out miraculously allowed him to relax a little.

CHAPTER 39

Tremaine pulled the Cutlass into Crystal Point, into the Malibu beach park. The lights the city had set up shone but didn't cast much light. A park really wasn't an accurate description. More of an area. An area with some grass and trees, benches, and a public bathroom. And if you headed due west, a boardwalk down to the beach.

Tremaine's was the only car in the lot. There were probably thirty other spaces, all empty. He had the love letters from Dean/Roger in an envelope in his pocket.

He sat down on one of the park benches and stared in the direction of the ocean, which he could hear clearly but couldn't see because his view was obstructed by the bushes and trees bordering the park.

Some time passed and the noise of the ocean drowned

out the sound of Evan's Jeep, but the headlights alerted him that the man he wanted to talk to was present and accounted for.

Evan got out of his Jeep. Tremaine looked at the circle of yellow on the parking lot cement that emanated from the parking lot's lights. As Evan passed through the semi-spotlight, Tremaine recognized him the way you recognize someone you've seen only once or twice before. Evan looked bigger than Tremaine remembered, his figure enhanced by a coat he wore to combat the chill of a Malibu night.

Tremaine stood as Evan neared and said, "Good evening, Evan."

"Tremaine, how are you?"

The two men stood face to face for a moment and then Donald Tremaine said, "I want to show you some things."

"All right," Evan said.

Tremaine and Evan sat down on one of the benches and Tremaine opened up the envelope that held the love letters to Kelly from a man who disguised himself to be a guy named Dean Latham. He kept them in his hand. He didn't show them to Evan. Not yet.

"Before Kelly was killed, she was having an affair with the man we talked about, Dean Latham."

"You told me that," Evan said with some of that same irritated edge from the phone call. "What are you trying to do, rub it in that my girlfriend found someone after me?"

Tremaine showed Evan the letters.

Evan looked at them. Didn't really read them, just processed what they were.

Evan said, "Look, I told you she was with other guys. I

don't know what this is. I don't know who this guy Dean Latham is. And I don't care. Don't tell me you had me come all the way out here to prove to me my dead ex-girlfriend was involved with some random guy?"

"No, I didn't have you come out here just to tell you that. Actually, I want to tell you my theory on the situation."

"Tremaine, I'm not necessarily interested in your ideas about the behavior of Kelly."

"Hear me out," Tremaine said. "It involves you."

Evan fidgeted on the bench.

Then Tremaine said, "Let's take a walk."

Tremaine and Evan headed out the boardwalk to the beach. It was dark and deserted, now the only light was provided by the moon and the stars. Tremaine guided them north toward a cluster of rocks he used as a marker when he surfed this part of the ocean.

"The man who wrote the letters to Kelly went by the name Dean Latham, but in reality, that wasn't his name," Tremaine said. "That was a fake name. In fact, it was a fake name created very carefully by the man himself. This man is dead now. His name was Roger Gale."

"What the hell are you talking about, Tremaine?"

The two continued walking on the beach. The waves pounded the shore, creating a wall of white noise that Tremaine had to talk over. They reached the cluster of rocks.

Evan leaned against one of the rocks and Tremaine faced him and continued. "Roger Gale, the ad man you said you'd heard of, was living a double life. Most of the time he was a successful ad man. But some of the time, dressed in a disguise, he was a guy named Dean Latham.

A man who was in love with your ex-girlfriend. Who, if you read those letters, was desperately in love with your ex-girlfriend. As in love with her as you were. As you *still* were up until the day she died."

Evan said, "What's your point, Tremaine?"

"There are several kinds of murders in the world, Evan. Sometimes people kill because they've just lost their cookies. Serial killers are an example of this. Guy who suddenly thinks it's his right to kill people and store their body parts in the fridge. That's called being crazy. Another reason people kill is out of desperation and fear. Gang murders are an example of this. Kids grow up so poor and hungry and angry and desperate that they begin to rationalize killing another man because they think it's the only way out. They cloak this kind of murder in a haze of bravado, but this kind of crime really comes from a place of fear—the fear that they're either going to die or get killed or never amount to anything worth a shit."

The look in Evan's eyes began to change. He had a glazed-over, almost hypnotized look as he listened to Tremaine's diatribe.

"Another kind of murder," Tremaine said, "is a crime of passion. This is the most interesting of all murders, if you ask me. You know why? Because so often it's the work of someone who's not a killer. This kind of murder comes from a place of love. Not necessarily healthy love, but love nonetheless. The love one person has for another. But when they see the person they love with someone else, it triggers something in their hearts that they simply can't control. And they'll do anything to satiate that feeling."

The waves pounded in the distance, and the moon's

reflection off the big mass of water provided enough light for Tremaine to see that the look in Evan's eyes had shifted yet again. From a state of hypnosis to one of anger.

Evan said, "Are you through?"

"No," Tremaine said. "But the next thing I'm going to tell you, you already know."

Tremaine stepped forward, moving toward Evan, who was now standing up, no longer touching the rock. This was the moment Tremaine had to trust himself, trust his instincts, trust his mind to have pieced together things properly, trust the fact that he was hired to connect dots, make educated assumptions, work on instinct and intuition.

Tremaine said, "You killed Kelly Burch, Evan, and you also killed a man you thought was named Dean Latham."

"It's true what they say, Tremaine—you are insane."

Tremaine was not deterred.

"You were still in love with Kelly, Evan, she did that to people. You tried to hold on to her, but you couldn't. But you never let go of your love. You couldn't do that either. And one day, you caught Kelly and Dean together and the sight of it made you sick, seeing her with another man. Seeing her want someone else, someone who wasn't you. So you shot Kelly and you hit Dean over the head, then you suffocated him. It was actually quite clever. You were smart, Evan. Because you didn't want two people both to have bullets in their bodies from the same gun, you suffocated the stranger. Then you found out it was Roger Gale, looked at his wallet, I don't know. And once you found out who he was, you knew exactly where to take him. Chainsaw, your company, has done work with Gale/

Parker. You knew exactly where the agency was. So you took his disguise off and took him there. And you know how you got past the security guards? You got lucky. They were screwing off, who knows? You probably found the code to the building's alarm on Roger Gale, then walked right in and out. The fact that Roger was found dead at his own agency was sure to confuse the hell out of people. And as far as Kelly's murder was concerned? She was a druggie—no money, no job, no family. Just another street murder. And nobody would ever connect the two. How could they? For all intents and purposes, the man Kelly was having an affair with didn't even exist."

Evan looked calm. He said, "That's the stupidest thing I've ever heard."

"You killed two people, Evan," Tremaine said. "And you did it with the gun you've got in your coat right now." Tremaine moved closer to Evan. "And I'm going to take that gun away from you, and then we'll match the bullet from Kelly's body with your gun, and you'll go to jail."

Tremaine kept walking toward Evan, and as he got closer, a combination of fear and anger and sorrow registered in Evan Mulligan's eyes.

Evan pulled a gun out of his coat pocket and pointed it at Tremaine's head. It was a silver and black Walther, now about five feet away from Tremaine's face. Evan looked at Tremaine as Tremaine looked at the barrel of a gun.

"Congratulations, Tremaine. You figured it out. Only problem is, what makes you think I won't kill you, like I did them? No one would ever know. No one's even going to hear the gun go off."

———

John Lopez moved from behind one of the rocks he was hiding behind to another, closer rock. He'd been there, waiting, the entire time. Listening as Tremaine pulled a confession out of the man now pointing a gun at him. Tremaine heard Lopez, Evan didn't, not listening for him. Tremaine made a slight movement with his right hand, unnoticed by Evan, telling Lopez, hang on one more second.

Tremaine knew Lopez was itching to pop out and hold his gun on Evan. But Lopez listened to Tremaine's sign and stayed still behind the rock, no doubt with his gun cocked, his body clenched and ready for action.

Tremaine said, "Put down the gun, Evan."

He stepped toward him, closer.

"Take one more step and I'll blow your head off, Tremaine."

Tremaine continued toward Evan.

"You're not going to shoot me, Evan. The only reason you killed those other two people was because your heart told you to. Your heart isn't telling you to kill me. You can't do it."

Sweat began to drip from Evan's face and his finger clenched the trigger of the gun, tighter, tighter. "You're a dead man, Tremaine. No one will know. No one's going to hear anything."

Tremaine, slowly, carefully, moved closer.

Evan said, "I walked into Kelly's apartment and a man I'd never seen before was on top of her and they looked at me and laughed. I've never felt anything like I felt at that moment. I drove home, so mad I couldn't see, and I got my gun. And I drove back to Kelly's getting angrier and angrier and angrier. And, almost without thinking, I was someone else, I shot Kelly in the face. And then I took the butt of the gun and I hit that fucker in the head. Hard, with everything I had. But I didn't even feel it." Evan paused and said, "I couldn't help it, Tremaine, I couldn't help it."

Tremaine was no more than an inch away from the barrel of Evan's gun.

Evan, sweating, shaking, said, "I'm going to shoot you, Tremaine. I have to. I'm going to shoot you."

"No, you're not," Tremaine said.

In one motion, Tremaine took the gun away from Evan and twisted him around, then shoved him forward, sending him down to the ground, his face now entrenched in the cold sand.

Lopez sprang from behind the rocks and threw some cuffs on the man Tremaine had pinned to the ground. Before he read the man his rights for killing two people, he turned to Tremaine and said, "You're not insane, Tremaine. You're fucking crazy."

CHAPTER 40

Sitting at Nina's house two nights later, Tremaine could feel the fatigue from the stress of the case still flowing out of his body. He had wine in his hand, Nina sitting across from him, and Lyle right there on the floor because Nina had suggested bringing him. It was nice, relaxing, and, as he talked to Nina about the final details of the case, he felt good. Good and tired and relaxed.

"Well, Donald, here we are," Nina said.

"Here we are."

"It seems like a long time ago that I was introducing myself to you."

"Indeed. The ups and downs of a case always seem to make the days a little longer."

Tremaine and Nina sipped their wine, the alcohol hitting them both in just the right spot. Lyle was on his best behavior as a guest in another person's house. Dead asleep.

"I had fun surfing the other day," she said.

"I did, too. You were good. Room for improvement, but you were good."

Nina smiled. That same smile that actually hurt Donald Tremaine.

They ate some dinner—Nina roasted a bird—and then she suggested doing something that Donald didn't see coming. She said, "Let's watch a movie."

"Good idea," Tremaine said.

"How 'bout *Insane Tremaine*?"

Tremaine laughed and said, "I'm afraid I don't have a copy of that one."

"That's okay," she said. "I do."

They sat in front of the TV, fresh bottle of white, both of them on a small sofa.

"It's been a long time since I've seen this," he said.

"Well, it'll be my first time, so I expect some quality commentary."

"I'll do my best."

What transpired over the next thirty minutes was nothing short of hilarious. For Nina, anyway. She kept replaying the section of the video that focused on his falls, and she seemed to laugh harder and harder at each near-death spill Tremaine took.

Tremaine gave Nina a look.

"I'm only laughing because I'm sitting next to living proof that you survived," she said.

"Fair enough," he said.

"You were in pretty good shape back then," she said.

"How about now?"

"Room for improvement, but not bad."

Then, Nina Aldeen looked right at Donald Tremaine and said, "Thanks for taking the case, thanks for figuring it out. I'm glad I know the truth. I feel like I helped do something good."

"You did."

He looked at her, saw in her face that, yes, she had done something good. She helped to find that lost piece of the puzzle—the killer, the truth—that had created a deeper rip in her family than just the fact that there had been a murder. And, in that same discovery, she'd gotten out of her head a little bit, and one step closer to recovering from her divorce.

But, Tremaine thought, *what other good things had she done?*

When was the last time he'd told anyone about Mandy Rice getting shot and killed? And when was the last time he'd put the details of his own divorce through a different filter, looked at them with a different perspective?

Tremaine said, "You know, Nina, you did something good for me, too."

"Yeah?"

"Yeah."

"And what was that?"

"Well . . ." he said. And there was the pressure in his chest, the heat on his face. The guilt he felt about Mandy and his failed marriage to Susan somehow still ramming around inside him. "It felt good for me to talk about some of the things we talked about during this. Why I quit the tour. Your divorce, divorce in general. It was good for me to talk about those things. To think about them. You know?"

"Yeah, I know."

Tremaine wanted to talk more, he felt comfortable enough with Nina to let just a little more out. "Some of that confusion will always be with me, but I'm a little closer to being okay with it."

Nina said, "Sometimes a missing puzzle piece isn't really missing, it's just being ignored. And the way you find it, and deal with it, is to look at it, and think about it, and talk about it."

Tremaine nodded. He continued to look at her. But not just at her appearance—no, at her everything. And in that moment, he got a quick, incandescent feeling of hope. He knew, in that tiny section of time, that he could, that he would, someday get back in the relationship game.

Someday. Yeah, someday.

It made him uncomfortable, uneasy. But somehow it was good. He knew for sure that it was good. Yes, in that moment, he was on a wave, but it wasn't a wave he could control. It wasn't a wave that he could slice and carve and shape. It wasn't a wave that he could maneuver on and ma-nipulate. It was a wave that took him wherever it wanted to go.

He remembered now Nina first arriving at his house, looking up at him standing on the roof of his trailer, hand shielding her eyes. He remembered her walking on the beach at night, sitting across from him at the Lobster, waving to him from the steps of Gale/Parker. And as he examined those memories, he was glad, he was grateful, that he'd been able to help her.

Or was it the other way around?

CHAPTER 41

A week later, Tremaine was up on the roof of his trailer reading a draft of Nina Aldeen's book, *Split Up*. Remarkable. Sad, angry, strong, inspiring, just like a book like this should be.

He had planned to start the book on his flight to Australia the next day, but he couldn't wait, the big manuscript sitting on a table in the trailer was just too tempting. He knocked out about a hundred pages, then stood up and looked at the surf. Looked to be about three to four, really good shape. Tremaine knew he was definitely going to get his fill of surfing Down Under, but, man, it was a nice Malibu afternoon. Warm, still, just right. And the waves looked good. It'd feel nice, it'd *be* nice, to be out there.

Tremaine went inside the trailer, gave Lyle a pat on the

head, put Nina's manuscript in his carry-on bag for tomorrow. He'd pull it out later that night and read more, he knew that, but he wanted to at least pretend he was going to save the lion's share of the book for the plane.

Tremaine looked out his window and saw Marvin Kearns walk by, dressed as a cowboy. He shook his head and laughed.

Then Tremaine looked at his surfboard bag, all packed and ready to go. He thought, do I really want to go through the trouble of unpacking just to grab a few waves, even though I'm headed to Australia tomorrow to surf for two months?

And then, in an instant, the board was on top of the Cutlass, and the Cutlass was parked at the break, and Donald Tremaine, backlit and silhouetted by the sun, was gliding across a perfect Malibu wave.

ACKNOWLEDGMENTS

I would like to thank my mom, my sister, Priscilla, Sarah Durand, Daniel Greenberg, Emily Krump, Michael Signorelli, and last but certainly not least James Frey. In many different ways, you have all been great.